PRAISE FOR CAROLINE MITCHELL

'It is no secret that I love anything this lady writes. I find that her style carries me along beautifully. From the very first moment I felt Rebecca's tension I did not breathe properly until I read the very last word. As ever I was entranced by the sharp characterisations that convinced me I knew these people personally. This book was thrilling, tense, exciting, dark and twisted in the best possible way. It is only now, the following day, that I am able to breathe normally again.'

—Angela Marsons

'A dark yet compelling domestic drama that had me hooked straight off. The tension built up and up, the fear and sense of dread layered throughout, and the ending had me breathless. I devoured every page.'

—Mel Sherratt

SILENT VICTIM

ALSO BY
CAROLINE MITCHELL

DC Jennifer Knight

Don't Turn Around
Time to Die
The Silent Twin

Detective Ruby Preston Crime Thriller Series

Death Note
Sleep Tight
Murder Game

Individual Works

Paranormal Intruder
Witness

SILENT VICTIM

CAROLINE MITCHELL

This is a work of fiction. Names, characters, organizations, places, events, and incidents are either products of the author's imagination or are used fictitiously. Any resemblance to actual persons, living or dead, or actual events is purely coincidental.

Published by Thomas & Mercer, Seattle

www.apub.com

ISBN-13: 9781503948983 (hardcover)
ISBN-10: 1503948986 (hardcover)
ISBN-13: 9781542046626 (paperback)
ISBN-10: 1542046629 (paperback)

Cover design by Tom Sanderson

Printed in the United States of America

First edition

Benjamin.

Love you to the moon and back x

'A gentleman is simply a patient wolf'

—Lana Turner

PROLOGUE
EMMA

2013

I am not a bad person, but I've done a very bad thing.

A sense of unreality washes over me, cushioning the consequences of my act.

I am a murderer. My soul is damned to hell.

My thoughts are speared by a seagull's cry as it glides across the dusky sky. It is mournful in its bidding, and I stand over the ditch, my knuckles white, gripping the shovel in my right hand. A trickle of sweat rolls down the curve of my back, cooled by the twilight breeze. From the bottom of the ditch Luke stares with empty eyes, the soil beneath his head absorbing his blood. My lips part to accommodate my heavy breath while my lungs drive the panicked rise and fall of my chest. Is he truly dead? Did I really kill him? Legs shaking, I cling to the shovel – the only thing keeping me standing in this desolate field. The breeze plays with my hair, blowing dark strands into my eyes and lips. I draw them back behind my ear as I struggle for clarity. Just how long have I been standing here? The cogs of my brain whirr, trying to snap back the pieces of the complex edifice that has toppled all around me. My gaze falls to the shovel where his blood still stains the blade. *You need to clean that off,* a voice inside me whispers. *But first, hide the body.*

My thoughts are cloaked in darkness as self-preservation kicks in. My husband will be wondering where I am. He might even come looking for me. I should check Luke's pulse, call for an ambulance. Deep down, I know it's too late for that now. The ditch is lined with freshly shed leaves from the trees that border the field: a suitable resting place, if only for tonight.

Pressing my boot against metal, I slice the shovel into the earth. I draw up a wedge of soil, pausing only for a second before flinging it on to his face. As the dirt hits his parted lips, my stomach rolls over, the gravity of the situation hitting me with the force of a punch. I fall to my knees and vomit noisily into a patch of dandelions. Digging my fingers into the earth, I try to ground myself, coughing and spitting until my throat has cleared. I dare not look at Luke's body as I stand and brush the soil from my jeans. Picking up my shovel, I fling dirt into the ditch until my biceps ache. My armpits are damp with sweat; the skin on my face burning with effort. Opposing thoughts circle my brain, like vultures ready to pick over the carcass of my actions. I have committed a mortal sin. Hot tears of regret trail down my face. A thought resurfaces, telling me that I had no choice.

Forcing myself to focus, I survey the shallow grave. I can still see flashes of skin. His nose, his brow. Patches of white shirt are visible beneath the soil, and the tips of his leather shoes peep upwards. I stifle a sob. I need to finish this, but my arms are weak and the shovel feels like it is made of lead. Darkness is closing in yet the sky is devoid of cloud, awaiting the infiltration of stars that will burn brightly long after I am dead and gone. Dropping my gaze to the ground, I try to assemble my thoughts. I will come back tomorrow and finish the job properly. For now, I need to get home. I drag across some fallen branches from a recent gale, throwing them over the ditch until it appears undisturbed. Not that anyone will see it. The only witnesses are the curlews and seagulls flying overhead. I rub my hands against the back of my trousers before tying my shovel to my quad bike. 'Tomorrow,' I whisper, repeating my vow to return. 'I'll come back tomorrow and bury him properly.' The breeze snatches my words, as if disbelieving my sincerity. Inhaling deeply, I force my shaking breath back to normality. The land will keep my secret for now. I mount my quad bike, my eyes on the gravel path home. Revving the throttle, I push everything that has happened deep into the recesses of my mind.

CHAPTER ONE
EMMA

2017

Red-nosed and laughing, Jamie ran towards me, his red wellington boots making a thunk-thunk noise as he scattered the fallen autumn leaves. My husband had a propensity for buying Jamie bigger sized clothes than he needed, saying he would 'grow into them'. I made a mental note to take our son for a proper fitting. Shaking a tissue from my pocket, I wiped the dribble from his nose.

'Swing me, Mummy!' he squealed, his impossibly blue eyes bright with an excitement that only a child could feel. At almost three and a half years of age, his senses had not yet been dulled by the world. Getting down on one knee, I tightened his blue duffel coat and fixed his gloves before allowing him to run towards the bucket swings. A veil of fog hung over the landscape, leaving the small children's playground too gloomy a prospect for the mothers and their children who frequented it in the summer. I had been coming here since my childhood. I was not going to stop now. The fresh air would serve as a sedative later on, giving me time to catch up with my work. I watched him run towards the swings, his little body wiggling from side to side as layers of clothing hampered his movements.

I jolted in response to the hand that touched the curve of my back. 'Oh! You gave me a fright,' I gasped, clutching my husband by the arm.

'And you're very jumpy,' he said, his kind face settling my nerves. 'I finished work early; thought I'd give you a lift home rather than have you walking in the fog.'

I kissed him on the cheek, his smooth skin a novelty. I had been sorry to see his beard go, but the onset of a few grey hairs had been the death knell for his facial hair. In his tailored suit and rich wool-blend coat, he looked every inch the businessman. He was not the only one who made an effort when it came to clothes. I put my contacts in second-hand designer wear to good use, sourcing the vintage style that had appealed to me since my late teens – a look which had caught my husband's eye when we first met.

'Just five more minutes,' I said, turning back to look at Jamie, who was grunting as he tried to hoist his leg into the bucket swing.

'Daddy!' Jamie squealed, and I watched as Alex swung him around before plopping him into the seat and giving him a hefty push. He was a strong and capable father but, all the same, I found myself biting my lip as my over-protective streak kicked in. Catching my worried glare, Alex brought the swing to a steady pace, despite Jamie's cries to go higher.

'I've got some good news,' Alex said, giving me a furtive sideways glance. It was enough to tell me that his perception of good news might be different from mine.

'You've not gone and bought that car, have you? Diesel engines are pollutants on wheels,' I said, my eyes following Jamie as he swung back and forth. Alex could pick his moments, waiting until I was distracted with our son before dropping any bombshells. He knew I would never argue in front of him.

'Give over,' Alex said, 'as if I'd dare.' His Leeds accent filtered through his words. He masked it in the office, changing the rhythm and tone to mimic his upper-class clients. I liked that he could be himself with me. 'No, it's about work . . .'

I took a sharp intake of breath. The fog was coming down so thick that I could taste it on my tongue.

Alex flashed me a smile. 'I've been offered the promotion . . .'

'In Leeds.' I finished his sentence, trying hard to hide my reluctance because I could not offer a reason as to why we could not go. At least not one I could disclose.

'Yes,' he said, giving Jamie one last push. 'They've given me the job.'

Opening my arms, I took him in an embrace, but inside my heart was dropping like a stone. 'Well done, love. I know how much this means to you.'

'Not just me.' He drew away, his dark eyes searching mine. 'To all of us. Living in Leeds is going to be a whole fresh start. You can branch out with your business, and we can enrol Jamie in a private school.'

'Push, Daddy, puuuuussh,' Jamie squealed, kicking out with his feet to gain momentum.

I fixed the smile that had slid from my face. My reluctance to move had been a bone of contention between us for what felt like a lifetime; all because I was not strong enough to face up to my past. 'Our house could take for ever to sell,' I said, clinging on to the hope that our departure would be delayed.

'That's my second bit of good news,' Alex said. 'I've got someone interested in the property.'

I should have known. My husband managed the Colchester branch of the estate agency that he worked for. Although he sold mainly up-market properties, they sometimes had enquiries from buyers with less cash to spare.

He hoisted Jamie up from the swing and spoke over his shoulder as he gave him a squeeze. 'They say it comes in threes; we should buy a lottery ticket on the way home.'

With Jamie in his left arm, he threw his right one over my shoulder and the two of us walked to the car. I should have felt safe, protected by his strength, but my mind was racing as news of the move sank in. I strapped Jamie into his car seat, my stomach clenching from the sudden sense of dread. I could not hide from the past any longer. It was time to go back there. To face what I had done.

CHAPTER TWO
ALEX

2017

'Beautiful, isn't it?' Sweeping a hand across the brooding landscape, I stood at the open back door. My words belied my thoughts. I could not wait to get out of this godforsaken place. I smiled sweetly at Mark and Kirsty, the young couple viewing our home. Not that it had felt like home to me. Despite Emma placing my name on the deeds, I had felt like an intruder from the day I moved in. It was quaint enough, with its weatherboard exterior and red roof tiles, but the interior needed a serious cash injection, and was a poor comparison to the show homes in which I spent my working day. It was hardly any wonder I was too embarrassed to invite my colleagues round.

Giving our viewers the full treatment, I glossed over the house's flaws using the words 'rustic', 'quaint' and 'charming'. 'You can put your stamp on it,' I said. 'Plenty of room for your personalities to shine through.' Their nodding heads told me that the tour of our three-bedroom cottage had gone down well. I glanced at my watch, a pang of guilt making itself known. It was the first time I had gone behind my wife's back. I wanted to tell her about the viewing, but she had sabotaged my efforts to move too many times before. Not that she'd ever admit that. I loved Emma with all my heart: clever, talented and perpetually enigmatic Emma. Life had never been dull in her company. The puzzling thing was that, deep down, I knew she wanted to move. Perhaps it was the guilt of leaving her family home that was holding her back. Then again, her father had died years ago. Whatever the excuse, this place had dug its claws firmly into her and refused to release her. But this time I was ready, and had an answer for every excuse. The viewing couple would not be the first artists drawn to Mersea Island. Mark raved about the network of creeks and boardwalks that crisscrossed the marshes, while his wife delighted in the shapes, textures and colours of the nearby beach. I nodded in all the right places, attempting to share their enthusiasm. It was all a lie. Where they saw striking abandoned boats on the foreshore, I saw rotting wooden skeletons jutting out of the slime. As they spoke of the Strood, they came up with romantic notions of the island's history. It was something I was all too happy to capitalise on.

'You can still see evidence of the Roman occupation dotted all over Mersea,' I said, having brushed up on the island's history the night before. 'The ancient causeway connecting the island is the only way on and off.' The Strood was something of which I was all too aware. I hated the sense of being trapped as the tide cut us off from the outside world. 'My father-in-law used to be an archaeologist. He had some fascinating stories. If you're interested, the Mersea Museum is on the west side of the island.'

'You don't find it a nuisance, being cut off by the tide?' Mark said.

I shook my head. 'The locals call it the "causy". It's what makes the island unique. As long as you're up to speed on the tide times then you should be OK.' Perhaps it was because I was a city boy, but settling in Mersea Island was never an option for me. God knows I had tried. It was Emma's idea that we move in to look after Bob, her father, before emphysema claimed his life. I could not stand by and watch him be placed in a nursing home, so I agreed. However, there was nothing to keep us here any more.

I led them round to the kitchen and opened the back door. 'The gravel drive is wide enough to accommodate several cars if you're holding an event.' I pointed beyond the log store and the numerous fruit trees dotted around our half-acre plot. 'See that gate behind those trees? There's a further four-acre paddock that comes with the house. You can't see it from here, but there's a wooden bench built into the big oak tree down the end. It would really extend your garden if you took down the back gate and opened the whole lot up.'

'Now that *would* be a big back garden,' Mark said, his nostrils flaring as he inhaled a deep breath. 'I love the seclusion. You could run around naked and there'd be nobody here to see it.'

'Not that we would,' Kirsty laughed. 'We may act like hippies but I draw the line at baring all.'

I flashed a smile, rubbing my hands together as they spoke. I had a good feeling about this, and knew an offer was on the cards. Impressed by my patter, Mark and Kirsty seemed happy enough to overlook the damp climbing the walls and the crumbling brickwork that needed attention. Their faces gleamed with excitement as I quoted a fair price. My colleagues would have asked for more, but my conscience would not allow it. I reasoned that my lack of ruthlessness afforded me a better reputation than some of the sharks conducting business in my office.

'My wife was going to turn the land into a giant vegetable patch, but she never got round to it.' I looked down at Kirsty's embroidered flat shoes. 'Do you have any wellington boots? It's quite foggy, mind; you might be better off coming back when the weather's cleared a bit.'

'There's no need. I've seen everything on the plans. It's just what we want,' Kirsty said, grinning.

'We can drive down there if you prefer?' I suggested for good measure. 'There's a laneway leading to the back of the land that's accessible by road. It's a bit bumpy, but we can take my car if you like.'

'No need, honestly,' Kirsty repeated, turning her gaze to her husband, pleading with her eyes.

'We've literally just put it on the market, so I'd advise you not to delay.' I had barely uttered the words before Mark spoke.

'Any movement on price?'

I shook my head. 'Sorry, we've priced it competitively for a quick sale. I've been offered a job you see, in Leeds. I can't afford to hang around. I have other people on my books, and it's bound to be snapped up. It's not every day that a property such as this—'

'We'll take it,' Kirsty breathed, clasping her husband's arm.

He rolled his eyes. 'So much for playing it cool. Yes, we'd like to offer the full asking price.'

I shook their hands in a firm grip. 'You've done the right thing. There's so much potential with this property, and it's easily worth the asking price and more. You're getting a bargain.'

'It's perfect,' Kirsty said, looking around the room as if it were Windsor Castle. Clearly she could see beauty where I could not. I felt comfort in knowing that they were the right buyers.

My dislike for Mersea Island was deep rooted. I had nothing against the residents, and the landscape could be breathtaking at times, but I could not stand the isolation. I could not escape the suffocating sense of claustrophobia when the tide rolled in and the island became closed off from the outside world. At night fog came like a blanket, so thick you could hardly see your hand. Emma used to laugh as she told me the old story of the ghost that haunted the Strood. I didn't believe in ghosts but she was voicing my worst fear. Some souls were destined to be here for ever and I did not want to be one of them.

In the past, Emma had seemed pleased when I showed her pictures of the properties we could afford, but this morning as I broke the news in the playground, I could sense her hesitancy. I had a choice: we could delay proceedings by weighing up the pros and cons, or I could carry on full steam ahead. After all, I wasn't just doing this for me.

Now that I had the buyers in the palm of my hand, I felt a mixture of relief and excitement. I only hoped that by moving on, my wife could leave the ghosts of her past behind.

CHAPTER THREE
EMMA

2017

'Careful with that,' I said to Josh as we unpacked a beautiful silk gown from our delivery. Purchased from Oxfam after being worn just once, it had been a steal. I loved my job and often found that immersing myself in work was the best way of getting through the day. Here in Something Borrowed, I could get lost amongst beautiful things and leave the real world behind. I was not the only person to love my shop; Josh did too. My retail assistant was twenty-six years old and, by his own admission, this was the longest he had ever held a job down. A firm believer in second chances, I had been willing to ignore his mediocre references when I'd offered him the position six months ago. Josh might not look like your typical wedding boutique assistant with his floppy auburn hair and black skinny jeans, but he had proved to be a godsend, setting up the online side of things as well as helping with the day-to-day running of the shop.

'So, have you spoken to your parents yet?' I asked, preferring to focus on his problems rather than my own.

He smirked, carefully smoothing the delicate material and giving the dress a little shake. 'I work in a wedding shop; I think that's a big enough clue.'

'We'll get you out of that cupboard yet,' I said, smiling as his laughter erupted. 'What?'

'Closet. It's closet,' he said, still chuckling as he carried the dress to the back room to await collection. Under the deal I'd negotiated with the local dry cleaners all my dresses were picked up and cleaned before going on display.

The old-fashioned bell over my door tinkled as Theresa pushed it open with her backside. We were fully staffed today as we prepared to present our winter collection to our clients. 'Skinny latte, mocha, and a disgusting green tea for you,' said my sister, laying them on the vintage ivory table.

'Much obliged,' I said, my words barely out before the doorbell rang for a second time. I groaned inwardly. The fact we closed on Mondays never stopped a certain client who had been coming since we opened. Given the nature of our business, we did not see a lot of repeat custom. Maggie was the exception to the rule and I did not have the heart to refuse her. At eighty years of age and four foot eleven, she could be swept away by a sudden breeze. She smiled, her bright-pink lipstick eclipsed only by the sapphire-blue eyeshadow courting her lids. Taking my tea from the table, I patted a chair for her to sit down. The interior of our bridal boutique was like something out of a wedding magazine. I loved the vintage ivory furnishings, the plush cream carpet and the scent of white roses dotted in antique vases throughout the store. French designer curtains cloaked two generous changing rooms leading to a platform surrounded by fairy lights and full-length mirrors. Everything fit for a princess on her special day. It was just as I had envisioned it when I'd first met my husband over nine years ago. Most men would have run a mile from a woman with a passion for wedding dresses. Instead, Alex helped me through my business studies course, encouraging me every step of the way. I felt proud that his faith in me had been rewarded. I never would have made it without his 'dream big' attitude to life.

I sat beside Maggie as she stared at it all, her eyes sparkling as they reflected the view. 'How are you, lovely? All ready for the big day?'

'I came to talk to you about that dress,' she said, a frown crossing her face. 'I'm not sure if it's for me. I heard you have some new ones and I was hoping to try them on.'

'Really? I thought you looked beautiful. What's changed your mind?'

Maggie rifled in her bag, pulling out a bent-up snapshot that I had taken during her last visit. 'They were laughing at me down the pub; said I was mutton dressed as lamb. Bastards.'

'Since when have you cared what anyone's thought of you?' I asked, seeing wisdom in her green eyes. 'Now where are you heading after here? Over to see Bernard?' I crossed my legs, tilting my head to one side as I took in her expression.

She gave me a knowing smile. 'Already been. He told me to pay no heed.'

'Makes sense to me. Besides, what do those old codgers down the pub know about wedding dresses?'

'True,' she said, gathering up her bags. 'I suppose you're right. I should be off. This wedding won't plan itself.'

'And I'd better get back to work,' I said, relieved that today at least, she was willing to see sense. 'Send Bernard my best.'

It was a spell that Maggie seemed content to stay under. For her, it was preferable to facing the truth. Bernard was not waiting at home, he was in Colchester cemetery, having died on the eve of their wedding seven years ago.

'You're such a soft touch,' Josh said after she had left. 'For a minute there I thought you were going to let her try on the new gowns.' Eighty per cent of our stock was upmarket second-hand, but at the start of each season I invested some money in the latest designs.

'I don't think Theresa's heart would take it,' I laughed, knowing that by the end of the session there would be more make-up on the dresses than on Maggie's face. I had a special selection of retired and bargain gowns just for her. 'She's a good soul, and if it makes her happy then there's no harm in it, is there?' I could empathise with Maggie. Some people went on living, even those buried in the ground.

CHAPTER FOUR
LUKE

2002

I inhaled the smell of freshly mown grass as the school lawn received its last cut of the summer. For me, it marked a new beginning, and as my Year 11 students filtered in through the classroom I pulled the window shut and offered them a warm smile.

'Good morning, class,' I said, raising my voice to gain their attention. 'My name is Luke Priestwood and I'm replacing Mr Piper, who's retired early due to ill health.' They seemed surprised but pleased to see me, and I glided over the lie. In reality, Mr Piper had been pushed. Last year's exam results in Art & Design had been shamefully poor. According to the head, I had been brought in to inject some 'fresh blood' into the class. That and my indisputable talent had landed me the job. My eyes roamed over the class. At twenty-three, I was freshly qualified and only seven years older than most of the people in the room. Not that I was intimidated. I watched the male students hitch up their trousers before taking a seat. Arseless and charmless, they paled into insignificance next to me. The chatter in the room quietened and I gazed down on their expectant faces. Already I could see the effect my presence was having on the female students. My morning gym sessions left me lean and toned, a vast contrast to the pot-bellied Piper, who could barely climb the stairs without coughing up phlegm. I licked my lips as a tinge of satisfaction made itself known. It felt good to be back in the school I'd been taught in. I felt like I had gotten somewhere in life. That I was in control.

I loosened my tie, my eyes roaming over the chattering female students. Sweet sixteen and never been kissed. There was little evidence of that here. They were the stereotypical gaggle of teens: layers of make-up, tight short skirts and the stink of cheap perfume lacing their skin. Beneath the confines of the school uniform, they held little mystery to me. The shrill ring of the bell jolted me out of my thoughts, signalling it was time for class to begin. I walked to the door, curling my fingers around the handle to push it shut. It met with resistance from the other side as one last student ploughed through.

She may have been a poor timekeeper but my new arrival was deliciously pert, with curves in all the right places. Laden with books, her bag slapped against her thigh when she came to a sudden stop. She briefly met my gaze, and I felt an instant spark of attraction as her cheeks flushed a furious pink. Her dark wavy hair was swept over in a sexy side parting, framing her face. She brushed an errant lock from her cheek, panting from the exertion of rushing to be on time. I regarded her with a look of amused curiosity. Inside I was thrilled that a gorgeous young creature would be subservient to me for the forthcoming year.

'Sorry, sir,' she mumbled self-consciously, before finding a table at the back of the room.

Tugging at her skirt, she took a seat, entwining her summer-tanned legs. Devoid of make-up and jewellery, she carried an innocent beauty as yet untainted by the modern world.

I began the class without a moment's hesitation, explaining my plans for the curriculum. She gave her name as Emma, and I struggled to keep my thoughts in check. She was jailbait and I was newly qualified. I could not afford to be caught up in an illicit affair. 'If you can take out your text books . . .' I said, clearing my throat as I tried to focus. But I knew that I was fooling myself. My mind was not on the history of art, it was on the brooding schoolgirl at the back of the room.

CHAPTER FIVE
EMMA

2017

My keys rattled as I locked the shop's front door. It had been a long day and I was dying to get home and kick off my shoes. 'I'll see you tomorrow, then.'

Theresa smiled, her shoulder-length blonde hair catching the last of the dying sun. 'No need to detour to the nursery, I'm picking Jamie up today.' Theresa was Jamie's godmother. With no other siblings, I had not had many choices when it came to candidates, but there was nobody better suited for the role than my big sister. At thirty-seven, she hadn't yet had children of her own and was more than happy to take on babysitting duties. She and Jamie made a fantastic team, and she spoiled him rotten during their time together. 'Are you sure?' I said. 'It's news to me.'

Arching one eyebrow, she gave me a conspiratorial smile. 'Alex asked me to babysit for a few hours. Looks like he has something in store for you.' Alex was an old romantic at heart and I loved his little spontaneous acts – even now, after almost a decade, he still had the ability to give me butterflies.

After rolling down the shop shutters, I thanked Theresa and left. But as I walked to the car park, my nerves got the better of me. Sure, Alex was no stranger to sweet gestures, but this felt different. Had Theresa misunderstood? Did Alex have something else in store?

After paying for my ticket, I entered the Osbourne Street multi-storey car park. My heels echoed ominously down the hollow concrete construction. Devoid of fresh air, it carried the stale smell of engine oil and diesel fumes that I could not wait to escape. Level C had been full when I'd driven there this morning but, apart from a rusted Mercedes in the far corner, my yellow Volkswagen Beetle now stood alone. A sudden sense of vulnerability sharpened my senses, hastening my steps. I didn't notice the newspaper nestled under my windscreen wiper until I opened the car door. Odd, I thought, plucking it from its resting place. I was used to seeing flyers but never a whole newspaper. In the absence of a bin, I threw it on to my front seat, locking myself inside my protective yellow shell. As the car engine rumbled into life and I put the car in gear, I gave the paper another glance. Why had it been placed on *my* car? Sighing, I threw the gearstick back into neutral while I unfolded the paper, smoothing over the creased pages to reveal the front-page headline. CRASH INVOLVING THREE CARS CAUSES MAJOR DELAYS. I frowned. I didn't remember hearing about that. It was only when I glanced at the date that I froze: 1 October 2013. The same date indelibly branded on my mind. The day I killed a man. I exhaled a painful breath, the blood draining from my face. It was a coincidence. It had to be. Maybe it was some kind of promo. Maybe they were on all the cars. My mind raced as it tried to provide me with answers, fuel to enable me to push my fears away. It was someone messing around. It had to be. Only two people knew the significance of that date – and the dead kept their secrets well. I breathed fast and deep, panic rising as the past returned to haunt me. I spun the car round, desperate for the open air. Through my windscreen, I caught sight of the CCTV camera, my glance falling guiltily back to the newspaper on the passenger seat. I could hardly afford to draw attention to myself, not when I had gotten this far. I lowered my window, depositing the newspaper in a litter bin on the way out. It was silly, I told myself, panicking like this over nothing. Just as I always had, I pushed my fears to the back of my mind, focusing on my journey home.

I didn't know what to expect when I walked through the front door. I adjusted my eyes to the darkness of our narrow hall, negotiating our uneven terracotta tiling, which was in need of repair. The smell of spicy food wafted from our kitchen and, despite my anxieties, my stomach grumbled in response.

'Hey, you, how was your day?' Alex said, looking relaxed in sweatshirt and jeans. His enviably clear skin still glowed from the Indian summer we had enjoyed before the cold autumn winds took hold. Taking my coat, he kissed me on the cheek. I slid my fingers beneath his jumper and he gasped at the contact of my icy skin.

'Sorry,' I said, chuckling as I withdrew my hands. 'Work was fine. I'm really pleased with the new lines. Well, all except one. It's a beautiful dress but it's got this whopping big footprint on the train.' I did not care about the dress, much less want to talk about it, but he would think something was up if I didn't share my day.

'I'm sure you'll work your magic on it,' Alex said. He was proud of what I had done to the business, though he had no idea just how lucrative it had become. Had he known, he would have pushed for a move long before now. The thought sent a frisson of worry through me. Had the person interested in the house come through? Was that what this surprise dinner was all about?

Alex opened the door to our dining room and I saw that the table was set. With soft music playing and candles flickering, he had transformed it into a warm, cosy space, but still there was a chill growing inside me and I could not hold back the question on my tongue. 'What's the special occasion? It must be good, you've bought oysters.'

'Fresh off the bay,' he said, avoiding the question as he poured me a glass of champagne. Oysters were my favourite food and I rarely went a week without indulging. Jamie called them fish bogeys, and Alex wasn't much better, reluctant to admit liking anything that my birthplace produced. I took a few sips from my glass, my nerves jangling as I waited for him to tell me what was going on. We ate in silence, my thoughts racing. It was not until we had finished our desserts that he let me in on the secret. He topped up my glass with the last of the bubbly and I wondered if he had been hoping for the alcohol to take effect before he broke the news.

'Here's to new beginnings,' he said, gently clinking his crystal glass against mine. 'I've sold the house.'

My hand raised in mid-air, I stared at him. '*Our* house?' I lowered my glass, unable to drink its contents. I knew this moment could come, yet hearing the words leave his lips made me feel sick inside.

'Yes,' he said, his tone forcibly light. 'I had a lovely couple view it today. Cash buyers. They want to restore it to its former glory.'

'Really? But there's so much to be done . . .' I said, amazed he'd accepted their offer without telling me. I should have been annoyed, but I'd made him put his life on hold for long enough. I knew I could not stay here for ever.

'They're artists; they fell in love with the setting more than anything. They're very keen.'

My face was a picture of calm but inside my heart felt like a jackhammer. 'Did they check out the land?' I said, praying the answer was no. What if they had? Alex said they were artists. People like that would immediately be drawn to the trees that bordered the paddock. What if they'd discovered my secret? The police could be on their way right now. I might never see Jamie again.

'No – it was raining and they didn't have any proper shoes. They offered the full asking price without seeing it. A dream sale.'

I knocked back the contents of my glass, the once pleasant bubbles now leaving a vinegary taste in my mouth. 'Looks like we're moving to Leeds,' I said, knowing Alex had probably already earmarked a property to buy.

'You're going to love it,' he said, the relief visible on his face as he reached over and squeezed my hand.

I offered him a tight smile, my mind on the body I'd buried in our back yard.

CHAPTER SIX
EMMA

2017

With Jamie home and tucked up in bed, it felt as if the whole house was sleeping. Alex snored softly, tired from a full day's work then coming home and cooking as well. I stared up at our low-beamed ceiling – the cobweb magnet, as Alex called it. At six foot two, he had to duck slightly each time he entered a room. Everything was small in our little L-shaped cottage; it was easy to see why he was fed up of it. It was not as if it were filled with happy memories for me either: my mother's departure, nursing my terminally ill father, and what had happened out back . . . It felt entrenched in misfortune. I only hoped that the new owners would have more luck.

Alex was quiet and thoughtful when we first met. Our friendship was firmly established before he made his feelings clear. He knew I was still recovering from what I called a 'bad relationship', although that was as much as I told him at the time. It was the little things that endeared him to me: smuggling food into the library when I was snowed under with studying, and knowing when I needed some time on my own. When I was struck down with a bad case of the flu it was Alex who nursed me through it. When I was snotty and dishevelled it was Alex who missed important lectures to stay by my side. Alex's continued support was a debt I was only able to begin to repay when his father died from heart failure, squeezing his hand tightly as the man he loved most in the world was lowered into the ground.

Alex gave me the courage to believe that I deserved a better life. Family was everything to him and, after we married, all he wanted was to seal our union with a child. Getting pregnant with Jamie had been worth all the sacrifices it took to get there. But now there was a cloud on the horizon, threatening to break a storm over our happy home.

The more I thought about what I'd done, the sicker I felt inside. The truth was rotten and festering. I pictured it as something ragged, dragging itself across the mudflats to make me account for what I had done. Lying in bed with no street lights to soften the night, it was easy to allow my imagination to run riot. I had been reckless, crazy. Christ! I still had the shovel in my shed. Why hadn't I gone back there, buried the body deep and disposed of the evidence? It was the same reason I stopped going to church after it happened. Because I could not face it, that's why. I forced myself to think about what I had done. Luke's body was out there, but what state was he in? It had been four years. Had he fully decomposed? Or had the wildlife picked his remains apart? My stomach lurched at the thought. And then a flashback, in glorious detail, making me sit up in bed and gasp for breath.

Alex stirred beside me. 'You all right, love?' His words were muffled, thick with sleep.

I smoothed his tousled brown hair. 'I was having a nightmare. I'm going to get a glass of water. You go back to sleep.'

But as I wrapped my dressing gown around me, I knew the truth was a nightmare from which I could not awake. I crept to the kitchen, working my way through my options, trying to view them as dispassionately as possible. I could return to the body and dig a deeper grave, yes, but what if the new owners had the site excavated? Then what? A chill descended and I switched on the kitchen light. An energy-saving bulb hung limply from its pendant, devoid of a light shade. The last time I had tried to fit one, it had driven a shock down the length of my arm right down to my toes. Alex seemed happy to allow the place to fall further into disrepair because it was another reason for us to leave. Shuffling to our wide, square kitchen sink, I filled a glass with water from the tap, forcing myself to focus. I needed a plan B. I could gather up Luke's remains, burn them, dispose of what was left somewhere safe. But how? I was a thirty-year-old woman who dealt in wedding dresses. I couldn't do this alone. *You murdered him quickly enough*, my subconscious rasped.

I took a shuddering breath. The idea of going back there made me sick to the core, but I told myself that the man I'd buried had been more of a danger alive than dead. I stared through the window at the moonless sky, comforting myself with the thought that Luke could no longer threaten me. But that was a lie; he was still reaching out from the grave, calling my name. There was no ghost haunting the Strood, just Luke. I had to go back there and deal with the body: only then could we move away and start again. A new home, a promotion for Alex and private schooling for Jamie – it was all we had ever wanted and it was within reach. I just needed to be strong enough to get through this.

I sipped my water, not realising I had bitten my lip until I tasted the warm tang of blood. I remembered the stained shovel, the blood oozing down on to Luke's shirt collar then into the soil for the insects to feast on. My breath sharpened. I began to think about the meal I had eaten that day and how it was lying in my stomach, working against me. Dark thoughts reached out like tentacles in my mind. I closed my eyes, willing myself to think sensibly. Tomorrow I would go to Colchester, place Jamie into nursery then ask Theresa to cover so I could finish work early and return home. If Alex found out, I'd say I was checking the fencing before the buyers returned. I'd dig up Luke's remains and dispose of them for good. This time somewhere nobody would ever find them.

CHAPTER SEVEN
EMMA

2017

The balls of my feet ached from standing in my heels. After a busy morning, I was happy to turn the Closed sign on the door for lunch. Not that I was complaining. Being occupied kept my mind off my problems. But I could not exercise avoidance forever. As soon as Theresa came to cover my afternoon shift, I had to go home.

'Something wrong with that?' Josh eyed me from across the circular table as I poked at my salad.

'It's a bit limp,' I said. 'I should have put it in the fridge.' Our staff-room was blisteringly warm. It comprised a small table and chairs and a kitchen counter with the usual appliances: microwave, fridge and sink. It smelled like a greenhouse: tropical plants took up most of the room, a joking reminder of Theresa's disapproval of the high heating bills. But I couldn't have my brides trying on wedding dresses with goosebumps on their skin.

'Want some of mine?' Josh offered, nodding towards his lunch box. 'Mum made loads.'

'No, you're all right. I'm just tired,' I said, listlessly prodding some beetroot with my fork. 'I had a really lucid dream last night, and it's been running around in my head all day.' This much was true, though I could not tell him the real reason behind my unease.

'Was it one of *those* dreams? I had this dream about Tom Hardy the other night . . .' he said, his blue eyes glinting as he flashed me a cheeky smile.

'Tom Hardy didn't feature,' I replied, wishing I could come clean. The more I came to know Josh the more I liked him, but there was no way I could burden him with the awful truth. I should have been confiding in Theresa, but I couldn't risk her judgement either.

'I was in prison,' I blurted, feeling my muscles tense. 'I'd done something terrible, but I didn't know what it was. I woke up crying because Alex wouldn't visit me.' I pushed my food away, the thought stealing what little appetite I had.

Josh swallowed the bite of cheese sandwich he had been chewing. 'That's a bit heavy. Where did that come from?'

'I don't know,' I said, using the lie to facilitate a conversation I was dying to have. If I didn't speak to someone soon I would explode. 'It got me thinking. What would you do if you were married to someone and they did something really bad?' To pose such a question to Josh was not out of the ordinary: we were forever discussing moral dilemmas to pass the time when the shop was slow. My heart beat a little faster as I waited for his response.

'Ooh, how bad are we going? Bank robbery? Kidnapping?' He rummaged around his lunch box, plucking out a Mars bar and a bag of crisps.

'Nobody robs banks any more. Hmm . . .' My fingers tapped the table as I pretended to come up with the act that had been on my mind all day. 'Let's say . . . murder. A one-off. In the heat of the moment.'

'That's tricky,' Josh said, his eyes thoughtful as he soaked up the challenge. 'I guess I'd stand by them, at least until I knew the truth. If I loved them then I'd like to think I'd stay, because someone I love could never do something like that on purpose.'

'Top marks,' I said. 'Me too.'

'Is this where you confess to murder?'

A flush rose to my cheeks as he broke the silence with laughter. 'Can you imagine it?' Josh said. 'You can't even kill a fly. I won't go calling the police anytime soon. Now that sister of yours . . . she's one to watch.' He gave me a wink as Theresa strolled in.

'What have I done now?' she said, shrugging off her rain-speckled coat and hanging it on the back of the door.

'Moral dilemma time. You've married the man of your dreams, but on your wedding night he's confessed to murder,' Josh said, embellishing my earlier scenario. 'The cops are coming to lock his sorry backside up. Do you dump him or hang around?'

'Dump him. Murder is murder.' Theresa finger-combed her windswept hair, her words delivered without a moment's hesitation.

'This is *the* man of your dreams we're talking about,' Josh said.

'I'd bang him first,' Theresa laughed, mulling it over. 'Maybe stretch to a few conjugal visits?'

I forced a laugh, the thought of prison continuing to make the prospect of food unappealing.

'Aren't you eating your lunch?' Theresa said, taking a look at my discarded salad.

'I had a big breakfast,' I lied.

'Really?' She narrowed her glare, as if she somehow knew better. But then she did. Theresa knew many things about me.

CHAPTER EIGHT
LUKE

2002

I smiled at my own ingenuity as I glanced at Emma, who was sitting on her own in her usual seat at the back of the class. Lunchtime detention was an excellent excuse for having her all to myself. Emma, on the other hand, seemed unimpressed at being kept in for failing to complete her homework. It was the first time it had happened, but it was time to progress things between us and I could only do that by getting her alone.

'Why don't you sit up front so we can chat?' I asked, standing from my desk. A recent haircut, a new set of clothes: I had made a special effort with my appearance in order to reel her in. Not that I knew who or what she found attractive; everything about her was closed off, hidden from view.

'Yes, sir,' Emma said, picking up the tin box containing her charcoal pencils.

'Well don't seem so thrilled about it,' I smiled, bending down to retrieve a piece of paper that had slipped from her grasp. 'Anyone would think you were being sent to the gallows.'

'Sorry, sir,' Emma said dolefully, taking her chair.

I leaned forward, grabbing the seat beside her. 'What's wrong? It's not like you to miss handing in your homework. I thought you enjoyed our classes?'

'I do,' she said, earnestly meeting my gaze. 'It's just that . . .' she pursed her lips, seemingly unsure of herself. Her barely brushed hair, her unironed shirt, her appearance gifted me clues.

'Having a tough time at home?'

'Yes,' she nodded, and I smiled inwardly as I detected a slight wobble in her chin. 'You live on Mersea, don't you? Is that the east or the west side of the island?' I asked, hoping the gods would favour me.

'The east,' she said glumly. 'Nothing around but sky and land.'

It was exactly the response I wanted. Had she lived on the west, she could have benefited from the close-knit community that inhabited it. As it was, my little Emma was all on her own. After checking the coast was clear, I briefly rested my hand on her back. 'You know what they say – a problem shared is a problem halved.'

'But the homework . . .' she said, glancing at the half-finished drawing of a drooping sunflower.

I removed my hand, marking the paper with my pen. 'Consider it done. A-plus, your best work yet.' I gave her a wink. 'We've got ten minutes. Why don't you tell me what's wrong?' I wasn't really interested in her pitiful home life, but her physical presence was intoxicating. It was not often I was graced with such innocence in a fifteen-year-old girl. Her attention drawn inwards, my gaze crept to her skirt, which had risen above her knees. I looked at her face, now twisted with the effort of discussing problems that seemed buried too deep to reach.

'Is it your family?' I said, sympathetically tilting my head to one side. 'You can trust me. I know what it's like to grow up feeling like you don't fit the mould.'

'Do you?' she said, a flicker of light reaching her eyes. I had hit the bullseye first time. Quickly I formulated a backstory, something that I hoped mirrored her own. I knew she came from a one-parent family, and was not part of the popular groups in school. 'Yes,' I said. 'I didn't have many friends growing up, and there was nobody I could confide in about what was happening at home. I felt isolated from everyone else, because their lives were so different to mine.'

Emma nodded sadly. 'That's how I feel too.'

I gave her a gentle smile, conscious time was ticking away. 'Mum did her best after Dad died, but she couldn't cope with bringing up a family on her own. That's why I had nobody to turn to when . . .' I paused for effect, it was best to leave these things vague. 'Well, none of that matters now. All I'm saying is that you're not alone.'

'It's why I couldn't do my homework,' she said, her voice low. 'Dad wasn't well and I had to call the doctor. Sometimes he finds it hard to breathe. He was meant to write a note but he was asleep when I left for school and I didn't want to wake him.'

So not only was my little Lolita isolated, she played nursemaid to her father too. Perfect. Such commitment afforded little time for outside friends. The bell rang in the hall to signal the end of lunch.

'I tell you what,' I said, 'why don't you stay behind after school for some extra art tuition? We can have a chat, work out a plan for improving your exam results. You're a talented artist, Emma; if we put in the extra work your pictures will be fit for the school exhibition this year.'

'Really?' she said, her face glowing from the compliment. 'Mum used to exhibit her drawings, they were hung on the walls of the craft shop in Mersea.'

'Well, there you go; you've obviously inherited your talents from her.' I smiled. 'Now, get moving, you don't want to be late for your next lesson.'

I watched her as she walked away, her step lightened from the effect of my words. Her desperation would fuel our blossoming friendship. Delicious anticipation beckoned. I had baited the hook, now all I had to do was land her.

CHAPTER NINE
ALEX

2017

'Congratulations, Alex – we'll be sorry to see you go.' Charles took me firmly by the hand, his gruff exterior temporarily lightened by his smile. His cheery disposition told me that his well wishes were genuine, and I returned his smile, feeling real hope for my future plans. It was a shame that his marriage to my sister-in-law had not worked out, but thankfully he had not allowed his personal life to colour his attitude towards me.

'Thanks, I've been waiting for this for a long time,' I said. The resignation of the divisional manager in Leeds had come just at the right time.

'Sounds like you're all primed for the role. You've sold your house, I hear?'

'And about to offer on another,' I said, hardly able to believe that the millstone around my neck would finally be disposed of. With a slap on the back, Charles told me to finish early for the weekend. For once, I didn't disagree. I'd put in enough unpaid hours to be entitled to a half day to sort things out. I had lots to do, and hoped we could move as soon as Mark and Kirsty signed on the dotted line. I'd narrowed the search for our new home to two really promising places, and I wanted to persuade Emma to come to Leeds for viewings. Both houses were stunning: four bedrooms, glossy designer kitchens and lots of room for Jamie to run about in. I couldn't wait to get him out of our ramshackle Mersea home. Emma used to tell me that the nearby beach made up for our lack of space. It was true that Jamie loved to go crabbing, searching the rock pools for the latest finds. He would come home, eyes bright, his tongue tripping over itself as he excitedly described his day's excursion. I consoled myself that there would be far more opportunities in Leeds for him as he grew up, and plenty of chances for trips to the seaside during our holidays. From an early age, I'd had my future planned out. I wanted a successful career, a happy marriage and, to top it all off, a child. It hadn't been easy to get to where I was now, but as I stepped out into the car park with the sunshine on my back, I felt truly blessed. It was only natural to want to move to a bigger home and be near my mum as she got older. Thankfully, Emma loved my mum and treated her as her own. Leaving the shop would be hard, but she was a brilliant businesswoman, and opening a new branch would be something for her to get her teeth into. So why, when there was so much to look forward to, did something seem to be holding her back?

Telling Emma had been easier than I'd expected. She had even agreed to visit Leeds to view some properties. But rather than soothe me, her calm exterior gave me greater cause for concern. She was an expert at hiding her feelings, selflessly keeping her problems to herself. It was why I had followed her out of our bedroom at 3 o'clock this morning. I hated spying on her but I knew I had taken a risk by pushing the sale of the house forward. A change in Emma's routine could be enough to send her spiralling over the edge. Any day now she could relapse, and the effect on our family could be devastating. As I felt her toss and turn beside me in bed the night before, the thought occurred to me that the wheels might already have been set in motion. Yet, I could not live a half-life any longer, too scared of saying or doing anything for fear of upsetting her. She had told me once that anything could serve as a trigger when she was low – an argument, a mishap at work, a perceived parenting failure – reawakening the voice within. But, from what I knew, that voice had grown quieter not long after Jamie was born. They say being a parent makes you a less-selfish person. For us, our precious Jamie was a glimmer of hope. Emma had had an odd childhood, so unlike mine, and it had taken me a while to get to grips with what she had been through. If I didn't push us to move forward, we would be stuck here for ever and resentment would eat away at my soul.

CHAPTER TEN
EMMA

2017

The keys of the quad bike felt cold and sharp in the palm of my hand. It was Dad's bike. Like everything else, he had left it to me after he died. His painful passing was granted by a lifetime of chain-smoking. After Mum left, he stopped caring if he lived or died. She'd been just twenty-two when she'd met my much older father. As a single parent, estranged from her family, she had struggled to cope with Theresa on her own. Dad had taken them both in and brought them back to Mersea Island. But their marriage had not been a happy one. Dad had said that Mum's was a spirit that could not be tamed. It was her Romany blood, he said, her wanderlust that drew her away. Pulling on my boots, I dismissed my thoughts, forcing my focus on to the task in hand. My head was filled with spirits of the past. It was a wonder I could function normally at all. I sat on the bike, the strong rumble of the engine beneath me. With Theresa covering, I had a couple of hours before I had to pick Jamie up from play school. I zipped up my jacket as I glanced warily at the sky. Pearl-grey clouds rolled above me, their bellies full of unshed rain. I needed to move quickly. I would get just one chance.

The wind burned my cheeks as I bumped along the torn-up path, my fingers tightly clenched around the throttle. I motored across the landscape, a chill driving its way down my back. It was accompanied by a strong feeling of déjà vu. Left unfertilised, the land had fallen prey to the ravages of time. Clutches of ragwort lined my path: a mass of dying yellow heads and ragged leaves, swaying in their last dance of the season. I parted my lips, tasting the faint kiss of salt in the air. My relationship with Mersea was a strange addiction. It was more than protecting the evidence of what I had done that kept me here. It didn't matter where I moved – I knew that this strange, haunting place would be a part of me for ever.

I eased off on the throttle as I caught sight of the oak tree on the border of our land. A mist clung around its leafless branches, draining the colour from the world. My stomach tightened and I drew in a sharp breath, slowing my bike further. I was not ready for this. My shovel rattled on the back as I hit a bump in the path, another reminder of what I had done. Taking a deep breath, I whispered a mantra to distract myself from the thoughts running loose in my head. 'I'm going to get through this, I'm going to get through this,' I repeated in a desperate prayer.

Before switching off the engine, I faced the bike for home, ready for a quick escape. Tugging at the rope, I untied my shovel from the back of the bike. Why had I kept it? Luke's DNA was surely embedded in its metal, in the wooden grooves of the handle. Perhaps I had left it there in the subconscious hope of being discovered. If only things had turned out differently. I caught the thought as it rose in the ether and wondered if I meant it. I had felt nothing but relief that Luke was gone. The realisation gave me the strength to carry on. I still knew the exact spot and I clawed away the obstacles until there was nothing but clear ditch to dig. There was something final about this moment, and my heart pounded in my chest as I disobeyed the urge to drop my shovel and run. I approached the ditch, expecting the scent of death to rise up to greet me, but there was only damp moss and rotting leaves. Goosebumps rose on my skin and I willed myself to get on with it. Slicing the shovel into the earth, I drew back a wad of soil, repeating the movement until my arms ached – just as they had done that day. I expected to glimpse a scrap of white material, a flash of a weather-ravaged jacket. But there was nothing. I dug further. Surely there should be something by now? Clothes, shoes, bone? Getting on my hands and knees, I burrowed my fingers into the earth. I did not know how I was going to cope with seeing the body again. Or what was left of it. Sweat lined my skin, and I raised an arm to hook back a loose lock of damp hair from my face. It was the worst kind of torture but I made myself push on.

Half an hour later, I was staring in disbelief at the shallow yet somehow body-less grave. Had animals dragged it away? I remembered his shoes peeping out through the soil. Where were they? Surely something had to remain? I checked my watch, gasping as I realised just how long I had taken. I needed to have a shower, get changed and pick up Jamie. Pulling off my gloves, I stared down at the red angry blisters that had formed on my skin. Only then did I feel the sharp sting of pain. It had been for nothing. My throat constricted as another emotion bubbled to the surface. Panic. There was no doubt I was at the right spot. Luke was dead. I had killed him.

So where had he gone?

CHAPTER ELEVEN
LUKE

2002

I straightened my posture as I sat at my desk. Parents' evening was a bit of a chore, giving up my free time to speak to mums and dads about a subject they were rarely interested in. But there was one student I was looking forward to finding out more about. I had purposely booked her father into the last appointment so I could take my time. Yet as the gasping, frail man entered my classroom, I wondered if I had got my times mixed up. This could not be Emma's father, surely? Emma had told me her dad was unwell, but just the same I had expected a more exotic parentage than this. I had allowed my imagination to run away with me; the old man now ambling in brought me sharply down to earth.

Parents were encouraged to bring their children with them so they could show them around the school and absorb the points brought up during the meetings. But Bob Hetherington was alone, and I wondered if Emma had been too embarrassed to tag along. His tall frame was slightly bent, his face a pallid grey hue. The deep lines on his face spoke of time spent outdoors. Slowly, he made it to my desk, walking with as much grace as he could muster. A strong smell of cough drops exuded from his breath as he introduced himself, wheezing into a handkerchief before shaking my hand.

After allowing me to talk through Emma's progress in class, he took a sip of the water I had offered, then crossed his legs. 'I came here without Emma because I wanted to speak frankly,' he said. 'She's come on in leaps and bounds since you took over. I'd like to thank you for everything that you've done.'

'Just doing my job,' I replied, knowing that my time with his daughter had gone way beyond that.

'It's meant a lot to me,' Mr Hetherington said, his eyes dropping to the handkerchief held tightly in his hand. 'I don't know if you're aware but my wife, Isobel, walked out on us a couple of years ago.' He delivered the words with a subtle shake of the head. 'It's really affected Emma. She's had . . . problems. The doctors said it's down to anxiety. I've tried to keep an eye on her, make sure everything's OK.'

I gave him a sympathetic nod. The head teacher, Mrs Pritchard, had filled me in on the extent of Emma's problems, after I made it my business to get to know her better.

Bob raised his tissue to his mouth and choked another cough. 'Mind you,' he said, clearing his throat, 'I don't think Emma's going to set the art world on fire. She's got her heart set on business studies when she leaves school. But I know you've been talking after class and she comes and sees you during her lunch hour.'

I felt a sharp surge of panic as he brought up our private meetings. The last couple of weeks, Emma had been bringing in her mother's old sketches, trying to emulate her style. I had put up with Emma's meanderings in order to draw her in, but it seemed she had let her father in on our little get-togethers. Was he going to tell me off? Report me to the head? I had done nothing wrong – at least, not yet. I tightened my grip on the pen I was holding. If Mr Hetherington wanted to make a big deal out of this it could make my life very difficult. I'd put a lot of time in, getting Emma on side, promising myself that she would be worth all the effort, but now I was not so sure.

'Anyway,' he continued, talking over the babble of students out in the hall. 'I just wanted to say thank you. I hope she's not making a nuisance of herself. She's been a lot less . . . troubled since you began teaching her class.' He sighed. His exhalation ended in a jagged cough. 'I've been a bit lost, raising two girls on my own, and my health isn't very good, as you can see.' Pulling the paper handkerchief back from his pocket, he wiped his mouth before continuing. 'Tizzy – that's Emma's sister – doesn't live with us any more, and Emma spends most nights in her room. Knowing she has someone to talk to has helped ease my mind.'

I nodded, my pulse rate returning to normal. Emma had told me about her sister and how a falling out of some sort had driven her away. She really was a lost, lonely little soul – which was good, because now she was starting to rely on me. I knew from my own sister's ditherings about boys how the female mind worked and had learned how to read the signs from an early age. The first person to arrive and the last to leave the class, Emma just couldn't keep away. The fact she had told her father about our blossoming friendship displayed just how naive she was.

'I'm glad she's feeling better,' I said. 'I'm always on hand to offer counsel, but Emma's a bright girl and she's growing stronger in her own right. I'm sure she'll be very successful in whatever field she chooses.' I wanted to ask more about her background but thought it better to rein my interest in. It was only a matter of time before Emma became attracted to me. Coaxing young women into my bed came as no trouble at all. Trust took longer; I had to build enough that she would lie for me if the shit hit the fan.

'Thank you, that's good to hear,' Mr Hetherington said.

'She often talks about her mother,' I said, giving in to the temptation to find out more. 'I think it's why she's so interested in art. A shared interest helps her feel closer to her.' I sighed for effect, lacing my fingers together. 'She used to blame herself for her disappearance, but we've talked it through. She's feeling a lot better about things now.'

Mr Hetherington shifted in his chair. 'Isobel was very unhappy. She'd been talking about leaving for months.' His eyes glazed over as he recalled a memory. 'She wasn't cut out for motherhood. Didn't bond with her children like most mothers do. Then she started drinking and, well . . . let's just say the girls are better off without her.' He rose, offering his hand once again. It was warm and clammy and I fought the instinct to wipe my palm on the back of my trousers after we shook. No wonder Emma was happy in my company, if this was all she had waiting for her at home. A doddery old man on his last legs in a bungalow in the wilds of East Mersea. I had seen it from a distance, when I followed the bus as it brought her safely home. My previous encounters with fifteen-year-old girls taught me they could be economical with the truth. But Emma was a good girl and had not let me down. She just needed some extra lessons in discretion before I advanced my plans.

CHAPTER TWELVE

EMMA

2017

Tiny needles of rain spiked my face as I waded through the greasy leaves and muddy track to cover the ditch I had just disturbed. I worked on autopilot, dragging the broken branches back into place. My breath ragged from exertion, I worked swiftly as I camouflaged my tracks. The icy wind had permeated my clothes, numbing my fingers and toes. My mind had been hurled into chaos as I tried to comprehend what had happened to Luke. By the time I returned to the house, I had only minutes to spare. But I had not expected to see my husband as I opened the back door.

I don't know which of us was more surprised. The shock on Alex's face told me how much of a state I must have looked with my mud-stained clothes and wild hair. He wasted no time in firing questions at me.

'Where have you been? I've been trying to ring you. Why didn't you take your phone?'

I glanced at my mobile on the kitchen table. In my rush to get going, I had left it there. I stammered as I tried to formulate an answer. 'S . . . sorry. I went for a ride on the quad . . . I fell off.'

'Look at your hands,' he said, turning my shaking palms over. 'They're bleeding. You're filthy.'

'I hit a bump in the road, fell into a ditch,' I said, relieved that my bleeding blisters were consistent with a fall.

Alex smoothed back my hair, his frown growing as he focused on my face. 'Sweetheart, you look spaced out. You could be concussed. Do you want me to take you to A&E?'

'No,' I said, gripping the back of the chair for support and immediately regretting it as my blisters cried out in protest. I was still trying to come to terms with what I had found. 'I . . . I've got to collect Jamie from nursery.'

'He's in his bedroom. I picked him up on the way home,' Alex said, still eyeing me up and down. 'I finished early and went to the shop, thought we could all go to McDonald's as a treat. Then Theresa said you'd left early and I tried to ring. I was worried when you didn't answer your phone.'

'Sorry,' I said, still feeling dazed. My face felt tight from where the mud had dried in. I pulled the scarf from my hair, which was wild and matted from the wind. 'I need a shower. I won't be long.'

'I bought you something to eat,' he said, pointing to the microwave. 'I've left it on a plate. Want me to heat it up? I can make you something healthier if you prefer.'

'I've already eaten,' I replied flatly. 'We can talk about the move when I'm changed. Why don't you show me the places you've got your eye on in Leeds.'

His face brightened, and I congratulated myself on coming up with a diversion. I peeped in on Jamie as I passed his room. His hair damp, he was already bathed and changed into his pyjamas and was sitting on his bed, cosied up to his army of teddies as he flicked through his new

Fireman Sam book. He could be an introverted little soul, enjoying his own company when the mood took him. I gently withdrew from the door, having caught sight of myself in the hall mirror: my appearance would only concern him.

I stood in the shower, streams of mud and blood swirling down the plughole. The palms of my hands felt as if they were on fire as I shampooed my matted hair. I ran the soap over the curves of my body, feeling a familiar anxiety bloom. I had gained weight; I could feel it. Despite my efforts it had crept on just the same. I mentally recounted the calories I had consumed this week against the exercise I had done to burn them. Not enough. It was never enough. I dropped the soap, cursing myself for allowing my self-deprecation to creep in. How self-centred could I be? At a time like this I should be focusing on my family and how I was going to get us out of the mess I had created. I would tell Alex I had been having one last look at the land. I should have been pleased: by the look of the ditch, it had been undisturbed for some time. It was over.

A familiar voice rose in my mind. *Who are you kidding? You should have dug deeper. It will never be over, you know that.* I swirled conditioner in my hair, my thoughts wrapping themselves around me like a python, squeezing harder until I felt like I was going to pop. Tilting my face towards the shower head, I stood under its hot spikes, feeling out of breath as I tried to comprehend just what had happened that day. Luke was dead. Dead and gone. But if by some miracle he had survived . . . my heart lunged at the thought. He couldn't be alive. Besides, he was not the sort of person who would just leave me alone. We were too far off the beaten track for anyone to have wandered on to our land and found him accidentally – even if they had, there were still the No Trespassing signs my father had erected dotting the adjoining field to warn them away. But I *had* dug deep enough to find him. So where was he? Was it really possible that he could be out there, waiting to return? I almost jumped out of my skin as Alex banged on the bathroom door.

'You all right in there?' His voice was husky, laced with concern.

I took a breath before responding, turning off the tap and grabbing my towelling robe from the hook on the wall. 'I'm fine, be with you in a minute.' I sighed, wishing my husband did not feel the need to monitor every minute of my day.

'I've made you a sweet tea. Don't let it go cold.'

Working a comb through my hair, I slipped on a pair of old jeans, wrapping a chunky knitted cardigan around me. I had barely eaten today and my stomach grumbled at the deprivation. I welcomed the discomfort. It made me feel grounded, alive.

Heat pumped from our Aga in the kitchen and I grudgingly sipped my tea, imagining the sugar-laden liquid infiltrating my system. Full-fat cow's milk and at least three spoonfuls of sugar, judging by the taste. I wanted to pull a face but Alex was watching me closely, his expression wrinkled with concern. For once it was justified. My old habits were rearing their head and I felt helpless to stop them.

'I think I know what's wrong with you,' he said, his fingers tracing the deep grooves of our thick oak kitchen table.

My heart skipped a beat. Had he followed me? Had I been talking in my sleep? Another emotion rose up inside me. Relief. I had carried this burden for such a long time. Perhaps Alex would be able to help. The fact that he was still sitting here with me spoke volumes. Maybe I should have trusted him with the truth all along.

'It's your mother, isn't it? You're worried that if we move she won't be able to find you.' He reached across the table, his fingers touching mine. His wedding ring glinted beneath the last rays of dying sun flooding through our kitchen window. I felt my bottom lip tremble. Tears welled in my eyes as he spoke, and he gave my hand a squeeze, the warmth of his flesh providing fleeting comfort.

'I was thinking,' he said, 'we could hire a private detective to try to find her. There's Jamie to consider too. He has another grandma. Wouldn't it be nice if he could get to know her?'

My lips parted as I exhaled a sharp breath of disbelief. It was the last thing I had expected him to say. The realisation that I was alone with my problems hit me all over again. Alone to deal with the consequences of what I had done. Disappointment fuelled my bitterness. Weren't we in enough of a mess, without bringing my mother into the mix as well? I took a deep breath as I tried to explain. 'I was devastated after Mum left. Sure, she wasn't perfect. She was temperamental and moody, and when she drank, she took her anger out on me. I still loved her though.' I lowered my head as two fat tears rolled down my face and plopped on to my cardigan. Withdrawing my hand, I dabbed my eyes with a tissue. 'But I don't want to see her again. I couldn't bear the pain of her walking out a second time. I won't do that to Jamie.'

'I can't begin to imagine what that must have been like,' Alex said. As he spoke, I could see my own hurt reflected in his eyes. They were dark, like mine, but open and honest. How could I ever tell him about Luke, knowing how easily he felt my pain?

Rain tapped on the window like tiny frozen arrows, the light from the sun now withdrawn. I stood up and switched on the lamp. I wanted to go to Jamie. I needed to cuddle him, to inhale his little-boy smell. But Alex was looking as lost as any child and I felt a sudden rush of love.

Standing behind him, I squeezed his shoulder. 'I know you're trying to fix things, and that's what I love about you. But Jamie has a lovely grandmother already. Let's just leave it at that, eh?'

The mention of his mother brought a brief smile to Alex's face. 'Mum can't wait for us to move. But I don't want to bring our problems with us. If it's not Isobel holding you back, then what is it?'

Silence fell, ominous and awful as I wrestled with my thoughts. This was my opportunity. I had to tell him now or not at all. I felt my throat tighten as I shrugged a response. 'Nothing. I just wanted to say goodbye to the land. It's been a while since I rode the quad bike and I was a bit out of practice. I won't be doing it again.' Despite my reassuring words, I could feel a layer of dread building up inside me. How much longer could I keep this all in?

'Are you sure you're OK?' Alex said, looking up at me as he touched my hand.

I wasn't.

'Yes,' I murmured, forcing the corners of my mouth into a tight smile. 'Are you going to show me these houses?'

CHAPTER THIRTEEN

EMMA

2017

As I crept through the hall, I listened for the slightest sounds. Creaking through the rafters, the rising wind made itself known, rattling our wooden front door. I wondered what it would be like to live in the new house that my husband had shown me. The weather would definitely be more forgiving. Our current home was often battered by the rising storms, standing desolate on the landscape. Tightening my dressing gown, I padded into our kitchen and turned on the lamp. It was more intimate than the accusing glare of the light bulb overhead. Just a slice, I told myself, knowing deep down that it was my compulsion that drove me, rather than the need for cake.

My eating disorder was my constant companion, surfacing in times of stress. A chubby child, I was berated by my mother, which in turn led me to find comfort in food. Now I gained control via the starving–bingeing–purging cycle whenever stress re-emerged. It was difficult to label what I carried inside me. Bulimia seemed too small a word to cover it.

I glided soundlessly to the fridge and opened the door. I had tried hard to fight the temptation as I starved myself that day. I had told myself that the pain of an empty stomach was good. It made me feel in control. But now the inviting glow of the open refrigerator was drawing me in, my eyes roaming the food I had bought earlier that day. Starchy cakes, sugary soft drinks and, stashed in the vegetable compartment, bars of chocolate, all ready for my midnight feast. No matter what happened today, I knew they would be waiting for me when I got home. 'Just one slice,' I whispered to myself, my mouth watering at the sight of the fresh cream cake. As if saying it aloud would make any difference. I was not in control any more. After starving myself, it was inevitable that a binge would follow. There was no point in trying to fight it. Closing the fridge with my elbow, I rested the large Black Forest gateau on the kitchen counter. My eyes widened, excitement growing at the thought of the sticky substance that was about to line my throat. I didn't need a plate. There was no need for such pleasantries now. Taking a knife from the drawer, I cut myself a generous slab. The first mouthful was bliss. I closed my eyes as I succumbed to the delicious cherry sauce and cream melting in my mouth. I swallowed it back, quickly needing more. Texture was important for when it made its second showing. Dense sponge always made a satisfying thud as it hit the toilet bowl. I licked my fingers, my gaze on the cake. I barely paused for breath as I cut a larger wedge. Moaning in satisfaction, I turned the second slice over in my mouth. By the third slice, I didn't bother with the knife, gorging with my fingers until it was all gone. I needed more. The McDonald's Alex had brought home, the chocolate bars, I kept going until I'd polished off the lot. I couldn't have stopped even if I'd wanted to. I washed it all down with a fizzy drink, belching to make room in my expanding stomach. At last, when it was all gone, I folded up the empty containers ready for the recycling bin. But my movements were sluggish and painful. I leaned across the counter, my head hung low. The skin around my stomach felt like a tight leather ball, over-inflated and ready to pop. A voice screamed in my head. *What have you done, you disgusting pig? Look at the state of you, how can your husband bear to sleep in the same bed?* I lurched to the toilet, ready for my next move. It would be painful because I had not done it in some time and no longer had the automatic reflex action, which meant I would have to shove my fingers down my throat. I knew how pathetic I must have looked but, strangely, I took comfort in the presence of my old friend. Bulimia felt like something I could rely on even in the toughest of times.

I did not hear Alex come into the kitchen and I certainly didn't hear him standing outside the toilet door. After cleaning up the kitchen counter, I had chosen to use the bathroom next to the utility room at the back as it was the furthest away from our bedroom. It was only when I had flushed the toilet for the third time that I heard him shuffle outside the door. My heart plummeted. Despite my old trick of leaving the sink taps running, he would have heard me throw up. Once, twice, three times: I had kept going until every crumb of food had been expelled.

'Emma?' he whispered, tapping his nails on the door.

I wiped the dribble trailing down my chin. 'What?' My voice was scratchy and brittle as I clung on to the toilet bowl, my hair hanging limply around my face. The familiar emotions of self-loathing and disgust returned. I felt exhausted, as if I had been through nine rounds in the boxing ring.

'Sweetheart, can you come out? I need to talk to you.' Alex spoke softly, his words gentle and reassuring.

'I'm on the loo. I'll be out in a second.' Guilt swept over me as I checked my watch. It was 1 a.m. We both had the next day off, but he must have been tired from work. What was he doing behind that door? Rolling his eyes? Wishing he'd never met me? Nobody asked him to follow me around. But the thought was fleeting. He monitored me because he cared. Now I needed to placate him, find a plausible excuse for my nocturnal behaviour. Would he believe me if I told him I was feeling ill? I doubted it. I had been lying about my illness since we met. It wasn't that I was a stick insect. I fell in and out of bouts of starvation and binged in between. Months could pass before suspicion was aroused. But Alex was wise to my ways. He knew the trigger points. I opened our bathroom window to dissolve the acrid smell of undigested food. It flew back on its hinges as the full force of the growing storm took hold. I sucked in a breath, relieved to see the glass remain intact. As I brushed my teeth, I welcomed the biting chill, avoiding my reflection in the bathroom cabinet mirror. Another wave of shame overtook me. *Look at yourself, you little pig.* My eyes flicked up and I saw my hair bunched in my mother's fist as she forced me to stare at my reflection. My eleven-year-old face stared back at me, tear-streaked and puffy as she squeezed my plump cheeks with her spare hand. Chocolate stained my mouth: evidence of my sinful act. Her breath stinking of spirits, Mother's slurred voice rebounded against the walls, her fingers squeezing harder as she called me a greedy pig. She had been right. Pink faced and sweating, I appeared just that.

Dropping my toothbrush in the sink, I recoiled from the memory. I rúbbed my cheeks, still feeling the haunting imprint of her fingers on my skin. But as I glanced back up, I saw another image, a reflection from outside. Luke, bathed in moonlight as he looked through our bathroom window, his face as gaunt and pale as when I buried him. I wanted to scream but the sound locked in my throat, and I felt like I was going to choke. I was paralysed with fear. Suddenly my breath returned. 'No!' I yelled, spinning around to the open window. My heart beat wildly as I turned to face him, the corpse of the man I had killed. I blinked to clear my vision, standing rooted to the spot. There was nothing there. Nothing but the light of the moon shining and the howl of the wind filtering through rain-whipped trees. I jumped as Alex rapped on the door, his voice more insistent this time.

'Emma, are you OK? Open up.'

'I'm coming,' I said firmly, taking a deep breath and pulling the bathroom window shut. Cruel in their bidding, my thoughts were quick to respond. *There's nobody there, you stupid fat cow.* It tailed off into laughter that I had heard far too many times before. Hands shaking, I fumbled with the door handle. I had to do something. I couldn't go on like this. It was time to tell my husband the truth.

CHAPTER FOURTEEN
LUKE

2002

She stood at the doorway, cautiously waiting for my acknowledgement. I kept my gaze on my desk as I pretended not to see her. Let her wait a few more seconds, show her who was in charge. The bell to signal the end of the school day had long since rung, and my after-school session with Emma had been approved by the head. She had noticed the positive change in Emma and kept a watchful eye on us both, but I had used the guise of extra tuition in order to gain her approval for our time alone.

Emma had looked hurt when I'd sent her away at lunchtime. I could not afford to have any suspicion cast.

With her shirt tails hanging out and her shoelaces undone, her appearance would have earned her a telling off from the head. But to me, she looked positively delicious. Her long dark hair was worn in a loose bun on top of her head, curly spirals falling loose at the side of her face. How someone could look both sultry and innocent at the same time was beyond me. I watched entranced as she played with the tips of her hair, sliding them through her parted lips. It was an odd habit sure to gain my attention. 'Come in,' I said, a ghost of a smile on my lips.

Closing the door behind her, she took a seat at a front-row desk, following my instructions to take out her latest work, as I took a seat beside her. It was all for show; art was the last thing on my mind. I kept up the pretence for a while, talking about the movement and flow of her latest piece. I had brought my class an unusual challenge: a finch that jumped from perch to perch in his cage. The task was to draw it while in mid-movement, and Emma had not done a bad job of capturing a likeness of the energetic bird. But she seemed to sense that she had not been summoned here for extra lessons. How could she not? The attraction between us was undeniable; I was slowly winning her round. I took a fresh sheet of paper and placed my palm over her hand, guiding the charcoal pencil over the page. I heard her breath quicken from the warmth of my touch.

'Sir?' she said, when I drew my hand away. 'Why did you send me away at lunchtime? Have I done something wrong?' She turned her dark liquid eyes upon me, and I was painfully aware of her leg touching mine.

I glanced up at the closed door, ensuring we were alone. 'No, of course not,' I said, smiling. 'It's just that I don't want people getting the wrong idea. People are beginning to notice how much time we're spending together. I am your teacher, after all.' In truth, the only person who had passed comment was her father. He may have expressed gratitude, but I had to remain on my guard.

'But we've not done anything wrong,' she said, heat rising from her collarbones to her cheeks. 'Talking to you, it's really helped. I've been eating better, looking after myself more. Where's the harm in that?'

I risked another glance at the door before resting my hand on her back. For a few blissful seconds I left it there, teasingly pausing over the outline of her bra strap. She smelled like a punnet of fresh peaches on a warm summer's day. I was intoxicated by her presence and the promise of what was to come. Rising from my chair, I allowed my knuckles to graze her cheekbone, unable to resist the temptation of touching her one more time.

'I value our friendship too,' I said. 'But we have to be careful. Not everyone would understand. I need your discretion if we're to spend time together.'

I watched as the angst visibly lifted from her face, forming into an expression of hope. She nodded. 'I won't say a word to anyone, I promise.'

'I thought you'd say that,' I said, walking to my desk drawer. 'Which is why I've bought you a phone. It's a pay as you go, nothing fancy. We can text each other whenever you want,' I licked the dryness from my lips. My heart thumped hard at the implications of my words. *Steady. Take your time*, I reminded myself, urging caution at every corner. 'I'd like you to put your name down to borrow the class camera for a week too. You know, for art projects, homework, things like that.' I quickly followed up. 'I'll book the darkroom, develop the photos myself.'

I handed her the phone, watching as she quickly stowed it away in her bag. 'Be careful,' I said. 'Don't show it to anyone, not even your dad. Don't text names. I'll know who you are. If you get caught with it then say it belongs to one of your friends.'

Emma nodded. 'I'll delete any texts that I send.'

I leaned against my desk and crossed my ankles. 'I was thinking, we should keep our meet-ups outside of the classroom. There's nothing wrong with bumping into each other if we're out for a walk, is there?'

'I hang out in Castle Park at the weekends around two. Sometimes I bring a picnic,' Emma said, packing away her pictures before swinging her schoolbag over her shoulder. 'I'll wait to hear from you then?'

I delivered a curt nod, before walking to the door and showing her out. She'd had enough encouragement for one day. The art of seduction was as much about the lead-up as the execution.

CHAPTER FIFTEEN
EMMA

2002

My heart throbbed a warm beat as I lay on my bed, trying to make sense of the day. *He's just being nice*, I chastised myself, wishing my pulse would slow the heck down. My emotions seemed too big, too overwhelming, yet the prospect of having more than a platonic friendship with my teacher frightened me silly.

I licked my lips, my mouth dry. Thoughts of Mr Priestwood crept further into my consciousness, and I blushed as I imagined him pressing his lips on to mine. In the background, Dad's television blared from the living room, and I wished I could mute the sound.

I took a slow, calming breath, telling myself not to become carried away. Just having someone to open up to about my problems had really lightened my load. But lately, silly daydreams were stealing my focus. I imagined us getting married, me taking his name. Emma Priestwood. Mrs Priestwood. Mrs E. Priestwood. I wrote it over and over, improving the curve and flow of the words. I thought of our children, whom

I would call Daisy and Teddy, and our home in the country, complete with a picket fence.

I sighed, running my fingers through my hair. It was a silly day-dream. I wasn't a child any more, and Mr Priestwood was no schoolboy. My stomach tied up in knots as I imagined us together. Men like him weren't content with holding hands and a peck on the cheek. He'd want a real kiss, with tongues and everything, perhaps even more. I pressed my palms against my cheeks to stem the rising heat. How my classmates would laugh if they knew of my naivety. Marsha Beckett had had sex with two boys by now, and I was pretty sure I was the only girl in class not to have had a proper kiss. That's if you didn't count the fumble with Samuel Clarke at the back of the bike shed last year, when he tried to suck off my face. It had felt like a slug attaching itself to my mouth, all wet and gross, and I had pushed him away. But something told me that Mr Priestwood wouldn't be like that. He was a man. He would know exactly what to do.

I could talk to Tizzy, isn't that what sisters were for? But I hardly saw her these days. Besides, she wouldn't understand. No, she wouldn't *approve*. My frown burrowed deep as I tried to make sense of it all. I'd gotten myself into a right state. *A something and nothing*, my mother would call it, but it felt very real to me. I wanted my friendship with Mr Priestwood to continue, but I saw how he'd looked at me, felt a tingle when he brushed his fingers against my cheek. He didn't treat any of the other girls that way, and they were all desperate for his undivided attention. And now the phone . . . I didn't know what to make of it. What did he want me to text? Sometimes he could be so forward, but other times he was distant and aloof. As for meeting him in Colchester, what was that all about? I had come to rely on his friendship, but did he really want something more?

A muffled cheer erupted from the football game on the television as my father's favourite team scored a goal. Dad thought Mr Priestwood had been a positive influence. If only he knew. I closed my eyes, allowing my teacher's image to seize my thoughts. A soft sigh escaped my lips. He was only seven or eight years older than me. It was no biggy. People fell in love every single day. It wasn't as if he was going to pounce on me, make me do anything I didn't want to. I slid my phone from under my pillow, the one he had given me in class. Giddy with nervous excitement, I began to type a text.

> Thanks for lessons today, really enjoyed them. See you soon.

My finger hovered over the 'X' as I deliberated whether or not to send a kiss. A mischievous smile crept on to my face. He was my teacher. Would I dare? Then I thought how his eyes had sought out mine, and how his hand had rested on my back. Biting my bottom lip, I added 'X' to the text and pressed Send. I pushed my face into my pillow, squealing a giggle of disbelief. I had done it. I had texted my teacher, and even added a cheeky kiss! Another giggle erupted in my chest, silenced by my pillow as it found escape. I stared at the phone as I awaited a reply, feeling out of my depth. As fun as it was to flirt, I knew that when it came to Mr Priestwood, I wasn't really ready for anything more.

CHAPTER SIXTEEN
ALEX

2017

'You're frightening me,' I said, feeling a rising sense of dread. With shaky legs, Emma joined me in the living room, her eyes darting from left to right. I had confronted her about her bulimia in the past, but I had never seen her as tightly wound as this. 'I'm not angry with you, sweetheart, just worried. We can sort this out.'

'You wouldn't say that if you knew.' Her words were jittery as she spoke. I laid my hands on her shoulders, stiffening as she flinched. I should have been paying closer attention. I frowned as I accepted my portion of the blame. 'Is it because we're selling the house? Because, well' – I sighed, trying to form the right words – 'we don't have to if it's upsetting you. How about we come to a compromise? We could get a bigger mortgage, hang on to this place too.'

'I don't want to keep the house,' she said, tear-stained and weary. 'I want to get as far away from here as possible.'

Her eyes left mine, and my head ached from trying to decipher her thoughts. 'Here, you're freezing.' Pulling a throw from our leather sofa, I wrapped it around her. I eyed my vaporiser on the coffee table. My nicotine habit was proving difficult to kick, now more than ever. Emma curled up beside me on the sofa, but she was still unable to meet my eyes. The house creaked around us from the force of the wind. The place felt cursed, and I could not wait to leave it. I wanted to challenge Emma about her eating disorder but at the same time I did not want to make her any more upset than she already was. 'What were you shouting about in the toilet? Have you had a scare? Is it your health? I know you're keeping something from me.'

'It's not my health. It's something I've done.' Taking a deep breath, her eyes met mine. 'If I tell you, our family can't go back to what it was before. In fact, it's better if you don't know. We can carry on with what we're doing, sell the house, and start a new life. I'll pull myself together in time.'

My heart pounded with ferocity. I was the head of the household. There was no question of turning my back on my family. 'Just tell me. I want to know.'

'Please.' Her eyes were soft and imploring. 'You don't need the burden of it.'

I took her hands in mine. They felt cold and unyielding, her fingers clenched as if she were holding her secret tightly in the palms of her hands. Slowly I opened her fingers, lacing them between mine. 'We took vows on our wedding day, remember? For better or for worse. Whatever it is, it can't be that bad.' I gave a soft chuckle of reassurance. 'No one died.'

Her eyes widened as she drew back her hands.

Her horrified expression made my mouth drop open of its own accord. 'Fucking hell, Emma, will you just tell me what it is?'

Composing herself, she glanced around the room. With Jamie fast asleep in his bedroom, there was only us there.

'All right, calm down. I'll tell you, but I can only do it once. I'll answer your questions at the end, so no interruptions either. Can you do that?'

I nodded dumbly.

'The thing is,' she went on, 'someone *did* die, and I'm the one responsible.'

I could barely take it in. Emma was no murderer . . . was she?

CHAPTER SEVENTEEN
ALEX

2017

'I was fifteen when it started,' Emma said, her eyes downcast as she revealed the truth. 'Mum had been gone two years and Dad had completely withdrawn into himself. Theresa . . . you know Dad used to call her Tizzy, because she was all over the place. She'd start a job and then a week later she'd quit. She'd go sofa surfing and we wouldn't see her for days. But after Mum left, everything changed. Dad gave her the deposit for a flat in Colchester. She got a job in the estate agent's and held it down. It was good for her, standing on her own two feet. But that's not how I saw it at the time. I really looked up to my big sister, I used to follow her everywhere she went. When she cut off all ties . . . I felt abandoned by everyone, adrift and unloved.'

I tried to imagine Emma at fifteen. I'd seen family photos of a sullen young girl, but Emma tended to keep them hidden away. It was as if she didn't want her past to taint our family. But it was too late for that now. I squeezed her hand, not wanting to interrupt her flow.

'I met Luke when he took over from the old art teacher.' She kept her eyes fixed on the woollen throw, unable to meet my gaze. 'In time, we got talking. He told me he'd had a difficult childhood. I felt he was the only one who understood. All the girls fancied him, but he didn't seem interested in anyone else but me.' Emma picked at the throw, dislodging loose fibres as she recalled the memory. 'We grew close. I felt special, having a proper grown-up man pay attention to me.' Briefly she met my gaze. 'He gave me a mobile phone so we could text each other in private. Then we started meeting up in Castle Park. It was nice, having a friend. He was nothing like the boys my age, all they wanted was a quick grope at the back of the bike shed. Luke valued my opinion, listened to what I had to say.'

'But things got heavy?' I said, feeling guilty for making her recall what was obviously a painful memory.

Emma responded with two sharp nods of the head. 'He was so intense. He said he was risking everything for me. In my mind it was romantic. What I didn't realise was that he was grooming me all along.'

Emma clenched the throw in her hands, wrapping it tightly around her. I opened my mouth to speak. As she took a breath to continue, I swallowed back my words, allowing her to carry on.

'He became really controlling after that, emotionally manipulating me into complying with his needs. He gave me the school camera and asked me to take some pictures that he could develop in his darkroom. I took photos of outdoor scenes for my art project. It's only now that I realise what the camera was for. I was so naive.'

'Bastard,' I said, my frustration growing. At least now I could understand why she had been so guarded when she'd met me. People had let her down for most of her life.

Her eyes glazed, Emma continued as if she hadn't heard me. 'Our relationship progressed and he pressured me for more. Well . . . I . . . I was just a mixed-up kid. Deep down, I knew I wasn't ready for it, but I would have done anything for him. It was only a matter of time before people found out.'

Her eyes flicked to mine and back to her hands as she struggled to find the words. It pained me to think of her being with someone else. 'So you ended it?' I said, trying to help her out.

'Yes,' Emma nodded. 'It was for the best. But as time went on, I'd see him wherever I went. Flowers came to the house, but there was never any card. I switched off the mobile phone and the house phone would ring all hours of the night and day. He began to scare me. It was like he was two different people. In the daytime, he'd refuse to acknowledge what he had done.' Still pulling at the threads, she sighed. 'I avoided him as much as I could. Weird things started happening, and it felt like someone had been in my room. Eventually I told the police, but Luke blamed me, saying that *I* wouldn't leave *him* alone. I tried talking to his sister, Noelle, but she wouldn't listen. Then he texted, saying he'd kill himself if I ever left him. I told him to leave me alone, that I didn't want to see him any more.'

I looked at my wife and it was as if I barely knew her. So much of her past had been a mystery to me, but I was beginning to understand. Her eating disorder had descended because she knew no other way of dealing with the chaos that enveloped her. She must have felt very much alone. 'Why was he so obsessed? You didn't sleep together . . . did you?'

A flush rose to her cheeks. 'We were never intimate, even though he tried. Things died down the following school year, but he was always in the background. When I was accepted into university I left home. I told my dad not to give my forwarding address to anybody.'

'And that was the end of it?' I asked, hoping she had meant a metaphorical killing earlier on, instead of a physical one.

'It was . . . until Dad's funeral. Do you remember how upset I was to get that bunch of sunflowers?'

I frowned as I recalled that day. I remembered commenting on the odd choice of funeral flower when Emma had burst into tears.

'He must have read the announcement in the paper,' she said. 'I knew it was him because they had significance. I used to draw them all the time. It was my favourite flower. I say *was*. I've come to hate them now.'

'It could have been your mum,' I said, but was immediately silenced by a darkened glare.

'It wasn't her.'

A gust of cool air blasted from the nearby window, and I shuddered as it ran down my back. Sitting in my T-shirt and boxers, I felt every inch of the cold, but I didn't want to move until Emma had finished telling me the truth. 'Why didn't you tell me?' I interrupted her again.

'You had to cope with so much when you took me on: my bulimia, Dad dying, and you were so upset when it looked like we'd never have a baby. I couldn't put you through any more.'

'But Emma . . .' I said, placing my hand on hers.

Slowly she withdrew, curling her hands beneath the throw, disappearing into herself. 'Please. Just let me finish.'

I met her gaze, sending her a nod to tell her it was OK.

'I blamed myself after things soured with Luke. Going to university was a form of escape. You made me believe in myself. Even after a year of me knocking you back, you still stuck by me.'

'I was crazy about you,' I said, the embers of old memories stirring inside. 'I still am.'

'I don't deserve you. I never have.' She sat with her shoulders hunched, her eyes wet with tears. It was as if the memory was bringing her back to the old days, to the person she once was.

'Dad's funeral was reported in the papers. It must have played on his mind, seeing a photo of me at his grave. A few weeks after that, he turned up here.'

I raised my eyebrows. 'Here? In our home?'

Emma slowly nodded. 'I was out by the oak tree – I'd decided to do some digging, make a start on the vegetable patch I'd been talking about. He must have followed me there from the house. We argued. He said that I had messed up his head, that it had been terrible for him after I left. The next thing I knew he was lunging at me, grabbing me by the throat. I couldn't breathe. It was muddy and he . . . he slipped. I thought he was going to kill me . . . I had no choice.' The whites of Emma's eyes flashed in the darkness, filling me with dread. She took a breath, panting now. 'I hit him with my shovel. I only wanted to keep him down long enough for me to get away. He fell backwards, into the ditch. That's when everything went quiet.' Emma's voice shuddered. 'At first I thought he was playing a trick. Then I saw the blood seeping from his head. I . . . I didn't mean to kill him. It wasn't my fault.' Her words were cut short as a sob caught in her throat. Her chin trembling, she took another faltering breath. 'I covered him up, told myself I'd go back the next day and sort things out. But after a couple of days I'd buried it so deep in my mind it was as if it had never happened at all.'

I shook my head. I had so many questions. Had she checked for a pulse? Was she sure he was dead? Did anyone else know? But she carried on talking, her voice barely a whisper.

'I wanted to tell you. But not long after, I found out I was pregnant. How could I have a baby in prison? We'd been so desperate for a child. I couldn't do that to you or our baby. So I put the past behind me and tried to forget about him.'

'Until now,' I said. All the pieces of the puzzle were coming together.

She nodded, wiping her tears with the back of her sleeve. 'I wanted to leave. But I was scared that the new owners would dig up the land and it would all come out. What good would come of that? He's dead. I hate myself for it but there's nothing I can do.'

As she drew her eyes away, I couldn't help but wonder if I really knew my wife at all.

CHAPTER EIGHTEEN
EMMA

2017

I finally drew the courage to look my husband in the eye. At least he was still here. I had half expected him to turn on his heels and walk away. He had paled in the aftermath of my confession. He was not the only one. I felt as if I had aged ten years. I stared at my lap, feeling empty inside, just as I had done after Jamie was born. But this time it was not a baby that had been expelled from my womb. It was a piece of myself that I had given away. Alex made no attempt to take my hands as he had done earlier. It was why I had withdrawn them when I began to speak. I could not bear to feel him pull away from me, as I knew he would. Alex was a good man with a strong moral code. He would struggle with what I'd done. But there was more than just me to take into consideration. My gaze fell on our family portrait above me on the wall. To the left, another framed picture, taken hours after Jamie was born. Our little king was now asleep in his bed, oblivious of our torment. I took a deep breath, trying to control the tremor in my body. I had thought it would make me feel better to offload the secret that I had carried for so long. It was as close as I could come to telling the truth. Judging by the look of disbelief on Alex's face, it was just as well I'd been circumspect. I don't think he could have taken any more. I sat in silence as he rubbed his face, washing away the ugliness of what I had shared. I looked at my watch. It was only half past one, but it felt as if a lifetime had passed before he spoke again.

He mumbled something about it all making sense, citing my reluctance to sell. As we talked it through, I was forced to recall how I felt after what I had done. He was searching in the darkness for a hint of regret, a flicker of empathy for the man I had killed. I had to provide him with the answers he wanted to hear.

'I was devastated by Luke's death. I blamed myself for everything. But it was a burden I didn't feel equipped to handle. When I came home, I forced the memory aside. That night I showered and scrubbed my body until it glowed pink. I remember you asking me if I'd been allergic to my moisturiser because my skin looked so sore.'

'I don't remember,' Alex said, with a slow shake of the head.

'Don't you see? That's what happens. Your mind casts away memories of no value.'

But my words were unconvincing. Being forgetful was one thing. Rewriting history was another. I was a murderer and I had learned to live with it. But I could not lose my family. I needed my husband to stay strong to keep me on the right path. As Alex stared into space unblinkingly, I wondered if it was too late.

I reached across the void and touched his hand. I had not realised I was crying until my tears tapped the throw which was wrapped around me. 'What do we do now?'

He cleared his throat. 'I need to go there.' His voice was cold and robotic. 'I need to see it for myself.'

Thoughts of returning to that place with my husband were too much to bear. 'See this,' I whispered. Opening the palm of my right hand I exposed the blisters on my skin. 'I didn't fall off the quad. I went back there, to the grave. I dug it up. He's . . .' I took a deep breath to calm my beating heart. 'He's gone.'

'Really?' He shook his head in disbelief. 'That can't be right,' he said, firmer this time. 'We have to figure out what the hell is going on. It can't have just disappeared.'

'He *is* gone,' I said, my fingers gripping my husband's wrist and making him wince. Fingers that had been down my throat less than an hour before. Had he realised what I had been doing? I relaxed my grip, grateful he wanted to help me out of this horrific mess. 'There's not a single sign that he was there. No clothes, no shoes, it's like it never happened.'

My words seemed to trigger a reaction as Alex opened his mouth to speak. He paused.

This was not the time for holding back.

'What?' I said, desperate to read his mind.

He turned away from me, facing the coffee table. His words came, slow and measured. 'Are you sure? Did it really happen?' His head hung low, his shoulders hunched, and he raised both hands to run his fingers through his hair.

A prickle of annoyance rose up inside me. 'What's that supposed to mean?'

'I don't know. I'm just looking for answers. It's so hard to believe.' Still, he avoided my gaze. Why wouldn't he look at me? Was he so ashamed of what I had become? Did he think that having an eating disorder made me a compulsive liar? My annoyance grew like a hot flame inside me, and I felt a stress rash break out on my chest. I had just poured my heart out and this was the best he could come up with? 'You think I made this up?' I spat the words. 'You think I'm mad, is that it?'

I did not notice his clenched fists until he banged on the coffee table, making me squeak as I jumped.

'For God's sake,' he roared, 'it's easier to accept that you're spinning some wild tale than believing you've murdered someone on our land. How am I meant to take that in? You won't even step on a spider! What are you not telling me?' He swivelled to face me, placing his hands on my arms and giving them a shake. 'Tell me! What really happened down there that day?' His eyes were filled with fury. I had broken him – driven him too far. This was a side of Alex I had not seen before. He could be overprotective sometimes, but he had never frightened me. His eyes widened as he registered the shock on my face, and he suddenly dropped his hands. As if someone had clicked their fingers, the fury faded. 'I . . . I'm sorry. It's a lot to take in.'

I wanted to tell him that I understood, that sometimes the basest instinct in our human nature takes control. When all you have is threatened, it's only natural to lash out. But my tongue felt like it was glued to the roof of my mouth, and I was concerned that his outburst may have awoken our sleeping son. I wrapped my arms around myself, feeling suddenly cold. Seconds passed, and all I could hear was the swish of the wind blowing down the fireplace, whose flames had been extinguished hours ago. With sharp snapping teeth, the chilling breeze invaded my territory. When I spoke, my voice no longer sounded like my own. 'If you want to leave me then I understand. You didn't sign up for this when you married me.' I doubled over, unable to keep my emotions in check any longer. I clenched my hands, biting into my fist as tears overtook me. It was a horrible, strange habit I had picked up as a child, a way to silence my tears as I cried myself to sleep at night.

At last, Alex wrapped his arms around my shoulders and drew me to him. 'It's over. It's going to be all right.' But his voice was brittle. He sounded scared, which frightened me even more. He gently took my hand from my mouth, my saliva forming in long threads as it stretched from my lips to my knuckles. I blinked away my tears, seeing the indentations of my teeth in my skin. Sometimes I really didn't know my own strength.

'Tomorrow,' he said, 'I'll go there alone.'

I could not speak. Could I bear to imagine my husband uncovering the corpse of the man I had killed? Just by telling him, I had made him an accessory to murder, risking our son being left parentless, unprotected.

Alex held me close, both of us stiff with fear. 'Are you *sure* he was dead?' he whispered. 'Maybe he was just unconscious. Perhaps he got up and walked away. Have you thought about that?'

How could I tell my husband that I would not let myself consider it because the thought of Luke being alive was more frightening than the thought of having killed him. If I told him that, then maybe he would wonder just how much of an accident it had been.

It was the first of many theories that he brought up. I barely remember getting into bed. I can only recall lying in the darkness, my head on my pillow as I stared up at the low beams of our ceiling. Silent tears streamed down the sides of my face, collecting in the shells of my ears. Finally, we both fell asleep.

I woke sometime later, the light of the moon strong and clear as the storm silenced at last. On the side of the bed was Alex, sitting with his head in his hands. Later I would wonder if I had imagined it. Perhaps I had imagined it all.

CHAPTER NINETEEN
LUKE

2002

I checked my texts one last time before I deleted them. It was a shame, really; a lot of pleasure could be gained from poring over Emma's coquettish meanderings. Emma. The very thought of her drove a delicious shiver down my spine. It was what was *unsaid* that turned me on; I loved to read between the lines. It had been frustrating to go at such a slow pace, given the urgency of my needs. Soon autumn would turn to winter and I wanted to be with Emma before we broke up for Christmas and the new year. I had become an expert by now, having played the game from an early age. I tended to go for the introverted types, the ones most grateful for my attention. Nightclubs were easy pickings. You just singled out the drunk girl that was separated from her friends. The one who was too young to be there, who looked a little lost in the crowd. But Emma was different. She had real feelings for me. I wondered what love felt like. I'd heard people talk about it, but I'd never experienced it for myself.

The classroom was a whole other level and I was ready for the challenge. The risks were monumental, but that's what made it so good. I knew the payoff would be worthwhile. I smiled as I scrolled through the texts. I kept mine to a minimum, to keep her on her toes.

Luke: Hey you, don't forget to finish your homework for Monday.
Emma: Already done! Looking forward to showing you. x
Emma: Miss you. Wish I had art every day, even weekends x
Luke: Miss you too. More than you know x
Emma: Really? x
Emma: I've no idea why you'd miss me! ;-)
Luke: Who wouldn't miss your gorgeous face?
Emma: You're not so bad yourself ;-)
Luke: I'm going to Colchester Castle this weekend. Maybe see you there about 1. x
Emma: Great! I'll bring my sketchpad. x

I arrived a few minutes late, so as not to appear too keen. She seemed as excited as a puppy when she saw me strolling towards her on the grass. Her grin lit up her face like a hundred-watt bulb, and all too late she tried to tone it down, though not before I caught something else in her expression – caution. The thought of getting closer to me both frightened and excited her. It was written all over her face. A shaft of golden sunlight beamed down on her spot and I noticed the two plastic cups and bottle of fizzy pop spread out on the picnic blanket amongst crisps, chocolate and shop-bought sandwiches. On her knees was her sketchpad, with some pencils next to her feet. She must have positioned herself carefully that day, out of the public eye as much as possible yet still visible enough for me to spot her when I arrived.

'Fancy seeing you here,' I said, squinting as I reached her.

'Sir,' she replied. 'Would you like to join me? There's plenty for two.' She eagerly cleared a space for me to sit down. I sat on the blanket, briefly closing my eyes as I tilted my face to the sun.

'What a gorgeous day,' I said, enjoying the fading warmth of the sun on my skin. The weather was predicted to turn, and a cold snap was forecast for the days ahead. Such was life. Everything bright and dazzling turned cold and grey in the end. I opened my eyes to find Emma's lingering gaze on my tight black T-shirt, which displayed my toned physique. Biting back my smile, I picked up the half-finished drawing of a nearby tree. It was mediocre at best but I looked at it as if it were a masterpiece.

'That's really good,' I said, complimenting the shading that outlined the scene.

Emma shrugged off my admiration. My eyes glided over her figure as she talked about composition and lighting and I pretended to sound interested. Her short-sleeved dress was slightly baggy for her frame, as if she had lost weight since she bought it. I liked that it wasn't too revealing. It would feel like I was unwrapping a present when I finally got her undressed. A couple more meetings like this and she would be mine. 'So why aren't you out with your friends on a lovely day like this?' I said, when she finally stopped talking about her picture.

'I could ask you the same question,' she replied, filling our disposable cups with fizzy drinks.

'I asked first,' I said. 'Fallen out with your boyfriend, have you?'

'I don't have a boyfriend, or friends for that matter. But I've told you that already,' she said sadly.

I nodded. 'You did, but I can't quite believe it. Someone as stunning as you, sitting here all alone. Do you play hard to get? Is that it?'

'Stunning? Don't make me laugh.' Her gaze fell to her cup. 'As for friends . . . I don't like hanging out in groups of people. I never know what to say. And boys . . . I don't know how to relate to them.' She gave me a sideways glance. 'You're the only person I can talk to. I don't want to be with anyone else.'

Silence descended and I watched the rise and fall of her chest as her inner turmoil quickened her breath.

I glanced around the park to ensure we weren't being watched before leaning in towards her face. 'If only you could see yourself as I do. You *are* beautiful, and one day you'll realise that.' My gaze roamed over her face, so young and trusting. Her lips parted as she leaned in towards me. 'I really want to kiss you right now,' I murmured under my breath.

'Then do,' she replied softly.

It took all of my willpower to draw back. Once, I might have given in to temptation there and then. But that was reckless and I knew from experience that now was not the time. 'I shouldn't have come. I'm sorry,' I said, rising from the ground. 'Your phone, can I see it?'

Hurt and disbelief creased her features as she stared up at me. 'I don't understand, have I said something wrong?'

'Your phone, have you got it?' I said curtly, ignoring her distress.

Silently she slid it from her handbag and passed it over. I checked the texts; there were only a few. She had been getting rid of them just as she'd said she would. 'This was a mistake,' I said, deleting the final texts. 'I can't trust myself around you, Emma. You're just a schoolgirl. It's selfish of me to expect anything more.'

She clambered from the blanket, an ungainly teenager again. Tears spiked her eyes, her face flushed with emotion. 'Please, sir, don't go.'

My features were torn but inside I celebrated a minor victory. 'I thought I could do this, but I can't. I want to have a deeper relationship, but I don't think you're ready for such a commitment.' I sighed, running my fingers through my hair as I scanned the park for onlookers. 'You're better off dating someone your own age – taking things slowly.' I handed her back her phone. 'I'll always be here as your friend. But I don't think we should be alone together.' I exhaled at her expression, which was aghast. 'You can't see it, can you? You're so unaware of your own sexuality. That's what makes all this so wrong.'

'I'm nearly sixteen,' she said, swiping away the tears now trailing down her face. 'I don't want to lose you.'

My voice softened at her obvious distress. 'And if you were a few years older and I weren't your teacher then maybe we could be together. But I have to let you go. I'm sorry, Emma. I'm only thinking of you.' Placing my arms around her, I gave her a parting hug. Deep down, I knew this was far from the end. Squeezing tightly, I allowed her to feel a teasing sense of security for a few seconds as she was encompassed in my strong grip. Then, dropping my arms, I turned and walked away.

CHAPTER TWENTY
EMMA

2002

Mug of tea in one hand, I glanced out through the crack in my bedroom door to check Dad wasn't about before making the call. The house still smelled of the fish supper we had shared an hour before. I had appreciated his efforts at talking to me, but our conversation soon ran dry. I knew I would have more luck with my sister, but it was proving difficult to get her to pick up. I felt so torn. I had vowed to keep things to myself, but I could not bear feeling this way any more.

I exhaled in relief as my sister answered the phone, reeling off the name of the estate agency where she worked.

'Tizzy, it's me . . . Emma,' I said, interrupting her flow.

A slight hesitation followed before she responded. 'Sis? Are you OK?'

'Yes,' I said, feeling foolish. 'I miss you. I was just wondering when you're coming home for a visit. I called at your flat when I was in Colchester, but there was nobody home.'

'Oh, did you? I'm in the middle of training and having to work weekends to make up for a staff shortfall too. Is there something wrong?'

'Oh nothing, just boy trouble,' I said, tears blurring my vision as I spoke. A physical ache rose in my chest and seemed to lodge in my throat. I hadn't realised just how much I missed Theresa until now.

'Ooh, has my little sister got a boyfriend?' she said, her voice teasing. 'Who is it? Timmy what's-his-name? Or that George boy you told me about?'

I winced. These were boys from the youth club in Mersea that I had spoken about over a year ago. 'No, it's someone in my class.' I wrapped my right hand around my mug, taking comfort from its warmth against my skin. Inhaling a deep breath, I tried to verbalise my problems. 'How do you know if a guy likes you? I mean, *really* likes you? It's so confusing. One minute they say they fancy me, but the next they're being totally vile.'

Theresa chuckled. 'Oh, you're gonna get that at your age, I'm afraid. Boys take a lot longer to mature than girls. What's he doing, blowing spitballs at you? Stealing your books?'

I stared unblinkingly into the distance, barely registering the view. 'Not really,' I said, wishing I could eloquently portray my feelings in words. I wanted to ask what it was like to have sex, and how it would feel the first time. I was clueless but not entirely stupid. I knew that's what Mr Priestwood had meant when he said he couldn't meet me alone. The concept of such intimacy frightened me, but the thoughts of losing him scared me more. I had heard girls in the school locker room talking about the ultimatums their boyfriends had given them: go all the way or get dumped. When I asked if they had given in, they had replied with a laugh and said 'of course'. I knew that locker room talk could be wildly exaggerated, but it made me wonder if it were my fault just the same. It was *me* that was slow on the uptake. Perhaps now it was time to enter the modern world.

'I've been getting on really well in art classes,' I said tentatively, as I tried to broach my relationship with Luke. 'Mr Priestwood's really nice. Sometimes I see him in Colchester too.'

'You're better than me,' Theresa laughed. 'I was bunking off school at your age – teachers were the last people I wanted to see.' A hint of caution entered her voice. 'Are you sure it's OK to be with him outside of class?'

I opened my mouth to speak, but was interrupted by Theresa's urgent whispers.

'Oh crap, my boss has just come in and he's funny about me using the phone. I'll pop over to see you as soon as I get some time off. Is that OK?'

'Sure,' I said, attempting to inject some cheer into my voice. The last thing I wanted was to be responsible for my sister getting into trouble at work. 'And, Sis, I'm fine, don't worry about me,' I said, wiping away my silent tears. 'I know what I have to do.'

CHAPTER TWENTY-ONE
EMMA

2017

I was awoken by the sound of giggling coming from the living room. I had not expected to hear it, given what had happened the night before. That was the beauty of having a child: life went on no matter what. Despite this, my heart was so heavy I could barely slip my feet into my fluffy slippers as I trudged out of my bedroom in my dressing gown. I took a soothing breath before pushing open the door of the living room. I had this. I was still in control. I thought about the breakfast my husband would insist I eat. The last thing I wanted today was food. As I stood with my fingers on the door handle, my stomach churned with the burden of my recent confession. I could not believe that I had finally done it. I listened to my husband and child laughing on the other side of the door, and smiled in spite of myself. I struggled to remember the happy days in my childhood, but then I had been hard to get through to. I did not want that for my son. He needed to know that there were people around him who loved him. People who would never leave him or let him down. I would have to pull myself together. Alex was still here, despite everything I had told him.

As I opened the living-room door, the sight of my son instantly warmed my heart. Sundays were family time and Alex and Jamie had already begun. They were sitting at the coffee table, their heads side by side as they played the pie game. A timer buzzed as a plastic hand laden with squirty cream threatened to splat the loser and a loud clacking noise sounded as each frantically pressed the button to guide the hand towards the other. I watched Alex ease off pressing the button, putting himself in range. Jamie was almost in convulsions he was laughing so hard. As the cream hit Alex's unshaven face, he looked so ridiculous I could not help but join in. Alex licked the cream and rubbed the remainder away with a tea towel. He caught my eye and a flicker of regret passed between us. It was still there, the horror of what I had done. But he was doing everything he could to make our son's life as normal as possible and I loved him for it.

'It's your turn, Mummy,' Jamie squeaked, and I knelt down to join him, squeezing my eyes tightly shut. By the time we had finished our game we had all experienced the joy of a cream pie. But I was the only one who had not tasted it. My memory of my encounter with the cream cake the night before made me feel sick. This time I kept my lips tightly closed as I wiped the offending substance away. It was all about maintaining self-control. Right now, that was something I needed more than ever.

Speaking in front of Jamie was not an option. Instead, we skirted around each other, ignoring the elephant in the room until our son went down for his afternoon nap. I had smothered him in kisses, absorbing his goodness to make up for the lack of my own.

Alex had his back to me when I returned to the living room. It warmed me to listen to my husband on the phone to his mother. We saw Louise for the usual holidays, as well as the anniversary of Alex's father's death. It would be nice to spend more time together when we moved to Leeds. I stood in the doorway, listening in to his call. There was no way my husband would reveal what I'd told him to his seventy-year-old mother on the telephone. The very thought was ridiculous. Just what would he say? *Guess what, Mum, my wife murdered her stalker and now his body's disappeared, but we're all fine, we had a game of pie face this morning.* No, if he were to confide in Louise it would be face-to-face. I felt my heart tighten. I had to convince him we needed to keep this to ourselves.

He hung up the phone and I came into the living room, trying to appear relaxed as I tidied up Jamie's toys. But we both knew it was all an act. I watched him as he stood poking some life into our open fire.

'Bollocks,' he said, pushing the blackened poker back into its holder. 'I've just remembered. I'm supposed to go to Leeds tomorrow to meet the team.' He stared unblinkingly into the flames. 'I can't just leave you.'

I hated seeing him like this, unable to meet my gaze. I stood beside him. I wondered if he had forgotten his earlier invitation to join him in Leeds or if he wanted to go alone. His muscles tensed as I placed my hand on his back. 'Of course you can,' I said, my hand resting on his woollen jumper. 'How else are we ever going to leave this place? Besides, it wouldn't do to call off sick when you're due to meet everyone.'

'I don't know,' he said, the flames reflected in his brooding eyes.

I rested my hand on his back, loath to take it away. I needed the contact. I needed a hug – but if he couldn't meet my eye then genuine intimacy would be a long way off. 'I'll be fine,' I said, softening my voice in an effort to show remorse. 'Theresa's meant to be coming over for a drink. I'll persuade her to stay the night.' But my words were hollow because I doubted she would. Theresa hated our house more than Alex did.

'Are you sure you'll be OK?' Alex said, turning to face me.

'All the stuff we discussed. It's in the past. That's where I want to keep it. Please. Let's not go back there any more. Can we just move forward? Act like it never happened?'

Alex appeared uneasy in his skin, his tension mirrored by the hiss and crackle of the fire. It smelled of damp bark and moss, like the land in which I had buried Luke. 'I want to drive up there,' he said.

I frowned. 'I thought you were going on the train?'

'No, I mean to where it happened. I want to see it for myself.'

I swallowed, my mouth dry. The room seemed to darken around me as I spoke. 'I'm not going back there. Just trust me. It's not a good idea.'

He lowered his voice to a level that only I could hear. 'What if the new owners dig it up? What if they find something?'

'They won't.' My face paled as I recalled Luke's half-opened eyes. The sweat trickling down my forehead as I shovelled dirt into his face. 'There's no trace. No shoes, not even a scrap of material. It's as if he'd never been there at all.'

'I know you don't want to talk about it, but he could have crawled out. It happens. In the old days some people had bells in their coffins, so they wouldn't be buried alive.' He slid his vaporiser from his pocket and inhaled, a modern-day Sherlock Holmes. The smell of fake tobacco rose up to greet me. My stomach lurched, not from the fumes but from the idea that Luke could still be alive. I thought about the apparition in the mirror. The newspaper on my car window.

'It's possible. I didn't take his pulse, and from what I remember, it was a very shallow grave. But he would have made himself known by now.'

'I wouldn't be so sure,' Alex said. 'If someone tried to kill me I'd get as far away as possible.'

Above me, the ceiling timbers creaked as another gust of wind rattled its frame. I knew what he was thinking. How can you *accidentally* cave someone's head in with a shovel?

CHAPTER TWENTY-TWO
EMMA

2017

Screeching on my windscreen, my car wipers grated on my senses. The inclement weather matched my mood: grey and overcast with a threat of worse to come. I checked my rear-view mirror for the hundredth time. Behind me was a view of the Strood. It was not uncommon to have traffic behind me as commuters made their way to work. But today was different. Today it felt as if the world was out to get me. After a restless night, I had come to one conclusion. Luke was alive. He had to be. That night I hadn't imagined his reflection in the mirror. He was coming for me, and he was looking for revenge. I'd had four years of peace. Four years of believing I had nothing to fear. But was I afraid of him, or the secrets he held? I glanced at my son on the back seat, my precious cargo. Dressed in his dungarees, he waved his Buzz Lightyear toy in one hand and Woody in the other, deep in his imaginary world. His thick blond hair needed cutting, but I couldn't bear to lose his curls.

I felt my resolve strengthen. Luke would not divide my family. My right eye twitched, a side effect of my frayed nerves.

'Are we here yet, Mummy?' Jamie said, scattering my thoughts. I blinked, barely able to remember the journey. Triggering the indicator, I steered my Beetle through the cement bollards of the car park. 'Almost,' I said, my eyes crinkling in the mirror as I gave him a reassuring smile. I had no qualms about leaving him in nursery school. It was run with the highest level of security; Theresa, Alex and I were the only people authorised to take Jamie out and I was able to log on to the CCTV at any time of the day to check how Jamie was doing. Alex had laughed at my paranoia but, unlike him, I had a good understanding of the evil in the world. I pulled into the parking space, checking left and right. Karma was coming to collect but it would not have my son.

After dropping Jamie off I drove to the shop and gave it a quick tidy up before turning the sign on the door to Open. Both Alex and I had vowed not to allow what had happened to interfere with our work. For Alex, his job was our gateway to a better life, while focusing on my business helped me stay sane. But today was not proving so easy. Feeling exposed and vulnerable, I tried to avoid the glare of high-street shoppers. I never realised how many men passed our doors, and I stiffened as each one took pause. The rain didn't help, with all the umbrellas, hats and pulled-up collars disguising faces. I could barely concentrate. Were they stopping to light a cigarette or seeing if I was still inside? Drawing up the nursery's app on my phone, I checked my son's progress for the fifth time. As the day wore on, my guilt intermingled with fear, making me start every time the telephone rang.

Our latest appointment arrived and I told myself to get a grip. A wedding-dress fitting was not the time for a glum demeanour. The bride-to-be was called Jennifer Delaney and Theresa was trying to find a way to alter her dress so that it would accommodate her growing bump. It had fitted perfectly six months ago, but her pregnancy had understandably changed her shape and now panic had set in. It was her own fault, given she had missed many of her fittings, but it did not stop me wanting to help.

'It's going to be a disaster,' she said, her pretty face in tears. 'Look at the size of me. I'm a whale.' Unfortunately for Jennifer, she was accompanied by her mother, who always seemed more than happy to put the boot in at every opportunity.

'You should have thought about that before getting yourself pregnant.' Her mother's features were sharp, accentuated by her voice.

I winced, instantly recognising her condescending tone, which brought with it a memory of the past. Theresa and I exchanged a glance as unspoken words passed between us. She had noticed the similarity to Mum too. Smiling at Jennifer, I guided her gently to one side while Theresa sat her mother down and distracted her by discussing the big day.

'I'm going to look a fool,' Jennifer wept, and I handed her a tissue. Hankies were always in plentiful supply.

I gave her a reassuring smile, the sort that I'd had cause to use many times before. 'Now listen to me, we have some beautiful high-waisted gowns that will fit like a dream.' I directed her to a mirror. 'See how gorgeous you are? You're going to look stunning, I promise.'

'Do you think so?' She sniffed, her tears testing her mascara.

'Your bump is so neat. You should have seen me when I was pregnant with my son. I was like a hippo. C'mon, follow me.' I felt a warm glow at the memory of my pregnancy and how thrilled Alex had been.

An hour later and Jennifer had left beaming because she had found a new dress to complement her shape. Even her mother was happy. Glowing with satisfaction, I barely noticed Theresa take a delivery at the door.

'Look at this,' Theresa said, sniffing the considerable bouquet. 'How lovely, although the silly sod forgot to write a card. Are you all right?' she asked, slowly approaching me. 'You've gone very pale.'

'I'm fine,' I said, taking the bouquet from her grasp. The sudden smell of sunflowers filtered up my nostrils, making my stomach churn.

It was taking me back to a place I did not want to go. Bringing the flowers out to the back, I dumped them in the sink. Alex *was* an old romantic, but after last night, sunflowers – any flowers, come to that – were the last thing he would have sent me.

'How do you know these are for me?' I turned to Theresa, who was standing right behind me, a curious look on her face.

'The delivery driver said. Why, what's wrong?'

'Nothing,' I said, my voice high-pitched from the effort to camouflage my emotions. 'I'm just curious. I don't think these are from Alex.'

Theresa raised an eyebrow. 'Ooh, lucky you. Perhaps it's a client.' She turned away, oblivious to my problems. Closing my eyes, I inhaled a calming breath. My sister had obviously forgotten about the relevance of the sunflowers. Their faces glowered at me, dark and gaping as if ready to swallow me whole. I ran the tap and plunged them into a vase, because I couldn't bear to bin them, despite everything. Was Luke sending me a warning? My pulse quickened as I thought about what might come.

In the distance, the dull ring of the telephone brought me back to reality. I strode towards it, grasping the old-fashioned Victorian receiver and placing it to my ear. 'Hello?' I said, holding my breath, awaiting a response. But there was nothing. Nothing but the heavy sense of dread rising in my chest. Then I heard it: a soft breath on the other side. A sudden wave of fear swept over me. 'Hello? Can I help you?' I almost choked on the words.

'No answer?' Theresa said, standing behind me. 'That's the third one we've had today.'

'Really?' I said, grateful my back was to her as I hung up the phone. Goosebumps prickled my flesh. I knew that it had begun.

CHAPTER TWENTY-THREE

ALEX

2017

I stood at my office window, absorbing the skyline. From the top of the high-rise building, the view over Leeds was stunning. The company had spared no expense in setting up the new branch of the business. I could not wait to get stuck in: dealing with million-pound properties brought generous commission, bringing me one step closer to our dream life. I inhaled deeply through my nostrils. The air felt better up here. I had my own personal secretary, a pleasant young twenty-something blonde by the name of Alice. Everyone had been welcoming, even seeming relieved to have a new manager take the helm. But at the back of my mind was Emma and the awfulness of what she said she had done. I was still struggling to comprehend it. The uncharacteristic act of violence that she had confessed to consumed my thoughts. I thought of my mother, with her soft permed hair, her homemade scones and jam. She was such a gentle soul; this would break her heart. I drove my hands through my hair, lost in thought as I tried to work it out. This wasn't a novel or a movie. We were talking about murder. Real-life murder. Carried out by Emma, who had taught Jamie how to feed bees sugar water when they were tired from their flight. Emma, who cried at the end of every Disney movie she had watched. How could she be capable of killing someone? And had he deserved such a fate? How could Emma – *my* Emma – kill someone, even if what she'd said was true? It was a question I had asked myself numerous times in the last few hours, and I was no nearer to finding an answer.

I closed the door on these thoughts. My focus had to be on my job for now. I rested my hands on the back of my leather swivel chair, staring at my glass-topped desk: it was equipped with all the mod cons, including a new Apple Mac, a far cry from the old PC I had been working on in Essex. Having grown up in Leeds and started off in the real-estate business here, I felt at home and knew many of the staff already.

I stiffened as my intercom buzzed, unaccustomed as I was to the alien sound. The soft, sweet voice of my secretary spoke. I could get used to this.

'Roger James to see you,' she said, and I smiled at the luxury of having my visitors announced.

'Thank you, Alice. Could you bring us through two coffees when you have a minute?' I said, remembering Roger's fondness for caffeine.

'Of course,' she said. 'I'll be right with you.'

'Alex, mate, good to see you!' At six foot one with a confident swagger, Roger was a man with enviable taste in suits. I made a mental note to ask him about his tailor now that I had come up in the world. He gave me a hearty handshake. We had known each other since back in the day – I'd been no stranger to bunking off school with him and his twin brother Jimmy.

Within minutes we were reminiscing about old times and what we were both up to now. I steered the conversation away from Emma, trying to focus on work.

‘So you don’t mind me being your boss then?’ I smiled, feeling my shoulders relax. Being in Leeds and chatting to friends was just the tonic I needed.

‘I’m made up,’ Roger said. ‘Besides, anyone’s an improvement on Hopkins.’

‘Thanks,’ I laughed, knowing he did not mean it the way it sounded.

‘Seriously,’ he said, flashing me a smile. ‘We have to call him *Mister* Hopkins. What a ponce. He’s only been in the game a few years.’

I grinned in response. ‘Not like us fresh-faced uni graduates hammering in our For Sale signs, then.’

‘Yup. And as for your secretary – you can thank Hopkins for her. Talk about perks of the job.’

I savoured my coffee as I sipped, the smell of freshly ground beans invigorating my senses. ‘I’m an old married man,’ I joked. ‘I don’t have the energy for that sort of carry-on any more.’

‘So that’s why you got rid of the whiskers? Too many grey hairs creeping in?’

Feeling the absence of my facial hair, I rubbed my bare jaw. ‘There might have been one or two. What can I say? All down to the pressures of work.’

Finishing his coffee, Roger threw me an envious glance. ‘Who would have thought it, us two ending up in the same office with you on that side of the desk. Fair play to you – maybe if I’d put in a few extra hours I would have made more of myself.’

For all Roger and I went back, I didn’t rush to tell him about the fact that I was Mr Second Choice, having applied but failed to get the job the first time round. I was pretty sure that if it weren’t for Theresa, I wouldn’t be sitting there at all. Despite her impending divorce from Charles, my boss in Colchester, she was still able to pull a few strings. Still, that was something Roger didn’t need to know. I would prove myself and make the team a huge success. I sank my coffee, filled with enthusiasm for what lay ahead. 'I've seen your sales figures, Rog, you're doing just fine. As long as you're happy to be working for me . . .'

'Like I said, goes without saying,' Roger said, placing his empty cup back on my desk.

Our meeting was interrupted as Alice announced my predecessor was on his way in.

As our office door opened, Roger straightened, fixing his tie. He nodded sweetly at the man entering before giving me a knowing look. Hopkins had short-clipped grey hair and was in reasonable shape. I guessed him to be in his late forties, and had heard on the grapevine he was an ex-army man. He carried an air of authority as he approached. Straightening my shoulders, I held in my stomach as he reached his hand to shake mine.

'So you're my replacement. Congratulations. I'm sure you'll get on better here than I did. This lot can't wait to see the back of me, can you, Roger?' He narrowed his eyes at my friend as he took his leave.

Roger coughed, giving him a sour smile. 'Of course not. But it's about time I got back to work. These properties won't sell themselves.'

'Who knows, maybe you'll sell the big one this month. You might be able to buy yourself a decent car instead of that pile of shit you're driving around.'

I winced. Roger's wife got through money at a frightening rate, and his lack of a decent motor was a tender subject. I made a mental note that as soon as Hopkins left, I would make it my business to get Roger a company car.

As the door closed, Hopkins turned to face me. 'I hear you can't wait to get stuck in.'

I smiled. There was no point in getting mardy with my predecessor if he was leaving soon. 'Yeah. I'm looking forward to working in Leeds again.' It was true. It was a vibrant and welcoming city, and my heart remained firmly in my home town.

'You're a native aren't you? What took you down to Essex?' Hands in pockets, Hopkins walked to the window, his gaze firmly on the streets below.

'The missus,' I said. 'But I've managed to persuade her Leeds is the best place to be. I'm looking forward to heading up the new team.'

'Oh, that reminds me, I've got a message for you,' Hopkins said, interrupted by the insistent strain of Queen's 'We are the Champions' ringtone playing in his pocket. He frowned as he silenced the phone call. 'Looks like I'm in demand. IT will sort you out with some passwords for the new system. Enjoy reacquainting yourself with the sights of Leeds.'

'I will,' I said, in an effort to be polite. 'You said you had a message?'

He raised a palm in the air as he made his way out. 'Oh yeah, I almost forgot. I've got the number of a potential client who insists that he'll only deal with you.'

'Me?' I said, frowning. 'I've not even started yet.'

'I guess word's gotten around. He said you and him go way back.' Hopkins rummaged in his inside suit pocket and pulled out a slip of notepaper. 'I tried to poach him, but he insisted he'd only speak to you.'

I raised an eyebrow at his shamelessness, curious as to the identity of my mystery client.

'You can't blame me for trying.' Flashing me a smile, Hopkins handed me a folded slip of paper. 'His name's Luke Priestwood. Ring any bells?'

CHAPTER TWENTY-FOUR
LUKE

2002

Morrissey sang a haunting melody from my car stereo system. The more someone ignored him, the closer he got. It was my favourite track from the playlist I had compiled. I loved nothing more than creeping into Emma's thoughts. Had she battled with her conscience? Such a good, caring girl, lying to her father and sneaking out of her room. Had the thoughts of our secret meeting kept her awake at night? It was convenient, Emma living in such an isolated spot in the countryside. Far from the glare of CCTV and with her nearest neighbour a mile away, I could pretty much get up to anything I wanted. I was no stranger to subterfuge.

You couldn't exactly call my new Ford Fiesta a passion wagon. The most exciting thing about it was the tinted windows I had insisted upon when it was ordered from the dealership. Sean Talbot, my friend and fellow teacher, called it the granny cruiser. It was all right for him to laugh; he owned a sportier motor far superior to mine. That's what happens when your mum pays for your car. You end up with something solid and sensible. Still, for as long as she was willing to throw money at me, I was prepared to take it. I smiled as I reread the texts on my phone, glad to be making some progress at last.

Emma: About the other day, I meant what I said. Text me. Xxx
Emma: Is it something I've done? Have I upset you? If so, I'm sorry. Xxx
Emma: Need to talk. Xxx
Luke: Sorry, didn't mean to upset you. That's the last thing I want. ☹
Emma: Can't stop thinking about you. Please call. Xxx
Luke: I only want what's best for you. Xxx
Emma: I'm almost 16. A grown woman. Please. Can we meet? Xxx
Emma: I'm free tonight. Are you about? Xxx
Emma: Please. Xxx
Luke: East Road on the junction of Ivy Lane at 9 tonight. Be discreet. X
Emma: I will. See you then xxx

I checked my watch. Five to nine. My car was tucked in behind the high ditch that afforded the neighbouring house some privacy. Not that I wanted to be peering in through their windows. Tonight was about discretion. The last thing I wanted was to draw attention to myself. Still, I couldn't help but feel a surge of anticipation as the flicker of the light on Emma's bicycle blinked in the distance. I knew she would be feeling it too. After tucking her bike away next to the hedge, she hopped into the passenger seat beside me. Her face was flushed from the exertion of pedalling, and she pushed the hood of her jacket down from her face.

'I'm boiling,' she panted, smiling in a sweaty apology. 'But I thought it best to wear a hood so I wouldn't be seen.' Plucking open the buttons of her blue coat, she revealed a knee-length tweed skirt with thick black tights and a black V-neck top underneath. I had to physically force my eyes away from her body, though she seemed oblivious to the stirrings she had caused. She looked at me in earnest as she shrugged off her coat, rolled it up and pushed it into the footwell. Her top gaped open as she leaned forward, and I almost had to sit on my hands not to jump her there and then. Talk about a body meant for sin. Hers was positively iniquitous.

'Phone,' I said eventually, reaching out my hand. She handed it over without question, used to this part of our routine. After deleting the last text, I handed it back to her. 'You wanted to talk?' I said, diverting my gaze through the window as my trousers began to feel a bit too tight.

Emma reached for me without a moment's hesitation and touched me on the arm. 'I've been thinking about what you said. I want to be with you. Properly.'

'I don't know,' I said. 'It could land us both in a lot of trouble. Can I rely on you to keep it a secret?'

'Yes, sir.' Emma nodded enthusiastically, brushing an errant strand of wavy black hair from across her face.

I responded with a laugh. 'I think we're beyond you calling me sir, don't you? I'm Luke, unless we're in school.'

Emma nodded, her fingers clasped tightly around her knees. 'I'll do whatever you ask. You're the only person I trust. I'd never let you down.'

Despite her mild perspiration, she smelled sweet. I turned on the air con, giving us both a chance to cool down. Finally, I met her gaze. 'I never wanted any of this,' I lied, 'but sometimes you can't help who you fall for.'

I almost felt sorry for her, the way all her emotions were laid bare. It was as if she had been waiting her whole life for someone to tell her they loved her. She reached over and threw her arms around me, excitement bubbling to the surface in her words. 'I feel the same way. You can trust me, you know that. I won't tell a soul.'

I pulled away, attempting a look of concern. 'Are you sure? Really sure you're ready for a serious relationship?'

'Yes,' she whispered, her long dark lashes inches from mine. 'But I hardly know anything about you. I'd like to find out more.'

'And you will,' I said. Another lie. Leaning in, I gently kissed her, introducing my tongue. Slowly we parted; her eyes flickered over my face and I knew she was looking for any signs of me getting cold feet. There was no chance of that happening. Not now we had taken it this far. 'You'd better get home, before it gets too late,' I said, keeping her hanging on a few seconds more.

'Can we meet again?' she said, bending over to reach for her coat on the floor.

I helped her pick it up, brushing my hand against her legs.

'Soon. But remember what I said. We've got to be discreet if we're going to make this work. Don't let me down.'

'You can count on me,' she breathed, boldly leaning over to kiss me one more time before making her way into the night. I smiled. Everything had gone as planned. It had been worth the wait, and I had something even better in store.

CHAPTER TWENTY-FIVE
ALEX

2017

I stood rooted to the spot as Hopkins left. All I could hear was my breathing, the sounds of city life muffled by the thick panels of glass behind me. Luke Priestwood. My stomach clenched as I made the connection. Luke Priestwood was the name of Emma's stalker. I had wheedled it out of her the night she confessed. Only this morning I had called a private detective to see if I could track him down. Now it appeared that I might not need to.

But that was too crazy, wasn't it? It couldn't be the same person. How could he have found me? And why say we were old friends? There couldn't be that many Luke Priestwoods around, could there? I remembered how she had described him: tall, sandy-brown hair, handsome.

I paced my office, no longer seeing the view as I recalled my wife's account. I pressed my palms on my desk, the surface cool on my skin as I slowly exhaled. 'Calm down. It might be nothing. Just ring the guy and see what he wants,' I whispered to myself. But the truth grasped at my throat like cold fingers of dread. Was he just fucking with me? How did he know I was here? Like a metronome, my thoughts ticked back and forth as I struggled to take it all in. If this were the same Luke Priestwood who had stalked Emma, then I would find out when I called. But what would I say? *So you're the guy my wife tried to kill. What's it like, coming back from the dead?* Standing over my desk phone, I thought about ringing Emma, telling her what I had found. As my fingers hovered over the dial, I thought about the consequences of such a knee-jerk reaction. She was miles away, where I could not help her. Fighting her eating disorder was taking all of her strength. This could tip her over the edge. And there was Jamie to consider. If by some miracle this *was* the same Luke Priestwood then at least he was a safe distance from Emma. I replaced the receiver. Tonight. I would ring him and, if he was willing, arrange to meet him after work. Best case scenario would be that he wanted to clear the air. Worst case scenario? If he tried to call the police now we would just deny everything. Against Emma's wishes, I had visited the alleged burial site, digging a few feet into the disturbed earth. There had been no sign of a body. It had come as no surprise because her story bothered me. There was something about it that did not ring true. If she wouldn't open up, then perhaps her sister would.

I stared out of the window at the view that now seemed drab and grey. The beginnings of a headache wrapped itself around me. There was nothing I could do but call the man and see what he wanted. As my intercom buzzed, I took a deep breath, keeping my tone light as I tried to disguise the dread that I felt inside. After a short exchange, Alice allowed the IT people inside. I watched as they set me up on the system and explained how it all worked. Personnel files, statistics and monthly reports were all at the tips of my fingers. Having command of my own team was something I had worked hard for all of my life. I thought of my family and the future I had planned. I could not lose this now.

CHAPTER TWENTY-SIX
EMMA

2017

'Put the kettle on, will you?' Theresa said, turning the sign on the door to Closed. 'I've got some nice cream buns in the fridge.'

I opened my mouth to say I wasn't hungry but her withering glance silenced my protests as she joined me in the staffroom. I filled the kettle with tap water, using it to give our thirsty plants a drink. Filling it again, I clicked it on and pulled two mugs from the shelves. As I busied myself making our drinks, Theresa's voice washed over me.

'Don't even *try* to tell me you've eaten. I've been listening to your stomach growling all morning. You're not leaving until you've finished that bun.'

If only she knew. Eating was only half the battle. The real struggle lay in keeping it down. I gave her a cramped smile. My sister had a way of telling it like it was.

'Here,' she said, pushing the offending cream bun before me as I sat down with our teas. My brain immediately made the calculations:

308 calories in a Morrison's cream bun plus a cup of tea with sugar and skimmed milk. I rounded it off to 350. I would need to run three and a half miles before I had even taken a bite. Unless I vomited, which would take seconds. It was a no brainer, I thought, knowing my sister would watch me as I ate.

'Look at those dark rings under your eyes. When's the last time you had a decent night's sleep? You look terrible.'

'Thanks,' I laughed, temporarily forgetting my problems. 'Whereas you look sickeningly well.' And she did. I was all too conscious of her forthcoming divorce, but she seemed to be taking it in her stride. 'We should have lunch together more often,' she said with a grin. 'It does wonders for my self-confidence. Now eat up. I can't have my little sister being skinnier than me.'

I wondered if the cake were worth the sacrifice that I would have to make later. My throat was still raw from my last bout of vomiting. It was too soon for another purge. I glanced down at my clothes, remembering the days when I used to secrete food in my pockets. Somehow, I didn't think my vintage winter dress-coat would stand up to hiding a cream bun.

But ten minutes of watching me pick at my food must have been too much for Theresa to bear. Having long since finished her bun, she leaned forward and took both my hands. 'Sis, I know there's more to this than you not eating. What is it? You've not been yourself all day.'

My eyes dropped to the table and I cursed my inability to hide my distress. Normally I was good at concealing things, but on top of my confession to Alex, the flowers and silent phone calls were proving too much. 'It's nothing,' I said, unable to meet her gaze.

'No judgement,' she said, squeezing my hands. It was what she said to me in the early days, when she was helping me through my bulimia. Such expressions of love made me want to cry.

I shrugged, swallowing back the words on my tongue. My bulimia was one thing. How could I tell my sister what I had done?

'I've relapsed . . . only once. I'm trying to keep it under control.' Our oversized wall clock ticked away the seconds, and I took a deep breath, gathering the strength I needed to continue.

'Right, what are we going to do about it?' Theresa jumped straight in, interrupting my flow. 'Do you want me to see if we can get you back in touch with your counsellor? Maybe see the doctor . . .' Her thoughts switched. I could almost see the cogs in her brain. This was how Theresa solved problems, flitting from one thought to another until she came up with the appropriate response. 'Is it the move? Alex's new job? Is everything going too fast?'

I shook my head. 'Hardly. It's taken him years to persuade me to go.' I met her eyes and I knew that she would not give up unless I gave her something to go on. 'The problem's not with Alex. It's me. Sometimes it feels like I'm being watched. The phone calls, the flowers. I'm scared that Luke is back.'

Theresa's lips thinned at the mention of Luke's name. She was one of the few people immune to his charms. It made me value our relationship all the more. So why couldn't I tell her what I had done? Because I knew it was wrong. What I did . . . what I *thought* I'd done, was commit murder. Even if Luke hadn't died, it was what I had intended at the time.

'Has he been in touch?' she said, scrutinising my face for the answer.

I shrugged, knowing how vague I sounded. 'No, not exactly. I was in the bathroom the other night and . . . I know this is going to sound crazy but I thought I saw him through the window. Then there are the silent phone calls and now the flowers . . . I'm feeling so panicky and I don't know what to do.'

'Oh, Sis. Have you told Alex?'

I nodded. 'He wants us to concentrate on moving to Leeds.'

Theresa frowned, her protective streak clearly evident. 'Alex is right. If you see Luke or feel afraid, just call me. I don't want you speaking to him. It's not safe.'

'As long as you promise not to report it to the police.' The very thought made me nervous. They were the last people I wanted involved. 'Promise me, Theresa, no police. It'll only aggravate things and I've got no proof.'

'OK OK,' she said, waving the palms of her hands in mock surrender. 'But you've got to stay in control of your eating. The more you panic, the worse things get. You've too much to lose. Your health, your husband, little Jamie. He needs you. They both do. Please, Emma. Eat something. For their sakes.'

'I'm fully aware of what I stand to lose,' I snapped, her crestfallen expression making me regret my tone. 'I'm sorry,' I said. 'I didn't mean to have a go.'

'Hey, it's me you're talking to,' she said, giving me a kinder smile than I deserved. 'Remember what I was like when I found out Charles was carrying on behind my back? I was in a right state, and you helped me through it. Working here in the shop, it's given me something to focus on. I don't know what I would have done without you.'

I nodded. In the circumstances, it was the least I could have done. Thanks to the prenup, Charles had left her virtually destitute, yet he had been the one in the wrong. I pushed the cream bun in her direction. 'You have this. If I start, I'll never stop. I've got some leftover salad in the fridge, I'll have that instead.'

'I can stay with you, if you like, until Alex gets back?' Theresa's voice was muffled as she took another bite. I envied her ability to eat whatever she wanted without putting on a pound. Not that it would have made a difference to me. I was never happy no matter what size or shape I was.

'I'm OK,' I said, checking the time. 'I just had a bad night. I've got rid of all the junk food in the house. Nothing for me to binge on there.'

But the expression on Theresa's face told me she was not convinced. 'And the face in the window? Aren't you worried about that?'

I was, more than she could ever know. I didn't know which was more frightening, the thought that Luke had been to my home, or the prospect that I was losing my mind.

CHAPTER TWENTY-SEVEN
ALEX

2017

In the former market man's pub, the smell of Theakston's ale carried me back to the days when I sat here with my father. He had brought me here on my eighteenth birthday to proudly buy me my first pint. I didn't much like the taste of it back then, but now that I was a father myself, I had come to understand the importance of the ritual. I could almost feel his presence as I sat amongst the shiny copper fixtures. Situated in Leeds city centre, Whitelock's location gave it an olde worlde feel and a unique charm. I could almost hear my father's voice, telling me to drink up as he set the world to rights. A pang of grief touched my soul. I wished he were here to advise me. But I was the man of the house now and tonight I had to be strong. Perhaps that was why I had texted Luke Priestwood instead of ringing and asked him to meet me here, in a public place. A small part of me hoped my dad would be here in spirit, providing me with some much-needed moral support. Could the person I was meeting be the same man who had terrorised my wife? I had to know. But how on earth was I going to broach the subject? I raised my glass to my lips. Alcohol was a good tongue loosener and, after the week I'd had, I needed a drink or two. Thoughts of Emma floated into my mind and I found myself dialling her number.

'Everything OK? I'm just ringing to say goodnight to Jamie.'

'Oh, I'm sorry, hun, he's fast asleep,' Emma said, her voice light and cheerful. 'He didn't have an afternoon nap so he went down early. I'll tell him you called when he wakes up in the morning. How's things?'

'Great. You should see my new office. It's three times bigger than my old one and has cracking views of the city. I can't wait for you to get here.' I smiled, pressing my hand against my ear to drown out the noise of my fellow drinkers.

'I've started packing some stuff already. Are you out? Sounds like you're in a pub.'

'Just having a few drinks with my new colleagues. They're a good bunch. I won't stay out too long.' We both danced around the elephant in the room. I wanted to ask if anything else had happened to make her worry – and if she had eaten today. But if she hadn't, she was hardly likely to tell me over the phone. I sighed, feeling the distance between us.

'Enjoy yourself, you deserve it. I love you,' she said, and I was just about to respond when my eyes were drawn to the door.

Somehow, I knew the man who had just walked in was Luke Priestwood. Looking from left to right, his eyes scanned the pub as he tried to find me. He was slightly shorter than me, with light-chestnut hair. I found myself sizing him up, assessing his strength. He was sinewy but not as broad as me. I could take him if I had to. I caught his eye, desperate to end my call. It felt wrong, talking to Emma while I was doing this. If he was the person I thought he was then the last thing I wanted was Emma hearing his voice. 'I've got to go, I'll see you tomorrow.'

It was only after I'd hung up that I realised I had forgotten to say I loved her too. There was no time to dwell, though, as he joined me.

'Mr Priestwood, is it?' I said cautiously, bracing myself as I rose from my seat. For all I knew the guy could be ready to pull a knife on me. My muscles tensed. I was ready for him if he tried.

But his expression was not that of someone who wanted to fight. He shuffled nervously before me, dipping his hand into his jacket pocket and pulling out his wallet. 'It is. Can I get you a drink?'

'No, thanks,' I said, pointing to my half-empty pint glass. I felt guilty enough just talking to him, never mind accepting drinks. I eyed him up as he leaned against the old-fashioned wooden bar. He was dressed casually in jeans and a jacket, his shirt pressed. Despite having been neatly folded, my Lacoste shirt still had creases from my overnight bag. I caught myself. Why was I comparing myself to this man? Because I was jealous of his former relationship with my wife? Had there *been* a relationship? From how Emma had described it, she had been easy prey.

A pint was laid in front of me, snapping me out of my thoughts. Luke delivered a half smile. 'I asked the barman for the same again. I figured we might be here for some time.'

I nodded, unable to bring myself to thank the man before me. 'What's this all about?' I said, before his backside had rested on his seat. 'Because you didn't contact me to buy property, did you?'

'No,' Luke sighed. 'It's a long story. One with a sting in the tail.' He sank back a mouthful of his pint. 'I've not come here to make trouble. I've told myself a million times to walk away. But then I heard Emma was moving to Leeds.'

'I don't understand,' I said. I felt my grip tighten around my glass. Our meeting was getting more surreal by the minute. Just what was going on?

'I live in York,' Luke said. 'But sometimes I come to Leeds.'

'Why did you call me? Why don't you get to the point?' I said, my anger simmering beneath the surface. It was difficult to equate the man before me with the person Emma had described. He looked harmless, like any bloke down the pub. How could this be the man Emma had been driven to kill? Something awful must have happened to push her to such an extreme. I lowered my gaze, determined to keep my emotions in check.

'I used to be her schoolteacher years ago, but I imagine she's told you that. Judging by the way you're glaring at me, I expect that's where the truth ended.'

I raised an eyebrow, trying to relax my facial muscles as they tightened around my frown.

Luke gave a nervous laugh, raising his palms in mock surrender. 'Mate, I come in peace. It's not what you think.'

'What do you expect?' I said. 'You've come here to relive your sick infatuation with *my* wife. Should I go to the jukebox and play "Don't Stand So Close to Me"?' I exhaled tersely. I had to distance myself if I wanted to hear him out.

Luke raised a cautionary finger. 'There's a lot of truth in that song. Especially when it ended with me almost being killed. Seriously. I'm trying to help you here, but if you're not ready to hear it, then I'll go.'

'Stay where you are,' I said, swallowing back the bitter taste in my mouth. 'Tell me everything you know.'

There was no doubt now. He was talking about attempted murder. He was talking about my wife.

CHAPTER TWENTY-EIGHT
EMMA

2017

It wasn't that I hated being alone. For most of my life, I'd preferred my own company, particularly when I was growing up in Mersea. But having three small bedrooms in close proximity did not offer much privacy. Every argument, every outspoken word could be heard. Our windswept bungalow jutted out of the landscape like a jagged thumbnail. Not many people wanted to live this far out, let alone on an island regularly cut off by the tide. I did not doubt that moving away would be the best thing for our son. He would miss the beach and the raw freedom of his surroundings, but I knew he would delight in our new home. I wanted him out there in the big wide world, but I wanted to be by his side too. The thought of being separated haunted my nightmares with terrifying lucidity. I did not deserve my beautiful child. Since confiding in Alex, I had wrestled with my conscience. But I was not a character from a horror story. Perhaps I was not even a killer after all.

A miserable growl emanated from my stomach. I hadn't eaten, apart from some salad Theresa had guilt-tripped me into and a chocolate digestive which I had taken a bite from then spat out in the bin. Hunger distracted me from my thoughts. Theresa would never understand.

For once, our house was steeped in serenity. The only sounds were the grandfather clock in the hall and the soft hiss and crackle as damp logs burned in the hearth. Alex always filled the void with the mundane chatter of a television show. Coming from the city, he had never gotten used to country life. I breathed in deeply, inhaling the scent of the pinecones I had picked with Jamie days before. I ran my hand along the long wooden beam my father had fitted years ago. It had been replaced after the fire. I thought about that day, how I'd hugged my knees as the flames danced around me. It was my father who had found me. Another horrific episode I wished I could forget.

I stared into the fire, my memories cracking open like festering eggs, the stink within leaking out. Alex had said that my nightmares were my subconscious mind trying to deal with what I repressed. If only he knew. Was I a product of my social environment or was I just born like this? I tried to think about Mum, to use my adult brain to analyse what sort of a person she really was. I'd been thirteen when she'd left. I focused hard, visualising her face, the memory blurred around the edges. I clung on tightly to the memories of her good days, when she was sober and Dad was around. Picnics at the beach, crabbing in the water, her skin freckled from the sun when we stayed out too long. But then there were the bad days when she was feeling neglected. When she drank too much and her moods raged like a storm. She was stick thin, unlike most of the mothers who picked up their children from school. I used to watch them, in their chunky knitted jumpers and padded coats, welcoming their children with warm hugs. I cycled home on my own from an early age. I withdrew from the heat of the fire – thinking of the past wasn't helping. I had to move forward. Move away and forget this place.

Picking up the poker, I jabbed at the logs, watching the sparks dance as they were sucked up the chimney and released into the violent winds. A sharp rap made me jump, and the poker clanged against the hearth as it fell at my feet. I held my breath, wondering if I had imagined it. Perhaps it was the crack of a log that misguided my senses into thinking it was someone at the door. We did not get callers this far out. It was after nine and Jamie was tucked up in bed. So who could be outside? I waited, crouching down to pick up the poker once more.

Crack! My head swivelled to the left as something hit the windowpane, making me freeze in my tracks. I had locked the doors, hadn't I? What about the windows? Were they closed too? My heart galloping in my chest, I rushed towards the glass, half expecting to see Luke peering through. It was just the storm, I told myself. Some debris had hit the door and was rattling the windows. But I didn't really believe that was true. After checking the locks, I stood in Jamie's doorway, watching his sleeping form. My heart melted at the sound of his soft snore. What sort of a mother was I when I could not keep my son safe? It had started, I was certain of it. Luke was back and determined to re-enact what had happened before. It would not be enough that he had invaded my mind. He would invade my home also. But it was not just me who would be put in harm's way this time. My family would suffer too. The sharp ring of the telephone made me grasp the doorframe. Tearing myself away, I forced myself to answer it, holding my breath as I awaited a response. But just as I expected, there was nobody there – at least, nothing except the faint sound of breathing on the other side. I ended the call and took the phone off the hook, checking the doors and windows one more time before peeping in on Jamie and going to bed. Around me, the house creaked and moaned in response to the gale outside. Taking a breath, I steadied myself. I could not give in to panic, not now. My fingers found the back of my neck, easing down the hairs that had prickled with fright. Bending on one knee, I checked beneath the bed, ready to shoot out of the room at a second's notice. There was nothing there, but I knew that may not always be the case. 'No,' I whispered, stumbling backwards as the walls closed in around me. The last thing I could feel were my knees hitting the carpet as I fell to the floor.

CHAPTER TWENTY-NINE
ALEX

2017

Luke lowered the phone from his ear and slid it into the pocket of his jeans. I had half expected him not to return from the toilet, and I watched his face closely for clues of his intentions.

'Girlfriend?' I asked, half hoping it was. I was conscious of the time. Soon the barman would call last orders and Luke had not told me why he had contacted me. Each time he was about to open up, we were faced with an interruption. Was he stringing me along or had booze addled his brain?

'Don't talk to me about girlfriends,' he said, taking a sip of his drink.

My thoughts darkened. I wanted to confront him, squeeze it out of him if necessary with my bare hands. I wasn't buying the nice guy act. If he *had* hurt Emma, then he would pay. I tipped my glass to my lips, barely sipping my drink. Alcohol brought out the worst of my temper and going off the rails was not going to help anyone. My mother's saying floated in my memory. *You'll catch more flies with honey than vinegar.*

She was always telling me off for my scowl, said if the wind changed then I'd stay that way. But she was right about one thing. I needed to keep my temper in check. Our area of the pub had cleared of patrons, and I was relieved that I could hear him without having to shout.

'You were about to tell me about that, weren't you?'

Luke nodded. 'Sorry. This is hard for me to talk about. But you need to know who you're married to.'

I forced a nod. I wanted to tell him he wasn't worthy to utter Emma's name. 'She said you were her teacher. Just how far did your . . . relationship go?' It was the question I had wanted to ask my wife. I knew she was trying to protect my feelings but keeping me in the dark was hurting me more.

'Too far,' Luke said. 'And I put my hands up to that. I was newly qualified, just a few years older than the class I taught. But I should have known better. Emma was your typical love-struck teenager. She was infatuated with me, there at every turn.'

'You're having me on,' I said, my throat growing dry.

He shook his head, a half-smile rising on his face. 'She told you it was me, didn't she? Figures. That's the line she fed everyone.' Lowering his voice, he tipped his head towards mine. 'She followed me everywhere I went, constantly texted me and gave me the eye. I was flattered, who wouldn't be? This attractive young woman coming on to me. She wouldn't take no for an answer.'

I stared in disbelief while, inside, my stomach kept turning over. He was talking about my Emma. He was lying. He had to be. And what the hell was I doing, betraying my wife by buying her stalker drinks? She would be mortified if she could see us now. But I needed to hear what he had to say. I sucked in a breath, 'So you slept together?'

Luke nodded. 'I gave in to temptation just once. She was a very troubled girl. I thought I was helping when she opened up to me. But she formed an attachment. They warned us about stuff like this but . . . Ach, I was very naive. One day she followed me to my dad's beach hut.

She made a pass at me and we got carried away.' He caught my tight-lipped expression. 'I won't go into details but I told her it could *never* happen again.'

I sat quietly fuming at the thought of her with another man. Would she have been that forward at sixteen? Her youth was something she didn't like talking about and pressing her for answers just caused upset. I couldn't help but wonder whether we might not have found ourselves in this situation if she had been more open about her past. Luke was feeding me an entirely different story than the one I had been given. If he was talking about Emma, it was not the woman I had come to know.

'I backed off immediately,' Luke said remorsefully. 'To be honest, I couldn't believe what we'd done. But it was too late by then.'

My cheeks flushed as I manufactured a response. 'What do you mean, too late?'

'God, even thinking about her gives me the chills,' Luke said, giving me a furtive glance. 'She became my shadow after that. Then the phone calls started, day and night. When I wouldn't respond, she broke into my house. I had to get a police injunction against her in the end.' He gave a dry laugh. 'She was like the Terminator. The injunction slowed her down, but it didn't stop her.'

'It must have escalated quickly if she tried to kill you.' I gave him a cold smile. I hated hearing him talk about Emma in that way. He was lying so I'd turn on my wife. I stared unblinkingly ahead, allowing his words to flow over me. Luke carried on as if he had not heard me.

'She became really nasty, told everyone that I'd pressured her into sex. It was her word against mine. Rumours started flying about and my contract was cut short. It was very hard to get anywhere to employ me because they wouldn't give me a reference. My teaching career was in tatters before it began.'

'I'm surprised you didn't go to prison for sleeping with someone in your care,' I said, showing little sympathy.

'There was no proof, and believe me, I've paid the price. All those years in university and the best I can get is a job in an art gallery on minimum wage.'

My eyes fell to his left hand, which had clenched into a fist. He caught my gaze and stretched his fingers before wrapping his hands around his pint glass. 'So you're bitter, and maybe you've called me here for some sort of closure. But Emma's no threat to you.'

'How do you explain this then?' He turned away from me, parting the back of his hair. I peered beneath the dim light at the raised scar on the back of his head and felt a sudden surge of dread.

I frowned. 'But you said you moved away? You must have come back at some point?'

Luke nodded slowly, lost in thought. 'I missed my family. I wanted to be able to go home without worrying it would start up again. I came back for a while, but I was still looking over my shoulder. So I decided to find her, confront her about what she'd done.'

Luke's finger trailed after the dribble of condensation on his glass. 'I followed her home one day. I guess I wanted to see how she'd feel if the tables were turned. Ten minutes after getting there she tied a shovel to her quad bike and rode to the paddock at the back of the house. I remember standing in the field watching her, trying to gather up enough courage to confront her for what she'd done. It seemed daft, being afraid of a woman. But deep down I knew things had the potential to get worse.' He took another swig of his beer before carrying on. 'And they did. She began screaming and shouting at me as if I was the one in the wrong. I turned to leave, but the next thing I was falling to my knees as I took a blow to the head.'

'So you're saying she purposely tried to kill you?' I said, confirming my worst fears. 'That it wasn't self-defence on her part?'

'Self-defence? How could it be self-defence when I was walking away?' Luke looked at me, his eyes wide with incredulity. 'When I woke up, I was covered in branches and a layer of dirt. At first, everything was black, and I didn't know where I was. The soil . . . it was everywhere. It blurred my eyes and was up my nose. The insects . . . crawling all over me, they were. They must have smelled the blood coming from my head.' He heaved a ragged sigh. 'I managed to claw my way up and I crawled out of the ditch. I was weak, my head was spinning. Scared the shit out of me, it did. I left after that, and didn't look back.'

'Did you call the police?' I said, knowing full well he hadn't.

'I knew it would aggravate things, and again, it was her word against mine. I just wanted to put the whole thing behind me. So, I covered the ground in, made it look like I was still there. I figured if she thought she'd killed me then she'd leave my family and me alone. They knew what she was like, so when I went to York, they promised to keep my whereabouts quiet.'

I realised he was staring at me, waiting for me to speak. 'Sounds like something out of a Stephen King novel.'

'Well, it's nothing to be proud of – being beaten up by a woman.' A smile touched his lips, but his blue eyes were cold. 'You're talking to a dead man.' He knocked back his drink, slamming the empty glass against the table. In the distance, a bell rang time.

'I'm not saying I believe any of this, but what do you want from me?' I said, as the few remaining drinkers made their way to the bar.

Luke masked a belch with his hand. 'I thought about moving again, after I heard you were coming to Leeds. But I'm tired of hiding. I want to be able to move freely, without worrying what Emma's going to do next. I could still go to the police but I prefer not to. In return for my silence, I want you to speak to her. Tell her that I don't want her coming to the art gallery. If she sees me out and about, she's to steer well clear.'

'I'll speak to her,' I said, 'when the time is right. But it works both ways. If I see you anywhere near my wife . . . I'll finish what she started.'

Luke rose from his seat, his expression neutral. 'You don't need to worry about that. The only reason I've kept tabs on Emma is to make sure she's nowhere near me.'

'Then we understand each other,' I said, touching his arm as he turned to leave. 'Just one more thing. When you came back to see her . . . when was that?'

'The date's branded on my brain,' he said, 'October 2013.'

CHAPTER THIRTY
LUKE

2002

My phone dinged with another text and I did not have to look at the screen to know who it was. My siren, my temptress, my Emma. She was still sulking as I hadn't mentioned her birthday the day before. Little did she know how much importance I had placed on her age. Silencing the engine, I plucked my phone from my pocket as I got out of the car. Whatever she texted, my response would be instant – this was not the time to be coy.

Emma: Everything OK? Sorry for being off with you. x
Luke: Silly. I can't treat you differently in school xx
Emma: :-P xxx
Emma: OK I forgive you. <3 xxx
Luke: Can't stop thinking about you. x
Emma: When can we meet? It's been ages. You promised. xxx :-(

Luke: I'm here. Waiting. And I've got your present ;-)

Emma: Oh! Where are you? Xx

Luke: Wouldn't you like to know. xx

Emma: Where? Tell me now!! XXX

Luke: At Dad's beach hut in Mersea. Remember where I told you? x

Emma: Yes! I'll be there in twenty xxxxx

I had already primed Emma by telling her about the place last week. She made it there in thirty minutes flat. I knew it was her from the on–off flicker of the light on her bike. It was late and the beach had long since cleared of dog walkers, the tang of salt on the cool, crisp November air. I had dangled the carrot. There would be nobody else here tonight. Just as I had planned. She found me sitting in the beach hut, apparently unaware of her arrival. 'Oh,' I said, opening the door. 'I wasn't sure if you were coming.'

'I wasn't sure myself,' she said, panting lightly as she stood in the doorway. 'Dad kept talking about some boring archaeology find on the news. In the end I said I was going to bed. I climbed out the window to get away.'

I chuckled in response, telling her to come inside. Dad's beach hut was sparse but fit for purpose, housing a small gas cooker, a square wooden table, some cupboards and two chairs. Deck chairs were stacked in the corner behind the door, as well as some sandy buckets and spades that had not been discarded by our neighbours' children when they'd used it for the day. I could not do much about the lack of heating, but I had cleared away any lingering cobwebs. In my experience, the appearance of spiders did not set a romantic tone.

'I'm sorry about before,' I said, offering a lazy smile as I gave her the once-over. She was wearing a baggy sweatshirt and denim skirt. I imagined the twilight breeze skimming the tops of her thighs as she cycled here to meet me in our secret meeting place.

'You were only looking out for me,' she said, catching my gaze.

I met her eye and smiled. I could not wait for ever. Soon we would be breaking up for Christmas and who knows how we would feel when the new term began?

'Your present.' I broke the silence by digging into my jacket pocket. The necklace was some cheap tat I'd picked up from the market, but she wasn't to know. I stood behind her to put it on, before she had the chance to have a better look. She could examine it later, when it didn't matter any more.

'Ooh, it's lovely,' she said, touching the tiny sunflower dangling from the chain.

A trickle of sweat ran down my back but, given the cool night, it was Emma making me perspire. 'Are you sure this is what you want?' I said. 'Really sure?'

Her attention on her necklace, she gave me an enquiring look, and it took several seconds for the penny to drop. 'Now?' she said, her words barely a whisper, and for a second I almost felt guilty for pushing her so fast. Almost.

'Hey, don't look so scared,' I said softly. 'Us, meeting like this, perhaps it was a mistake . . .' I made my way towards the door.

'Wait,' she said, blocking my path. Leaning forward, she kissed me on the cheek. 'Don't go.'

Turning around, she closed the door and pulled across the bolt. The air seemed charged between us, and I parted my lips as my breath quickened in her presence. She knew why she had been summoned; nobody had forced her to come. Her earlier sulk in school would have stoked a feeling of guilt that she would be keen to dissolve. I reached forward, pulling the elastic band from her hair and allowing it to tumble down on to her shoulders. She gazed at me with a trust I did not deserve.

'I love you,' she whispered, and it did not come as a surprise.

It seemed only fair I should reciprocate, as saying anything less could put a dampener on what was to come. 'I feel the same. You're the only one for me,' I said, and at that moment it was true. Pressing my lips upon hers, I kissed her hungrily on the mouth, my hands claiming her face, her neck, her shoulders. Her eyes were misty when we drew back for air and I questioned her a second time. 'Are you sure? Really sure?' I said, and felt a swell of satisfaction when she replied with a sudden nod of the head. 'You haven't done this before, have you?' I said, stilled by the fear lighting up her eyes.

'It's what I want. More than anything,' she replied. And that was how we progressed from our first kiss to something so much more.

CHAPTER THIRTY-ONE
EMMA

2002

Cycling home from the beach hut, I struggled to see the road. I didn't know why I was crying. My relationship with Luke had been sealed. We were a couple. It was too late to turn back now. I blinked hard in order to clear my vision. My tears were hot with frustration and shame. I had wanted Luke to treat me as an adult and he had. I wanted to keep him and this way I would. Nobody had put a gun to my head. So why did I feel so used?

Slipping into my room, I quickly undressed before pulling my long white nightdress over my head. Theresa had not followed up on my mention of meeting my teacher out of school, and there was no way I could tell her what had happened now. She still treated me like a twelve-year-old for starters. She'd be mortified if she knew what I had done. I kicked my clothes under the bed. I didn't want to see them, the memory of my intimacy with Luke invoking further shame. It was no fairy-tale moment as I had imagined; indeed, it was over before it began.

Tugging my clothes to one side, he had bitten my shoulder as his excitement mounted, and I had held on to the cold hard table, shocked and bewildered as he took control. Afterwards, the awkwardness between us was crippling, our professions of love a tainted memory. I had fixed my clothes, Luke checking his watch as he told me I should hurry home. My fold-up bicycle could have fitted in the boot of his car, but I was too embarrassed to ask for a lift. We were OK, weren't we? Once again, I found myself wondering what I had done wrong.

I lay in bed, listening to the wind creeping through the old fireplace, staring at my mobile phone. After ten minutes of willing Luke to text, I took things into my own hands. It was a one-line text, in the hope of further communication.

Goodnight, love you xx

But no response was returned. Thirty minutes later I pulled back the covers, wishing I could have a bath to ease the physical discomfort. Pacing the floor, I wished my sister were here to comfort me. I missed her so much it hurt. It had been so lovely earlier in the week, when we'd met up in town for my sixteenth birthday dinner. But a pizza restaurant was hardly the place to bare my soul. I touched my sunflower necklace, trying to comfort myself. I had Luke now. We were a couple. I would never be alone again. Lifting my feet on to the chair, I hugged my knees, waiting for a reply.

CHAPTER THIRTY-TWO
ALEX

2017

After my conversation with Luke, everything I did was on autopilot. Leaving the pub, finding my key and sliding it into the hotel room door, even getting undressed. I didn't remember anything because all my attention was on my son. Ever since Luke mentioned his relationship with my wife, suspicion had lurked in the back of my mind. Those blue eyes . . . they had triggered a spark of recognition. I could not focus on who was telling the truth because something far more troubling was plaguing my thoughts. I kicked off my duvet, allowing the air conditioning to chill my bare skin. I thought about Emma and Luke together and imagined our family being ripped apart. I didn't want to believe Luke's story and felt disloyal for its presence in my thoughts. Emma had not mentioned a sexual liaison between them, but there was an undercurrent of tension when she talked about that day. Luke's parting shot was in the forefront of my brain. October 2013. It suggested just one thing. Betrayal.

I rose from my bed. There was no point in trying to sleep tonight. I switched on the kettle on the hotel room desk, tearing open the decaf coffee sachet into a cup. As I emptied the capsules of milk I saw Jamie's face, the child we never thought we could have. Our fertility problems had consumed our marriage, and the strain on our relationship had been immense. It was nature, part of the driving need to reproduce. But it was my fault, not Emma's. My weakness.

I thought back to when she fell pregnant. It had felt like our marriage had been given a reprieve. We would have done anything to make it work. She had gained weight, turned her back on her eating disorder, at least for a while. Wearily, I took a sip of coffee, briefly closing my eyes as I remembered the argument we'd had about a sperm donor at the time. I'd found her searching for clinics and donors online. When I'd snapped the lid of the laptop shut she had jumped as if it were a crocodile about to bite her. I desperately wanted a child but she simply could not see how small the suggestion of a sperm donor made me feel. Then, like a miracle, we conceived and Jamie was born the following June. Had she instigated contact with Luke? Slept with him just one more time? She knew every inch of her fertility cycle – but only because I had piled the pressure on. I could not accept the doctor's prognosis of a low sperm count. I took another mouthful of coffee, trying to commit Luke's words to memory. He instigated the injunction, not Emma, as she had implied. Why would she lie about such a thing? Backgrounds could be checked – couldn't they? The same could be said for being in trouble with the police. Luke's version of events was similar to Emma's – but turned on its head. I felt disorientated, as if I was walking through a hall of mirrors. Had Emma gone off the rails after her mother left? Or was Luke lying, deliberately playing me to turn me against my wife? Wasn't that what stalkers did? Tore apart their victims until there was nothing left? My thoughts tortured me.

I checked my watch. Jamie would be sleeping now. I pictured him dressed in his Superman onesie, his tousled blond hair falling over his face as he slept. Everybody said he looked like his mother. But I couldn't see any of Emma in him. And his eyes . . . as blue as the sky. A throwback from a grandmother who had long since passed. At least, that's what Emma had told me. A wave of nausea made itself known. I sat up on the bed, planting my bare feet firmly on the floor. The world felt like it was tilting, and I dug my fingers into the mattress as I clung on for dear life. I had to get to the bottom of it. Grief swept over me, preempting the results. In my mind, I had lost a child and a wife. What if Emma left me? My name was on the birth certificate but what rights did I have? Could I live with not knowing? If a DNA test proved Jamie wasn't mine, where did that leave me then? I thought of my relationship with my father, his steady influence on my life. Jamie needed his dad. Emma *was* troubled at times – how would she cope on her own? Despite it all, I still loved her.

CHAPTER THIRTY-THREE
EMMA

2017

Postman Pat filled the air with a cheerful jingling tune as I replayed the latest episode for Jamie, who was nicely tucked up in his pyjamas under a blanket, a bowl of jelly on his lap. I had spent the evening cuddling him on the sofa, but as Alex pushed his key in the door, I could already feel the panic rising in my chest.

I met him in the hall, away from little ears. 'You're an hour late; I was worried sick,' I said, despite his text telling me he had been delayed. It was only seven o'clock in the evening. I knew the train journey was horrendously long, but it did not stop me getting anxious as I awaited his return. Last night I had quickly come to, waking up on my bedroom floor. I knew it was the lack of food that had made me dizzy and faint so I had forced myself to eat some spoonfuls of dry cereal before bed. Spooked by the storm outside, I squeezed in beside Jamie, listening for every sound. Only as dawn filtered through his window blinds did I relax.

'But I texted you. You said it was OK.' He took one look at my face. 'Is everything all right? Is Jamie—'

'He's fine.' I cut off his sentence. 'But I'm not – I didn't get a wink of sleep last night.' I looked him up and down. His crumpled clothes and the shadows under his eyes told me he hadn't slept much either. 'Had a good night, did you?' I hated feeling this way, irritable and snappy. Alex worked hard and deserved a break. But last night had felt like a year without him. I rubbed the back of my neck, still feeling cold prickles after the silent call.

'It was OK,' he said, turning his gaze away from mine. 'I could murder a coffee.'

'Jamie's in the living room.' I sighed.

He threw me a smile, pressing his lips against my cheek in a belated greeting. But it was not before I caught the shadow crossing his face. I thought back to last night when I said I loved him, and he hadn't responded. Just who had he been with? He had lots of old friends in Leeds – men and women. Was that why he couldn't meet my gaze today? I inhaled a breath, telling myself not to be so paranoid. I had enough things to worry about, without adding infidelity to the list.

'Daddy!' Jamie exclaimed from the living room as I put on the kettle. 'We're adopting a polar bear!' I walked to the open door, listening in on their conversation.

'Really?' Alex said. 'Where's he going to sleep then?'

'No, silly,' Jamie giggled. 'He doesn't live here. I get a teddy instead. I'm going to call him Snowy.'

I smiled. Jamie had just begun getting pocket money and had chosen to spend it on a donation to the WWF. Silently I padded back to the kitchen, feeling a swell of pride.

Twenty minutes later Alex followed me in, drawn by the smell of cooking which had carried into the hall.

'You said you had a restless night?' he said, gratefully taking his coffee.

'Yes,' I said, guarding my words. The last thing I wanted was to sound like some neurotic. 'It was stormy. Jamie was asleep and the television was turned off. I heard a bang, and then something rapped against the windows.'

'It's not surprising you're jumpy,' Alex said. 'But it was probably the storm. There's always debris flying about.'

'I had a silent phone call,' I said, glancing over my shoulder after I turned his omelette in the frying pan.

Alex shrugged, his gaze on anywhere but me. 'We're so exposed here. The phone lines probably went down. You won't know yourself when we move to the city. I've spoken to the vendor about that house I showed you online. It's even nicer in real life. I wish you'd seen it with me.'

I plastered on my brightest smile, but inside I was horrified. 'I trust your judgement. Put an offer in. The sooner we're away from here the better.'

Alex leaned his head to one side as he looked at me. 'It's really creeped you out, me being away, hasn't it? Next time you're both coming with me.'

I dragged my nails down my arm, feeling anxiety crawling beneath my skin. 'I feel like I'm being watched. A bunch of sunflowers were delivered to the shop for me.'

'Sunflowers? Perhaps they were from one of your clients,' Alex said, masking a yawn.

I nodded, frowning at his apparent lack of concern. 'You don't seem that bothered.'

'What? Sorry, love, I'm just tired and hungry. I didn't sleep too well myself.'

'I'll make you some toast to go with this,' I said, growing annoyed as I plated up his omelette. Why was he being so blasé? I turned to face him, my eyes narrowing. 'The flowers. The phone call. It's him. It has to be.'

Alex picked up his knife and fork. 'I think you're worrying over nothing.'

An open window was not enough to release the smell of cooking from our tiny kitchen, and I fanned the back door open and closed until fresh air invaded the room. I stood silently, my mind working overtime as I waited for the toast to pop up. I had lied to cover up my eating disorder in the past. Was I like the boy who cried wolf now? I couldn't bear to see that look of disbelief on my husband's face again.

'Aren't you going to join me?' Alex said, briefly touching my hand.

'Sure,' I said, remembering my fainting attack last night. I had been slipping, losing myself to my eating disorder as I fought to regain control. I could not allow it to happen again.

'Good,' Alex said. Despite my reservations, there was concern in his eyes. 'There's too much here for me.'

I popped the toast on to a plate and plopped down in the chair. 'I'm just worried. I don't know what he's going to do next.'

Again, he dismissed my fears with a shake of the head. 'Babe. We're leaving. It's not as if we can go to the police. Don't let it bring you down. Now c'mon, get some food inside you. Please.'

I nodded dumbly, taking a fork from the drawer and spearing a piece of his omelette. I'd added cheese, ham and tomatoes, but it tasted like cardboard on my tongue.

CHAPTER THIRTY-FOUR
EMMA

2017

An hour of fussing over Maggie had taken the edge off my morning, soothing my anxiety and calming my thoughts. Helping others was what I loved most about my business; it made me feel like I was worthwhile. As Maggie twirled in her latest choice of bridal gown, her smile lit up the room. Feeling a warm glow, I watched her sway before the mirror as she sang 'I Could Have Danced All Night'.

Josh handed me the camera. 'One for the scrapbook,' he said, with a smile to match my own. The photographs had been his idea, and he had hooked up our digital camera to a Bluetooth printer that delivered images in seconds. Every bride was given one when she chose her gown. That and a glass of Prosecco set us apart from other businesses in town. Thankfully, Maggie didn't drink, or she would have gotten through several bottles by now.

Coming down from her cloud, she stood before me, flushed from her exertions. 'I like this one; it feels swishy when I move.'

'Lace suits you,' I said, handing Josh the camera as I escorted her to the changing rooms.

Minutes later she was out of her dress and back in her regular colourful clothes. I handed her the photo to add to her collection. 'Here you go. Don't you look lovely? Bernard's a very lucky man.'

'He was,' she said, with a sense of finality. 'This is my last visit. I won't be coming back.'

'But . . .' I was just about to ask why, when she silenced me with a gaze.

'I know there's no wedding, I always have. It's time to join the real world.' She smoothed down her hair. 'Still, it was nice while it lasted, and sweet of you to indulge me.'

'I don't understand,' I said, still not wanting to burst the bubble.

'My son's paid a visit. He's got it into his head that I'm senile. I don't want to go into a home.'

'But Bernard . . .'

'Is buried in the graveyard. I'll still visit him, have a little chat, but I know there's no wedding. Still,' she chuckled, 'it was nice to pretend.'

'You do know you can come here anytime, don't you?' I said, following her to the door.

She shook her head sadly. 'As the saying goes . . . the past is a nice place to visit but not a good place to stay.'

As I saw her out, I wondered if I would be echoing her words when I was eighty.

'You OK?' Josh said, handing me a cup of green tea.

'Ta,' I said, feeling my throat constrict as I spoke. 'Yeah, I'm all right, just feeling a bit sorry for Maggie.' I looked him up and down. 'You look nice.' Gone were the ripped skinny jeans and sweater. In their place was a pair of smart black trousers and a white shirt. I was going to make a joke about him having a court appearance but given my own predicament, decided to hold back.

'I thought I'd smarten myself up a bit,' he explained. 'You know, I was thinking – perhaps we could do a line in hire for gay weddings.'

'I thought we already did – if both brides hire dresses. Why?' I said, giving him a wry grin. 'What are you after? Rainbow colour fabrics like the gay pride flag?'

'Sounds good to me,' Josh said, with a twinkle in his eye.

I flashed him a smile. 'What I want to know is . . . how come you get a lovely rainbow flag?'

'I'll make you a flag if you like. What colour would suit your lifestyle?' Josh said.

'Black,' I said morosely. 'No, make it grey.'

'Like an old pair of knickers too long in the wash?' Josh grinned. 'I can't see it catching on.'

I chuckled into my cup as I took a sip of tea. 'You make me laugh,' I said. 'Did you actually have any sensible ideas or were you just trying to cheer me up?'

Josh clicked his fingers. 'Oh yeah, I thought we could get a photography shoot done of same-sex couples, use them for promo in selected websites and wedding magazines. We could open the business up to a whole new stream of clients. People will travel if they know we cater for everyone.'

'Sure thing,' I said, admiring his business acumen. 'Do your research, work out how much budget we need for marketing and I'll have a look.'

'Ooh the boss lady is loosening her purse strings. There's a first time for everything, I suppose.'

I was just about to respond when there came a familiar jingle from above the shop door. 'Saved by the bell,' I said with a smile.

As I immersed myself with my client, I came to a decision. Maggie was right. The past was not a good place to live. I could not allow it to eat into my soul any longer. Josh had come on so much since I'd given him a chance. I could move to Leeds knowing my business was in capable hands. It was time to give myself a second chance too. But the only way of doing that would be to find Luke and face up to what I had done. There was one person who would know where he was. His brother had moved away, but he had a sister who, so far as I knew, still lived in Colchester. For a long time I had dreaded bumping into her on the street, and hoped I had changed enough that she would not recognise me immediately. But the days of hiding were behind me now. I thought of Jamie, my marriage, and everything I could not afford to lose. It was time to find Luke and put the ghosts of the past to rest.

CHAPTER THIRTY-FIVE
EMMA

2002

Holding my breath, I pressed my finger on the stiff plastic doorbell. Luke's house loomed large and imposing. It was a mansion compared to the tiny cottage I lived in. I cast an eye over his car parked on the gravel driveway, appreciating the scent of the chrysanthemums bordering the path. I felt like I was in a game of knock down ginger with my sister, ready to run at the first sign of life. My grip around the bouquet of sunflowers tightened. They had cost me all my pocket money due to them being imported, but you couldn't put a price on love. I sniffed the flowers, thinking what a beautiful bridal bouquet they would make. I spent a lot of time daydreaming about weddings, when my thoughts weren't tied up with Luke.

The sight of his shadow behind the frosted glass made my heart trip over itself in my chest. Wearing my brightest smile, I took a deep breath as he opened the door. 'Hi,' I said breezily, even though my limbs were trembling as I stood.

'Emma? What the fuck are you doing here?' Luke said, craning his neck from left and right before dragging me inside.

'Steady.' I emitted a nervous giggle at the strength of his grip. 'You're keen.' But as he slammed the door behind me, Luke's face relayed he was anything but. From a side room I could hear the sounds of the television and I wondered if we were alone. He was wearing a tracksuit, the zip half undone, revealing his toned chest. The same chest I had run my fingers over just a couple of nights before. Tearing my eyes away, I was taken aback to see the spike of annoyance in his gaze.

'I'll repeat the question, will I? What are you doing, turning up at my house?'

My smile fell as I absorbed the frosty reception. 'I . . . I heard you were sick. I thought I'd bring you some flowers to cheer you up.'

'How did you find out where I lived?' he said. 'What if my mother had answered the door? You're lucky she's out, or there would be hell to pay.'

My fingers twisted into the bindings tying the bouquet. 'You weren't answering my texts. I was worried.'

'Worried about what?' he said, running his fingers through his hair. 'And you haven't answered my question. How did you find out where I live?'

I responded with a half shrug, my throat dry. I couldn't allow myself to cry. I was an adult now. 'I'm sorry,' I said. 'I thought you'd be pleased to see me.' I held out the flowers, but Luke just laughed in my face.

'What did I say when we met? I'm not a kid, Emma, and this won't do. I don't want you coming here again. So you can take your sunflowers and go home.'

'But I haven't got any bus fare left,' I said. Naively, I had hoped he would give me a lift.

Rooting around in his pocket, he produced three pounds and shoved it into my hand. His lip arched in a sneer. 'Here, get yourself a few sweets out of the change.'

'Why are you being so nasty to me?' I said, hurt inflaming my words. 'I don't understand.'

Luke sighed, as if he were speaking to an errant child. 'Look. What we had was fun, but it's over now. Best you accept that and move on.'

The tears I had been valiantly holding back forced themselves to the surface. 'I don't understand.'

Patting me on the back, Luke steered me towards the door. 'Best not to dwell on it. Off you go, and remember, not a word to anyone.'

Paralysed with disbelief, I stood frozen on the step as the door slammed behind me. The flowers fell from my grasp, my limbs barely able to make it up the gravel path. What had he meant, 'Best not to dwell on it'? What had I done wrong?

CHAPTER THIRTY-SIX
LUKE

2002

'Here, you look like you need it,' Lorraine said, shoving a freshly made coffee under my nose.

'Cheers,' I said, gratefully accepting it from her grasp. Sitting in the staffroom, I had chosen my moment carefully, wearing enough of a hangdog expression so she would ask me what was wrong. She was known as a caring soul, a busybody in my opinion, always ready to stick her nose into other people's business. But on this occasion I wanted to turn it to my advantage; feed the rumour mill before it turned on me. Lorraine smoothed her long black skirt, her beaded necklace jangling as she sat. She had had her blonde hair cut short recently, giving her a pixie look.

I thought about Emma, wondering if she had taken off her sunflower necklace and noticed the 'Made in China' stamp on the back. I hung my head, hiding my smile. How I would have loved to have seen her expression as she realised she had been played. At least I'd managed to dump her before Christmas and spared myself the expense of another piece of tat.

'All right, mate? Students been running you ragged?' Sean Talbot's heavy paw clamped down on to my shoulder, spilling my coffee on to my hand. I shook my fingers to disperse the droplets, shaking my head in mock protest. Now the second of my fellow teachers was here, the stage was set. I had deliberately robbed myself of sleep, and would put the dark circles under my eyes to good use. A few years older than me, Sean was a giant of a man. He was dark haired, often unshaven, but very popular with staff. I had made it my business to befriend him from the onset: donating spare concert tickets, buying him an extra round in the pub. It had been worth the cost of my generosity to keep my name clear.

'Have you got five minutes to spare?' I said, knowing their classes didn't begin for another twenty.

'Of course, luvvie,' Lorraine said, wearing a concerned smile.

I got up and closed the staffroom door before sitting back down. 'Only this is a delicate matter,' I said. 'I'm not sure how to handle it.'

'Go on then, spill the beans,' Sean said, loudly slurping his coffee.

'It's one of my students, she's developed a bit of a crush on me.' I exhaled, like a kettle too long on the boil, tensing my body for effect.

'Let me guess, Vanessa Baker? The one that wears her skirt up to her backside?' Sean said. 'I think she fancies all her teachers, that one. You just have to be careful not to say anything that might be taken the wrong way.'

'That's just it,' I said. 'It's not Vanessa. It's Emma Hetherington, the last person you could accuse of being a flirt.'

'Emma?' Lorraine piped up. 'She's so quiet. What makes you think she's got designs on you?'

I exhaled loudly, shaking my head. 'I suppose I've only myself to blame. She's a real talent. I was giving her some extra art lessons, but lately she can't stay away.'

'She's had problems at home, poor girl. She's been very isolated since her mother walked out on her. I've been trying to get her involved in some clubs after school but she acts as a carer to her father too,' Lorraine said.

'I know, she's confided in me a lot. At first I thought I was helping, but now when I'm in town I see her everywhere I go.'

'You don't think she's following you, do you? Maybe you should report it to the head.'

'That's the last thing I want to do. The poor girl's just started coming out of her shell. From what she's told me, she doesn't have many friends in her life right now.'

'Yes, mate, but you're not her friend, you're her teacher,' Sean said. 'You need to keep things on a professional level, otherwise you'll come unstuck. The same thing happened to me last year. Remember Jenny?' He turned to Lorraine and she responded with a knowing nod.

'She found my mobile number,' Sean said. 'She started texting me after school. My girlfriend went ballistic, gave her a piece of her mind.'

'What do you think I should do?' I said. 'I don't want to go to the head with this, not yet.'

'Put an end to those extra classes, at least until things cool down. Don't leave yourself vulnerable. Keep the classroom door open during lunch, so if she wanders in, everything is open and above board. I'll talk to her again, see if I can get her involved in some group activities.'

'But if she starts stalking you or acting weird, you're going to have to report it to the head,' Sean interjected. 'Don't leave yourself open to allegations. Get there first, before she does.'

I nodded. He was voicing my thoughts. The part about Emma following me was a lie. But I had received three texts already this morning. She was too clingy for my liking, and not worth putting my job at risk for. It was time to nip this dalliance in the bud, before things got out of hand.

CHAPTER THIRTY-SEVEN
ALEX

2017

If betrayal had a smell, it would be that of tar – the kind that sticks to your shoes in the heat of midsummer and bubbles like a living thing on the road. Emma and I had offered each other weary smiles as we pretended everything was all right. I had shrugged off her concerns that someone had invaded our home, tapping on the window while I was away. She must have imagined it. How could this be possible, when Luke had been in the pub with me that night? I felt sick at the thought – and at the prospect of what I was about to do. Involving our son in our troubles was the last thing I wanted, but I desperately needed to know the truth. Jamie squealed with delight as I lifted him in the air, pretending to drop him, only to take him in my arms again. I inhaled the scent of liquorice shoelaces on his breath, allowed only on the condition that he brush his teeth afterwards. Plopping him on our bathroom counter, I wore my best smile. I had locked the door. Emma would be horrified if she knew what I was about to do. But then how many times had she visited our little bathroom to force herself to vomit when she had eaten just minutes before? The scent of lemon bleach and floral air freshener gave her away every time. If only the rest of her secrets were as easily deciphered. Reaching across the counter, I carried out my own form of betrayal.

'Ready to brush your teeth?' I said, watching Jamie's eyes roam to the DNA testing kit in my hands.

'What's that?' he said, his childish lisp melting my heart.

'It's a special way of cleaning your teeth. First, you open up . . .' I gently held his chin between my finger and thumb, dropping it open to insert the bud. 'Then I give it a little wiggle like this.' I moved the swab left to right as instructed. 'Then, hey presto, you're now ready to brush your teeth.'

Jamie's tongue roamed over the inside of his gum where I had gathered his DNA. 'But what *was* that, Daddy?'

Daddy. The word speared my heart. My smile wobbled and I fought to keep my tone bright. 'It's just to check that you've not eaten too many sweets. We'd better not tell Mummy, she might not let you have them again. What say you give your teeth a good brush now, have them all nice and clean?'

I set him down from the counter and ruffled his hair. Pocketing the kit, I had never felt so low. I said a silent prayer that it would give me the answers I wanted.

'Smells nice,' I said, inhaling the aroma of white wine sauce as I stepped into the kitchen. Pots and pans bubbled on the Aga, filling the room with steam. The extractor had packed up long ago, and I had not got round to fixing it. I opened the back door, allowing the breeze to sweep the steam outside.

Emma sniffed, tears streaking down her face. 'Onions, they get me every time,' she said, nodding towards the chopped pile. 'It's chicken, cauliflower cheese and some nice new potatoes.' She rinsed her hands under the tap before drying them on a tea towel. 'What are you looking for?'

I continued to rummage in the kitchen cabinet drawer. 'Car keys. I swear I've just left them here.'

'They're on the hook in the hall. You're not going out are you? Dinner will be ready in twenty minutes.'

'I thought I could get us a nice bottle of wine to go with our meal,' I said, blurting out the best excuse I could think of.

Emma closed the back door, rubbing her arms as the intrusive breeze plucked goosebumps on her skin. 'I've got some, I was using it for the sauce.'

I glanced at the wine label. 'I'm sure we can do better than that. I won't be long. I promised Jamie I'd pick him up some ice cream.'

Emma raised an eyebrow. 'Ice cream and sweets in one day?'

'It's OK, Mummy,' Jamie piped up from where he was colouring at the table. 'Daddy's got a special way of checking my teeth.'

'Oh yes?' Emma raised an eyebrow in my direction. 'A dentist now, are we? Is there anything you can't do?'

I laughed, kissing her on the cheek. 'You know me, I'll give anything a go once. The pot's boiling over, by the way.'

Her attention diverted, I grabbed the keys from the hall and made my way to the car. That was close. Too close. I made a mental note to tell Emma we had been flossing if she pressed me about it. Not that she would. She'd be too busy throwing up. I caught the unkind thought as it shot across my consciousness. What had happened was changing all of us, and I hated the direction in which I was being taken.

After posting the sample and picking up some groceries, I headed back home. I could have left it until tomorrow, but I wanted to make the post. The three hundred pounds I was paying for a quicker result would be worth every penny. There was no way I could have waited. I hated putting on a pretence that everything was OK. Jamie was mine, he had to be, and the sooner I got a positive result confirming this, the better, because the alternative did not bear thinking about.

CHAPTER THIRTY-EIGHT
EMMA

2017

Blinking in the darkness, I lay next to Alex, his shallow breathing the only sound in the room. It was one of those utterly black nights when the sky was thick with clouds, the moon and stars extinguished from view. My darkest memories crawled out of their box, clawing at my insides as I recalled what I had done. I imagined our oak tree, its bare branches stark against the grey, lifeless landscape. Dad sitting on the bench he had built at its base, staring mournfully into the skyline as he thought about Mum. It was a haunting scene in my memory, coming to me with greater clarity now the lights had been doused in every room of our home.

It had been Alex's idea to turn them off, citing a migraine that had come on after supper. But I knew from his sideways glances that he could not bear to look at my face. I closed my eyes as tiredness washed over me, my throat still sore from bringing up the food I had so carefully prepared. So much for my resolve. Had Alex really gone to the shops before dinner, or was it just an excuse to get away? The thought swam with all the others in a murky distillery of gloom.

Falling into sleep, my dream returned me to my childhood. I was four years of age, squirming as I awoke in damp flannel sheets. I had wet the bed again. I knew that Mummy would be mad. I blinked in the darkness. Eyes open or closed, it all looked the same. My room was blacker than the night outside. I slid from between the sheets, landing the balls of my feet on the harsh wooden floor. My heart fluttered like a hummingbird as my wet nightdress sent a chill through to my skin. Mummy told me if I got out of bed that the ghost of the Strood would get me. But I was more afraid of my mummy than the ghost. I reached out with my fingers splayed, blindly patted the blankets until I found the bedpost, which led me to the wall. Grasping the edge of the thick polyester curtains, I pulled hard until a chink of light filtered through my small box room. My gaze fell to the floor, half expecting a decaying hand to shoot out and grab me by the ankle. Grunting, I tugged the blankets on my bed, but they were too thick and heavy, and hot tears fell down my cheeks as I realised I couldn't change the sheets by myself. The more I pulled, the heavier they became. A whine growing in my throat, I climbed on top of the bed and curled up on my pillow.

With a slow creak my bedroom door opened. My heart pounding hard, I stuffed my fist into my mouth, trying to hold back my scream at the sight of the long reedy shadow bleeding through. Was the ghost really coming to get me? A hand reached out, flicking the light switch on the wall. Bright light flooded my bedroom, stinging my eyes and chasing the shadows away. It was my father. I jumped from my bed, wrapping my chubby fingers tightly around his neck as he crouched down to speak to me. I took comfort from his earthy smell. I knew Daddy went away to dig for treasure, but archaeology was too big a word for me to fully understand. Frowning, he took in the messy bed, the damp nightdress.

'Have you wet the bed again? Why didn't you tell Mummy?' he said.

My words came in choked sobs as my four-year-old body shuddered in response. 'Muh . . . Mummy said the ghost would get me if I le . . . left my bed.'

Undoing my fingers, he rose from his position, his leather shoes creaking on the floorboards as he walked. Picking up the empty jug on the dresser, he gave me a curious glance. 'How much have you had to drink?'

I stood open-mouthed, but my words would not come.

He knelt for a second time, his voice soft and coaxing as he told me I had done nothing wrong.

'Mummy said I had to drink it all,' I said. My voice was barely a whisper.

As his frown returned, I realised it was Mummy who was in trouble, not me. It gave me a certain satisfaction that I wasn't the only person who got things wrong.

Quickly, Daddy changed the sheets and dressed me for bed. Tugging at my curtains, he opened them wide and left them that way. I liked it when Daddy was home. I scooted to the edge of the bed. The stale scent of urine hung in the air, the damp mattress soaking through the freshly laid sheets. Muffled voices filtered from my parents' bedroom as my father asked my mother why she had insisted I drink so much before bed.

Mum denied it, of course, calling me an attention seeker and a liar. I knew what those words meant because I had been called them before.

I had come to hate the sound of her angry voice. It was a rough, grating noise, echoing like a trapped crow in the room. I wished that Daddy didn't have to go away, so Mummy could be happy all the time and wouldn't drink the brown stuff from the bottle that made her so mad.

'You've been drinking again, haven't you? For Christ's sake, Isobel, she's four years old,' my father said, and I wondered what my age had to do with it.

The bedsprings bounced and squeaked as if to signal it was the end of the conversation. I imagined my mother turning around to face the wall, grasping handfuls of blankets in her bony fists.

A light switch clicked off, and the sound of change rattled against the floor as my father undressed. It was a comforting noise. But morning would bring more disapproval after he left. I whimpered, tears pricking my eyes.

'Emma,' a voice said from so very far away. 'Emma. It's OK. It's just a dream.'

I blinked in the darkness at the hand gently shaking my shoulder. Disorientated and groggy, it still felt as if I were a child, back in the room where Jamie now slept. 'What?' I murmured, taking a slow breath.

Alex stretched to switch on his bedside lamp. 'You were crying in your sleep. Are you all right?'

I touched my cheeks, which were wet with tears. No wonder the dream felt so real. I steadied my voice, vowing my son would never hear the harsh whispers that had been a backdrop to my childhood. 'I'm OK; sorry I woke you.'

Seconds ticked by as we lay in the dark, my past circling around us like a kettle of vultures. Slowly, Alex's hand reached across the void and cupped mine.

I squeezed it back. 'It's going to be OK,' I whispered. 'We'll get through this.'

But my voice contained more confidence than I felt.

CHAPTER THIRTY-NINE
EMMA

2017

Spikes of rain hammered my car windscreen, making me curse the inclement weather. It felt like a lifetime since I had enjoyed the sun on my face. It would have been better to stay at home and talk things through with Alex, but Josh had been unable to cover my shift at work. Not that I expected customers in this weather. For once, my diary was free of appointments, and I was very tempted to tell Theresa to shut the shop for the afternoon. But I had forced myself out of the house just the same. Besides, it was bring your teddy to school day today, and Jamie could not wait to participate in the indoor picnic they had planned for lunch. I was all too aware that I was running late as the clock on the car's dashboard showed 11 a.m. By the time I got the buggy out of the boot and put Jamie in, he would be soaked. I pulled up the handbrake and turned round to face my son. 'I'm just going to get a parking ticket from the machine. It's just over there,' I pointed. 'You stay here in the warm, and I'll be back in a second.'

Jamie nodded, staring out at the rain. I rooted through the glove compartment for change. Like many family cars, the space was stuffed with a half-eaten packet of sweets, wet wipes, receipts and old coins. Taking the keys from the ignition, I shoved them in my pocket before pulling out my red umbrella and opening it through the crack in the door. 'Back in one second,' I said once again. 'You can watch.'

Like a meerkat, Jamie's head bobbed as he tried to get a clear view of outside. 'But I can't see, Mummy,' he said, straining against his straps towards the breath-fogged pane.

Turning back in my seat, I clicked the button of his seat belt, allowing him enough freedom to watch me get the ticket. 'I'm going to lock the car, OK? You stay inside and watch Mummy. I won't be a second.'

Hunching my shoulders, I pulled my collar up and faced the rain. It pattered hard against the thin fabric of my umbrella, and I activated the car's central locking system before tottering through the puddles towards the ticket machine. I had the sense to wear trousers today, my billowing blouse kept dry beneath my long fleece coat. I rifled through my change, depositing it into the machine. I was just about to turn round when the sudden screech of car tyres filled the air, chilling me to the marrow of my bones. Time seemed to stop in that second and I was snapped back into reality as I heard a child's cry. Jamie. My child.

'No! No, no,' the syllables fired from my mouth as my umbrella fell to the ground. My eyes flitted from my car door that was wide open and the 4 × 4 parked awkwardly nearby. I sprinted towards it, my eyes fixed on the small hand jutting out on the concrete, and the teddy bear thrown to one side.

'Oh my God!' The driver's screams filled the air as she scrambled out of her Range Rover, almost tumbling over herself in her haste to reach my son.

'Jamie,' I cried, falling to my knees, searching the puddles for a reddish tint of blood. Raindrops splattered his face and he blinked, his little hands clawing the air like a tortoise that had been flipped on to its back. The tall thin figure of the driver loomed over us, her hands on her mouth. Her long blonde hair trailed down the sides of her face as the rain dripped down its length. 'He ran straight in front of me. I didn't see him . . . I . . .'

But I was too busy dialling 999 as I tried to shelter my son from the rain. It was an automatic reaction and I struggled to find the words to call for help.

'Mummy,' Jamie cried, apparently none the worse for wear.

'It's OK, sweetie, you're going to be OK,' I said, my heart feeling like it was going to beat its way out of my chest. My left hand holding the phone, I patted down my son with my right, unable to believe he had escaped with his life.

'He ran out in front of me,' the woman repeated, her voice trembling above me. 'I didn't hit him. I braked the second I saw him. He . . . he tripped over his own feet.'

'What's your emergency?' A voice said on the other end of the line. I blurted out my location, requesting an ambulance as I told the operator my son had been knocked down. Jamie was crying, and warm tears fell down my cheeks as I realised what I had almost lost. I touched his face, checked the grazes on his hands from where he had fallen. Reaching out for his teddy, I drew them both near as I sat in the icy cold puddle, rain driving down my face. I craned my neck to stare at the driver, her face white and frozen in shock.

'He . . . he came from nowhere . . . I didn't hit him . . . I swear.' Her words were disjointed, raised against the fury of the rain. Mascara streaks began to tear down her cheeks, her fingers touching her lips as if caressing the words for comfort. I glanced back at my car – to the back door that was wide open. I had locked it when I left. I was sure of it. So how did he get out? A memory reignited in my brain, old and rusted. Harry the golden retriever, lying bloodied and lifeless on a day just like this. I heaved for breath, feeling my grip on reality loosen a notch.

Sitting in the back of the ambulance, I took comfort from the fact that no injuries were found. I had not expected the presence of a police officer as paramedics checked Jamie over. After catching his breath, Jamie was able to tell them that he had tripped over and fallen, but had not been hit by the car. He seemed excited by the prospect of being in an ambulance, and his eyes grew wide as a uniformed officer joined us, introducing herself to him with a smile. PC Bakewell seemed far less enamoured with me, however. After obtaining my details, she informed me that an automatic referral would be made to children's social services.

'Why?' I said, suddenly feeling small under her disapproving gaze. An efficient-looking woman with short brown hair, she turned over the page of her notebook and wrote down my details.

'I only took my eyes off him for a second,' I said, panic lacing my words. 'The child lock was on in the car. Somebody must have opened the door from the outside.' The thought hadn't entered my head until that second when I blurted it out. My eyes opened wide with the revelation. 'Yes, that's it. Someone opened the door of my car and let him out. He was running across the car park to see me.' I hesitated as I tried to work it out. Had I activated the central locking? If I had, then how could somebody have opened the car door?

PC Bakewell raised an eyebrow in a manner that suggested she was thinking the same thing. 'Did you see anybody else around?'

I frowned. 'No. Have you asked the woman driving the 4 × 4? She might have seen something.'

But the police officer stared unblinkingly, seeming unimpressed. 'It's a public car park. There's bound to be people hanging around. Besides, why would someone do that? Just how long had you left your child alone?'

I pursed my lips, feeling them strain over my teeth as I sucked hard. I thought about Luke and what would happen if I told the police the truth. It was him. It had to be. He was watching me, waiting for me to fall. I shook my head. 'I don't know – seconds,' I said wearily, watching as my child was given the all-clear. I wanted to draw him close. To smother him in kisses and never let him go. I could blame Luke all I wanted. This was my fault. Right now, I was the biggest threat to my child.

PC Bakewell smiled at Jamie, lowering her voice as she gave me words of advice. 'Visibility is very bad with all this rain. Your son could have been killed.' The tone of her voice told me she placed the blame solely on my shoulders. 'I've seen too many incidents like this with horrific outcomes. Don't take your eyes off your child again.' She looked at me with eyes that spoke of the memories of incidents she preferred to forget. 'Anyway' – she offered up a brief smile – 'I'm glad that luck was on your side. Don't let it happen again.' After a quick word with the paramedic, she bid me goodbye. Jamie was going to be OK, but I would not be going into work today. After I had promised to make it up to him with ice cream, we headed home. I needed to tell Alex what had happened before he heard it from anybody else. I looked at the keys in my shaking hand and I wondered if I could trust myself to drive. After tucking Jamie into his car seat, I slid behind the steering wheel. I caught my reflection in the mirror, barely recognising the person staring back at me. My eyes were bloodshot, my face chalk white with shock. This would not be the end of it. Social services would now have a record of my carelessness and I would have to explain myself all over again. How had I allowed my child to toddle across the car park in the pouring rain, resulting in him almost being run over? What sort of mother did that make me? What sort of person? After all we had been through to have our beautiful child . . . I pushed my key into the ignition. I had to force these feelings away and concentrate on calling home to break the news. Alex could barely look me in the eye as it was. Had it been an accident, or had my past reared up to greet me once again?

CHAPTER FORTY
ALEX

2017

My phone's ringtone drilled into my brain, resurrecting the sense of dread that had been keeping me company all day. I was plagued with a premonition that had made it near impossible to catch up with my work from home. It seemed crazy to worry about such a simple thing as Emma taking Jamie to nursery, but when I came home from Leeds she was so paranoid and upset, I wondered if there was more to her state of mind than she was letting on. I could not bear to confront her about Luke, at least not until I had the DNA results in my hand. Now, as her name flashed up on the screen, I knew I had been right to feel worried.

The first thing she told me was that she was at the shops with Jamie, picking up ice cream before they came home. This deviation from the usual routine quickened my pulse, and I could tell from the tremor in her voice that, despite her reassurances, something was very wrong. Slowly she relayed what had happened, her voice growing hushed as she told me about the accident. Jamie piped up in the background, asking her to hurry up so he could eat his ice cream at home. I stood, my heart in my throat as the papers I had been holding fell to the floor. Emma calmly spoke as if she had been reading the words from a prompt. I took a breath, grounding myself as I absorbed the news. 'Are you sure he's OK?' I said, imagining Jamie in the back of an ambulance while I was casually browsing over figures between puffs on my vaporiser.

'He's fine; we both are,' she said as I strained to hear over the beeps of the checkout till in the background. 'He's been checked over by the paramedics as a precaution, and he's none the worse for wear. Can you get the heating on? Light the fire? We're soaked through. I've promised him Ben & Jerry's and his favourite programme on TV.'

I peered through the window and watched the rain hammer down. 'Why didn't you call me when it happened?' I said, unable to comprehend the logic. 'I should have been there. He must have been terrified.' A frisson of annoyance rose up inside me as Emma continued to reassure me in a ridiculously calm tone. What had she said to the police and paramedics? Now we had a social services referral to worry about too. Mum would be horrified. This sort of thing may have been the norm in Emma's family but . . . I pulled away from the window, bitter seeds of disgust blooming inside me. How could she leave me in the dark when our son could have been killed? Or did she think that I could wait, given that I was not his natural father?

'I'm sorry,' she said. 'Look, this isn't the time. We're both soaking wet, and we need to get home. We can talk about it then.'

My fury remained long after the call ended. Jamie was little more than a toddler; why hadn't she been watching him? I had accepted that Emma had her own struggles to contend with and was not always as focused as she should have been. But this was different. This involved our defenceless child. Was she fit to look after him at all?

◆ ◆ ◆

As we lay in bed that night, I stared up at the ceiling wondering what had happened to our happy home. Had it ever really existed at all? I turned towards Emma, touching her hair and smoothing it. 'Are you awake?' I said, knowing she was.

Her steady inhalation of breath paused as she considered her response. After a couple of seconds she turned to face me, her eyes wet with tears. I felt a soft, warm pang in my heart at the sight of the woman I loved so upset because of something I had said. Our argument had been whispered, so as to protect our son. But that did not stop my words cutting her to the bone. I had witnessed the pain in her eyes as my accusations found a home. We had been through some tough times, and she had done a terrible thing, leaving Jamie alone in the car. But I was her husband and the day I took my vows I had sworn to stay with her through thick and thin. What sort of a man was I, abandoning her when she needed me the most? 'I'm sorry,' I said, 'I shouldn't have taken my anger out on you. Jamie is fine. That's the most important thing.'

She nodded, biting down on her bottom lip as she held in a sob. The light of the moon filtered in through our window, displaying the remorse etched on her face.

'We'll get through this,' I said, wiping away her tear with my thumb. 'What's done is done. We have a whole new life in front of us, you, me and Jamie. He needs us to be strong.'

'That's all I want,' she said quietly. 'Our little family. I promise. I won't take my eyes off him again.'

At least she wasn't trying to shift the blame any more. That's what had riled me in the first place. Instead of being sorry for leaving him, she had used Luke as an excuse rather than face up to her responsibilities. It was Luke who had opened the car door, just as it was Luke who had made the silent call and rapped on our window the night before. It was a good job I had not told her about the dead mouse I found in the kitchen today, or she would have blamed Luke for that too. Had Emma convinced herself that everything was his fault? According to Luke, the only person I should be worried about was my wife, who had some serious mental health issues. I had tried to question Jamie tentatively, but he had clammed up, no longer willing to speak about it.

'Do you think you forgot to lock the car?' I said, keeping my tone gentle so as not to sound like an accusation. 'Is it possible you might not have pressed the central locking button?'

'It was pouring with rain,' she said. 'I was fiddling with my umbrella as well as the change for the car park. I'm sure I locked it. I heard it click.'

I interlocked my hands behind my head as I lay on the pillow, trying to make sense of it all. 'You might have pressed the button to open the doors by mistake? That makes a clicking sound too.'

Silence passed between us, and all I could hear was the soft brush of the wind against the windowpane. Somewhere in the distance, an owl shrieked. A wave of tiredness overcame me.

'I don't know,' she said eventually. 'I'm tired of talking about it. I just want to go to sleep.'

I felt the gap between us widen. It was almost like a physical shift as Emma drew herself away to the edge of the bed. Up until then, I had always been the one who fixed things. But now I lay there, my head full of dismantled thoughts that I could not repair. Emma was upset because I had not sided with her straight away. But it was such a big ask when my head was still filled with revelations. She said she had killed someone yet their body was gone. She claimed she had been stalked by Luke, yet the man I'd met was polite and charming, and said Emma was dangerous and unhinged. I had cast his words aside as I didn't want to believe them. I'd told myself that, when we moved, everything would be OK. But we were building up to something; I could feel it. Jamie could have died due to Emma's lack of care. I was out of my depth. I needed to speak to somebody who could advise me what to do. Theresa. If anyone knew the truth about Luke and Emma it would be her. She was the one person I trusted to tell it like it was.

'He's out there,' Emma said, just as I was drifting off to sleep. 'He's out there waiting for me, and there's nothing I can do.'

I blinked, checking the bedside clock. It was three in the morning. 'Emma?' I said listening in the darkness for her response. But she was asleep, having another bad dream. I closed my eyes, wishing we could escape this living nightmare.

CHAPTER FORTY-ONE
EMMA

2003

My heart thumping double time, I closed the toilet cubicle and pulled down the seat before dumping my schoolbag on the floor. Tears pricked my eyes, my limbs shaking from humiliation. It was bad enough that I'd not heard from Luke over Christmas, but this latest betrayal was too much. I heard the swish of the main door open and tried to mask my sniffles into a tissue. A sharp knock on my cubicle door made me jump to my senses.

'Come out, Emma, I need to talk to you.'

It was Luke. What was he doing in the girls' toilets? I held my breath, unsure. His anger was apparent by the tone of his voice, but I had a right to be angry too. I blew my nose, blotting the mascara beneath my lids. I had returned to school after closing time, knowing he was staying on late to mark our work. Foolishly, I thought I could win him over. 'I don't want to talk to you,' I said, rising from the seat just the same.

I had barely slid the lock across when he pushed open the door and dragged me out. 'You're hurting me,' I said, wincing as his fingers bit into my flesh.

'It's nothing compared to what I'll do if you don't drop this.' Spittle laced his words as he pressed his face close to mine.

My eyes roamed over the other empty stalls. He was taking a chance, coming in here where anyone could walk in. But an after-school football match had driven any stragglers outdoors. I recoiled from his grip, the fury in his gaze telling me that rational thought was not present. A bright-pink flush had risen from the neck of his shirt collar, and his eyes bulged in their sockets as his anger became clear. For the first time in my life, I was scared of him. 'I saw you . . . with her.' My words trembled as he loomed above me, his muscles taut beneath his shirt. I had gone to his class in the hope of speaking to Luke alone. Finding him alone with another student had been the last thing I had expected to stumble upon. I knew the girl by sight; her name was Sophie. She must have been only fourteen or fifteen, yet he was leaning over her, his hand guiding hers across the page as she drew. Her long blonde hair shadowed her face, but not enough to disguise the blush rising to her cheeks. I had forgotten my previous promises of discretion as I launched into a tirade. Her eyes wide, the girl had looked at me as if I had lost my mind.

Luke lowered his voice to a menacing whisper as the caretaker's whistles echoed from the hall. 'I'm a teacher. It's what I do. Now, I've tried asking nicely. If you don't stop this ridiculous behaviour I'll take things further.'

'Like you took things further in the beach hut?' I asked, hurt casting an edge to my words. 'I know why you're doing this. You're scared of getting too close because of what happened to you when you were young.'

Taking a step back, his anger seemed to evaporate at the mention of his shared secret. A cold, thin laugh escaped his lips. 'Do you really think that's why I can't stand you any more?' Placing his hand on my shoulder, he pushed me towards the mirror. 'Look at yourself, with your greasy lipstick and cheap perfume. You're pathetic. Why the hell would I be interested in you?'

My stomach churned as I was faced with my reflection. The cosmetics were a Christmas present from Tizzy, and I'd worn them in an effort to win him back. But my attempts at applying it needed practice, and under the strip lighting of the school bathroom I was reminded of a scene with my mother all over again. The night she left, shoving my face into the mirror, telling me what a pig I had become. Tears streaked down my face as I bore the brunt of Luke's cruelty, each word slicing into my soul. But he was not finished yet.

'You threw yourself at me, because you thought sex was the only way of holding on to what we had. But in offering it up on a plate, you lost all my respect.'

'No,' I blurted, swallowing back my tears. 'You said if I didn't have sex that you'd finish it.'

'Really? Are you sure? Because sex didn't come into the conversation as far as I was concerned.'

'Wha . . . what?' I stuttered, barely able to believe what I was hearing.

'When I said I wanted a serious relationship, I was talking about baring our souls, not our bodies. I asked you to the beach hut so we could talk.'

'No,' I said, searching the corridors of my memory for the truth. 'You said . . .'

Luke shrugged. 'I was scared at the prospect of opening up; most victims of abuse are. But you turned all of that on its head when you locked the door and made it clear what you were really after. I was hardly going to say no.'

I pushed my hands to the side of my forehead, trying to extract the memory. Had he actually mentioned sex or had I misunderstood what he'd said? 'Please, Luke, I'm sorry. I must have taken what you said the wrong way.'

'Yes. You did,' he said. 'And while you may think little of your reputation, it's a different case for me. This is my job. My livelihood.' He reached for my throat, grasping hold of my sunflower necklace and giving it a tug. I winced as it snapped under his grasp, and he pocketed the remains. 'So quit with following me around and leaving flowers in your wake. You're dumped. Get over it.'

'You . . . you don't mean it,' I said, gripping the edge of the sink as he turned away. 'Luke. Are you listening to me?'

'It's Mr Priestwood to you,' he replied haughtily, before walking out the door.

CHAPTER FORTY-TWO
LUKE

2003

I felt the heat of the headmistress's glare long before she summoned me. It felt like a branding iron on the back of my neck. I resisted the urge to turn round until she cleared her throat. I had made it my business to leave my classroom door open after the students had left my class. Such efforts at transparency had come too late and I could tell by the look on the head's face that word of my run-in with Emma the day before had been spreading.

'Luke. Can I have a word?' was all she said, and I was brought back to the days when I was the apple of her eye. Back then, being summoned meant extra praise for working hard throughout the year. It was why I had returned here, to the same school I had attended. I didn't need to put in the effort of creating a friendly facade when the groundwork had already been done. And now, not even a year into my new role, I was being called to her office for a telling-off. My ego had led me to this point, an inability to resist a schoolgirl's adoration. I may have been the teacher's pet once myself, but I was not beyond reproach.

As we marched to her office I was grateful that most of my students had gone home. I tried not to think about Emma as I steadied my breath, but it was an impossible task. I knew without a doubt that she was the reason for the stringent beckoning, and I had my story prepared.

The head teacher's office had not changed much over the years. It still housed an old-fashioned Teasmade in the corner that appeared to be more for decorative than practical use. Mrs Pritchard used the recently refurbished staffroom with the rest of us, taking advantage of the Dolce Gusto coffee machine which was always on the go. A large round clock still kept time on the wall behind her desk, and the same wooden photo frames now held updated snapshots of her brood. On the windowsill a dusty-looking bonsai plant absorbed the sun through glass that was long overdue a clean. Tiny beads of sweat broke out on my forehead as I sat in the airless room. Having been forced to spend time with my family over the holidays, I had looked forward to returning to work. The question was, would I be staying? By the look on Mrs Pritchard's face, I was not so sure.

She clasped her fingers together, her heavy bosom fighting against the constraints of her blouse as she leaned towards me. 'I've called you here to ask you about one of your students – Emma Hetherington.'

I remained silent, my face impassive as I waited to hear what I was being accused of.

'There's no point in beating around the bush so I'll come straight out with it. What is the nature of your relationship with this young woman?'

I inhaled a calming breath through my nostrils as I prepared my explanation in my head. 'The same as with all of my students. She turns up for class – I teach her. Why?'

'Because that's not what I've heard. Apparently there was an incident after school last week and you've been seen together in town.'

'Colchester's not exactly London. I often bump into students when I'm out.' I sighed, leaving enough of a gap to make it appear as if I was wrestling with my thoughts. 'Can I be honest with you?'

'I'd prefer it if you were.'

I rubbed the side of my neck. 'I wasn't going to say anything. I'm fairly new to this role and the last thing I wanted was to be knocking on your door with my problems.'

'Which are?' She arched an enquiring eyebrow.

'Emma's got a crush on me. I've done everything I can to dissuade it, but she's totally infatuated. It's even gotten to the point that she's followed me about in town. If I've been seen talking to her outside of school, it's only because I've been gently warning her off.'

'A crush?' The head folded her arms and gave me a look that suggested she was not quite convinced. 'You should have spoken to someone if this has gone so far.'

'I did,' I said, relieved that I'd had the hindsight to talk to my colleagues in the staffroom. 'Lorraine Rugman and Sean Talbot. I mentioned it to them before Christmas.'

'Hmm,' she said. 'Best you don't leave yourself open to allegations. I'm going to monitor the situation, see how it pans out. Hopefully Emma will get over her infatuation soon.' She gave me another thoughtful gaze. 'You're sure you've not done anything to . . . encourage her?'

'I approached you about Emma's after-school art revision and you approved it. The minute I had an inkling of her feelings I brought them to an end.' I exhaled an exasperated sigh. 'Last week I was talking to one of my students after class. Emma burst in and created a scene. I followed her to the toilets to make sure she was OK, but she was in a dreadful state. She said she didn't want to see me talking to any other girls. I told her she was being ridiculous, that I was a teacher and I treated all my students the same.'

'And that's all you said? Because she's been off sick all week.'

'I've got a girlfriend. I've no intention of risking my career over a silly schoolgirl crush.' It was a lie, but a fictional girlfriend would suffice. After making me sweat for a few seconds, Mrs Pritchard delivered a warm smile.

'You understand why I had to ask, don't you? You've got a bright future ahead of you. I'll be making a record of our conversation and noting your concerns. If there's anything I can do, my door is open.'

I leaned across the table and reached out to shake her hand. 'Thanks. I appreciate your support.' I said my goodbyes, knowing that as far as Emma was concerned, I was playing a dangerous game. My footsteps echoed as I strode down the corridor to my classroom, inhaling the smell of gym clothes and well-thumbed books. A door slammed in the distance as the last of the students hurried to class. How I loved this arena, and the prospect of being delivered a batch of fresh-faced teenagers each year. But for now, my focus was on Emma because I was not quite finished with her yet. My chat with the head had made me realise Emma's work wasn't up to scratch, and wouldn't be making the art exhibition after all. I would enjoy teasing her tomorrow, my little puppet on a string.

CHAPTER FORTY-THREE
ALEX

2017

Inhaling the comforting scent of freshly ground coffee, I pretended for just a few minutes that everything was under control. A shaft of long-overdue sunlight flooded in through the window of Costa Coffee, and I basked in its heat as I queued, waiting for our drinks to be made.

'Alex?' Theresa spoke, touching me on the forearm.

A smile graced my lips. 'Thanks for coming. I ordered you a coffee.'

'I haven't got long, I'm afraid.' She eyed me warily. Her shoulder-length blonde hair was tied back into a short ponytail, and she looked smart and efficient in the black trouser suit she wore for work. I joined her at the quietest table I could find. As I passed her the shortbread biscuits, I thought of how nice it was not to receive a look of disdain in return. Food had always been a battlefield for Emma, its very presence bringing instant unease. Theresa took a bite, her little finger wiping away the trail of crumbs from the corner of her mouth.

'It's Emma,' I said. 'I need your help. She's relapsing, and I don't know what to do.'

'Is this about what happened to Jamie?' she said, her eyebrows knitted in concern.

'Partly,' I said. There was so much more to Emma's eating disorder than food alone. It stole her concentration, making her physically and mentally unwell. I listlessly stirred my coffee, feeling the burden heavy on my shoulders. 'I caught her throwing up in the toilet again the other night. She goes from bingeing to barely eating at all. I'm worried it's taking her focus from Jamie. He could have been run over yesterday.'

'You need to be there for her.' With the pad of her finger, Theresa picked at the leftover crumbs on the table and deposited them on her plate. 'What happened with Jamie was an accident, but if you treat her like she's some godawful person, that'll cause her to relapse even more.' She brushed the crumbs from her fingers, finally meeting my eye. 'Emma's suffered from anxiety all her life. It's like this tireless voice in her head, always judging, always pointing out her flaws. You need to be louder than the voice, tell her what an amazing person she is.'

I frowned. How could I tell her that after Emma's confession? Such a declaration would feel like a lie. 'What happened to Jamie . . . he could have died. I should have been there. Why didn't she call me?' The memory stabbed my heart. 'I've never done anything to make her scared of me.'

'You're looking at it from the wrong perspective. It's not about you. It's about what's going on in here.' Theresa tapped the side of her forehead. 'Besides, you need to be talking to each other, not me.' She gave me a look that suggested she knew more than she was letting on. I knew I was pushing the boundaries of our friendship, going behind Emma's back for advice.

'She's not sleeping,' I said, my voice wracked with concern. 'And when she does, she's plagued with nightmares. She's paranoid too, thinks the world is out to get her. I've searched online. Apparently, eating disorders can be sparked by mental health problems. What if there's a more serious underlying cause? I can't relax when she's with Jamie. I'm scared of what might happen when they're alone.'

'What are you going to do? Keep her under house arrest?' Theresa said.

I thought of how difficult I'd found it to let Emma take Jamie to school that morning. 'Of course not. I just want to keep both of them safe.'

Theresa nodded glumly. 'I've spoken to her about her eating, but I'm not sure if she's in control any more.'

My throat felt tight as I swallowed and I took a mouthful of coffee to ease the passage of my words. 'I knew she had problems when she was young but I didn't realise the full extent. And all this stuff with Luke. She thinks he's coming to get her. Do you think he could be stalking her again after all these years?' I wanted to tell her about my meeting in Leeds, but I needed to gauge her reaction. She was Emma's sister, and her loyalty must surely be with her.

Theresa took my hand. 'Come on now, that's silly talk. Luke's not back – Emma's just being paranoid. You're a strong man, Alex; you'll get through this.'

I squared my shoulders. Theresa was right. I had to find a way to fix this. 'I'd hoped that, when we moved, we could start again. But the nearer we get to leaving, the worse things become.'

'You can't walk away from your demons,' Theresa said, her eyes glazing over. 'They'll catch up with you in the end.' She seemed to snap out of her trance and took a deep breath. 'I don't make a habit of interfering in people's relationships, but I'm not going to stand by and let everything fall apart.'

I rubbed my chin, feeling two-day-old bristles. I was in dire need of a shave. 'She got a silent call when I was in Leeds. She said you had some sunflowers delivered to the shop too. She thinks history's repeating itself and Luke is to blame for Jamie almost getting run over.' At the mention of this, Theresa's face turned grim.

'She told you all that?' She frowned. 'You don't want her going back there. What happened with Luke affected us all.'

'Well, she told me *something*,' I said. 'And I hate to say it, but I'm not sure how much of it is the truth.' I repeated Emma's account, apart from the murder, of course. I desperately wanted Theresa to say it was true, that her sister had been a victim in all of this. Perhaps then I could move on, forget about what Luke Priestwood had said, and put all thoughts of Jamie not being mine behind me.

Theresa sipped her coffee, her elbows at right angles, her body tense. As I finished the story, I searched her face for answers. Her jaw was set tight, her gaze on the table. I knew without asking that my wife had been lying to me.

'The thing is,' I said, 'I've heard other things about Emma and Luke, and it's a completely different account. Believe me, I'd love to forget the whole thing. But now it's affecting our family – even social services are involved. I have to keep digging until I find out what's going on. This is where I need your help. Nobody knows Emma like you do.'

Theresa shifted in her seat. 'I can't bear to see what's happening to the three of you. But if you tell Emma what I've said, she won't confide in me again.'

'We both want what's best for her. Please. You have my word. Whatever you tell me is strictly between us.' I realised my voice was pleading, and in a way, I was dreading what she was going to say.

Theresa opened her mouth to speak, then paused as a group of noisy teenagers passed our table in search of somewhere to sit. Chairs rattled as they took a seat in the corner, and when they were finally out of earshot, she spoke. 'There's someone very important that we have to remember in all of this, and that's Jamie. I don't want him growing up like Emma did, in a disruptive household with a mum and dad arguing all the time. It was easier for me because I was hardly ever there. I'll always regret not watching out for Emma. But it's not too late for Jamie. He's entitled to a normal upbringing, and I don't want to see him suffer.' She leaned forward, narrowing the gap between us. 'I've watched Emma bounce back all her life. But with all of this going on, I don't think there's any more bounce left. You're right. She needs help.' Theresa rested a hand on my forearm. 'You've got to get away from that house.'

'I will, but first of all, I need to know what happened with Luke.'

She nodded her head solemnly. 'Will you promise to stand by her? To keep the family together? I can't bear to think of her raising Jamie alone.'

'Of course. You know how much they mean to me. I wouldn't be meeting you if I had any intention of leaving.'

Theresa drew her hand away and took her jacket from the back of her chair. 'Then I think it's time you knew the truth. But not here. Let's go for a walk.'

CHAPTER FORTY-FOUR
EMMA

2017

His eyes wide with excitement, Jamie had revelled in our bus excursion to Colchester. I felt compelled to use public transport, much to Alex's relief. I saw the way he had been looking at me, observing my behaviour for clues that I was going mad. I regretted my confession and all the intimate moments when I had discussed my eating disorder, telling him about the voice in my head. Everybody heard voices, and most were like mine, brutal and unkind. I only had to listen to my clients in the bridal shop as they chatted about diets and body image to know where their harshest critics lived. But I had to maintain control. What happened to Jamie must never happen again. As I walked into town, PC Bakewell's words rebounded in my memory. I would not be so lucky the next time around. For now, Jamie was safely ensconced in nursery school, seemingly none the worse for wear. A flush had risen to my chest as I explained our near miss to Mairead, the nursery head. She had treated me with compassion, offering to hold another teddy bear's picnic to make up for the one Jamie had missed. Such warmth had not been extended by my husband. I knew he was trying not to blame me for the incident in the car park, but I sensed an underlying resentment just the same.

The problem with having something precious was the very real fear of losing it, and as I checked my phone, I was more aware of that now than ever. I opened up the 'friend finder' app to check Alex's whereabouts, praying that I was wrong. He had said that he would be spending the day in his old office, tying up loose ends before returning to his new role. But the map on my phone stated he was in Costa Coffee in town. I bit my lip as I sent a text.

> Jamie's fine. He loved the bus ride. Did you get to work OK? Love you. XXX

The response was almost immediate, stopping me in my tracks.

> That's great! Yes, no problems. Up to my eyes in it. Speak soon. XXX

My husband was lying to me. Slowly I slipped through the Odeon cinema entrance so as not to be spotted as I cast an eye over the coffee-shop patrons. The two businesses worked in tandem. Alex and I'd had many happy dates here before Jamie was born. But today's visit was one he had not seen fit to disclose to me. He was taking a chance coming here, relying upon my routine of opening the bridal shop on time. I peeped around the corner to find him sitting on the sofa, his back turned to me as he sat with a blonde woman in an armchair. I tried to make out her features, but from my vantage point, I could only see the top of her head. As their hands touched from across the table, I felt bile rise in my throat. He did not touch colleagues like that. This was too intimate a meeting to be work. My insecurities grew. Was he having an affair? Why else had he lied, saying he was at work? Had my inadequacies pushed him away into the arms of another? Just how long had this been going on? Questions fired in my mind like poison arrows, making me feel sick to the core. Picking up a free newspaper, I slid into a nearby seat. Time was against me. Customers would complain if I opened up late. I peered over the paper, fury blooming inside me as I watched Alex lean in for a hug. It was only as the woman leaned forward that I realised the mystery date was my sister. What was she doing with Alex? Confusion wormed its way into my brain. She hadn't mentioned this to me. I watched transfixed as they parted, she patting him on the shoulder then Alex touching her arm. I lowered the paper and checked my watch. It was time for me to go.

I had to get to work and act as if it were a normal day. I would decide what to do once I had listened to what she had to say. I did not know which was worse: the thought of them plotting about what to do with me behind my back or finding comfort in each other's arms. Slipping outside, I could not stop myself from following a little longer. Swerving busy pedestrians, I kept my distance, wondering if Alex and Theresa were making a detour to the shop. Perhaps I had got it wrong. Maybe they were planning a surprise, to take me out for the day. Theresa linked Alex's arm through hers as she tottered down the street in her new trouser suit and heels. My face soured as they walked the path to Colchester Castle. The place I used to go with Luke. The lilt of laughter carried on the air, and I realised that it was coming from Alex. I had not heard him laugh like that with me in such a long time. I turned away, tears stinging my eyes. Why were two of the people I loved most in the world meeting behind my back? My arms swinging by my side, I strode towards my shop in haste. I would put on a brave face, pretend nothing had happened and wait for them to come to me with the truth.

CHAPTER FORTY-FIVE

ALEX

2017

A sudden stab of guilt hit me as I replied to Emma's text. I hated deceiving her, but it was nothing compared to the web of lies that she had spun around me. A web I was trying to battle my way through. I told myself that my secret meeting with Theresa was for her own good. All I wanted was to get to the truth. It was my job to help us move on and rebuild our lives. I knew that parenthood meant more than DNA and bloodlines, but I could not bear to discover that someone else had more claim on my son than I. Reaching across the table, Theresa had offered a sympathetic hug, having only an inkling of the tangled mess my marriage had become.

'Do you mind if I take your arm?' Theresa said, wobbling slightly as she got to her feet. 'It's these daft heels. They're far too high for me.'

As we made our way down the winding cobbled path, she recalled stories of Emma and the lengths she used to go to when sourcing her bohemian look. Such comments brought comfort, and I laughed as she reminded me of the unique young woman I had fallen in love with in Leeds.

'It's all down to Mum, you know,' Theresa said. 'Whether she knows it or not, Emma's emulating her style. I remember, growing up, Mum used to wear lots of tunic blouses, floppy hats, maxi-print dresses, all that stuff.'

This was news to me. 'But why would Emma want to copy your mum if she gave her such a hard time growing up?'

'It wasn't all bad,' Theresa said sadly. 'Emma only focuses on the bad bits because she punishes herself for Mum leaving. Mum was difficult to live with, and when she got drunk things would get a lot worse. But she could go weeks without a drink. She used to bring us crabbing down the beach, show us how to paint. Dad used to go away on his digs for weeks at a time. That's when she'd get lonely and hit the bottle. I wish . . .' Theresa sighed, our conversation taking on a more serious tone.

'Go on,' I said, as we turned into Colchester Castle.

'I wish I could tell Emma that Mum leaving isn't her fault. Maybe if she realised that, she wouldn't feel so tormented by the past.'

'It's not your mum she's worried about,' I said. 'It's Luke Priestwood. Right now I'd like to focus on what happened with him.'

'Well, this is where it all started,' she said, relinquishing her hold as she found a bench in the expansive grounds. Sitting here, with the birds singing and the sun warming our backs, it could almost be taken for a spring day. But my time in the sunshine was short lived, as Theresa opened up the wounds of her past.

'After Mum left, Emma went through a rough patch. I wasn't at home very much. Neither Dad nor Emma were coping very well. Then one day Dad told me Emma had a new art teacher, and he had really turned things around.' She stared into the distance as a cool breeze played with loose strands of her hair. 'He was in his twenties, good looking, the sort of man that girls swooned over back then. I think that's why he liked Emma. She was quiet and cautious. He befriended her and she began to open up to him. If you ask me, their problems began the moment he agreed to meet her here.'

I glanced around at the castle grounds, busy with visitors making the most of the sunny day. I tried to imagine a younger version of my wife, sitting on this bench, pouring her heart out to Luke. The image would not come. 'For a teacher to meet a pupil after school . . . it was very reckless of him. She was young and vulnerable. I can't help but think he took advantage.'

'You're right,' Theresa said, her voice tinged with regret. 'And I blame myself for not picking up on it earlier on. She told me she was seeing him outside school, but when I brought it up with Dad, he said their meetings were above board.'

'But they weren't,' I said. 'Were they?'

Theresa shook her head. 'Emma fell for Luke very quickly. I'd moved out and Dad was so distant . . . it was hardly any wonder she attached herself to him.'

'Luke shouldn't have agreed to it in the first place. Any fool can see that.' I tried to keep my emotions in check. Meeting with a pupil was nothing compared to Emma trying to kill him.

'He must have got a kick out of it, somewhere along the line.' Theresa sighed at the memory, her gaze distant. 'I only had to mention his name and she would turn bright red. It was obvious she had a huge crush on him. I thought it was harmless. Dad made it sound like Luke was counselling her and, for a while, she seemed happier.'

My heart sank as she echoed Luke's words.

'I knew something had happened because a few months later he cut off all contact with her. Suddenly, all she wanted to do was to follow him around. I had no idea how long it had been going on for, until it all came out.'

'So you're saying that she followed him? What about the flowers that were sent to the house?'

'Oh, we got flowers all right. At first Dad thought they were from Luke. We all did. That's until we found out she was sending them to herself. Thank God we weren't into social media back then is all I can say. At least her lies were limited to the people she told in school.' She gave me a sideways glance, regret written all over her face. 'Want me to keep going?'

I nodded, reminding myself that it was all in the past. Emma was a different person now. I would make her well again.

Theresa took a breath, her hands lightly clasped on her lap. 'She used to stalk him at school. Whenever anyone spoke to her about it, she'd put the onus back on him, saying he was stringing her along, that he loved her and wouldn't leave her alone. The more Luke tried to push her away, the more obsessed she became. It was almost tragic.'

Tragic? If only she knew. My thoughts streaked through my mind. Or did she know? How much had Emma told her? In the distance a group of mothers and toddlers assembled, one of the children shrieking as the red balloon she was holding was taken by the wind. I watched its ascent as it bobbed from left to right, its destination orchestrated by the unpredictable weather.

Theresa crossed her legs, clasping her hands around her knee. 'Perhaps fantasising about Luke gave her a break from her own thoughts. Maybe it was easier to live in that fantasy world. She got over him in time. University helped. Having new friends and facing different challenges really brought her out of herself. That was the last I heard about Luke until Dad's funeral. Maybe it *was* Luke who sent the flowers that time. I don't know.' She shrugged.

'But why?' I said. 'The phone calls, the flowers. Why has it started up again?'

'I don't know. Maybe stress is the trigger. Having you and Jamie in her life has really helped her pull things together. I'm hoping when you move she'll come back to herself again.'

'Or she could go the other way,' I said, thinking of the extent of my wife's lies. It was as though we were talking about a different person. I didn't know her at all. Yet I needed to ask Theresa outright – to hear her say the words aloud. I inhaled a deep breath, the warmth of the morning breeze giving me strength. 'Did they sleep together? Was that why she stalked him? Because that's what you're telling me, isn't it?'

'I think so.' She nodded. 'And I feel bad for not believing it at first. But you have to remember, Emma was just sixteen. Luke took advantage of her, used her for sex. That's when things turned nasty. Despite everything he'd done, Emma wasn't ready to let him go.'

So, Emma was the stalker, not Luke. He had been telling the truth all along. Thoughts raced through my head as I journeyed to my office, each one accompanied by a streak of fear. Theresa loved Emma as much as I did, and I knew she would never lie about their past. Her account had made me wonder if I had been married to a stranger all these years. Could Theresa have got it wrong? My shoulders fell as I realised I was coming up with excuses, rather than believing what was staring me in the face. But as I reached the office, it seemed that Theresa was not the only source of information. As I sorted through the pile of post on my desk, I found another part of the puzzle which was entirely impartial. The blood drained from my body as I read the postmark of the envelope. Jamie's DNA results. A hard ball lodged in my throat as I picked up the envelope. Was I strong enough to cope with what was inside?

CHAPTER FORTY-SIX
LUKE

2003

My meeting with the head teacher should have been the end of it. Yet I knew I could not leave it there. Having Emma in my life was like a scabbed-over wound I couldn't resist picking at. I knew from our chats that her dad went to the pub to meet up with his cronies on a Thursday night, leaving her all alone. I had been careful to park my car away from prying eyes. Dressed in black, I was barely visible against the greying landscape, and I crept to the back of the bungalow to check Emma was alone.

I held my breath as I glanced through the small square window, watching as she stirred a bubbling pot on the stove. How many times had she done the same to me? I had seen her, creeping around the perimeter of my home on the CCTV. Annoyance rose up inside me as I watched her cooking without a care in the world. Her hair was tied up with a red scarf, and she looked like she was humming a tune as she turned to scoop up a handful of chopped garlic cloves and plop them into the broth. Her long flowing skirt swayed as she moved; she appeared as if she came from a different era, an oddity in this world. But I knew what she was capable of and I could not stay away. I tapped on her window with my knuckle, taking pleasure in making her jump out of her skin. Gripping the kitchen counter, her expression changed from fear to wonder as she realised it was me. Patting her hair and brushing off her skirt, she whirled around in a panic, taking the pot from the stove before making her way to the back door.

A sudden puff of garlic-infused steam escaped into the night air as the door creaked open and I wasted no time in walking inside. 'Are you alone?' I grunted, surveying the kitchen.

She nodded, her eyes wide with anticipation. After all the times I had warned her off, she must have felt as if she were dreaming, finding me in her kitchen, the two of us alone. Any other woman would have been enraged by my treatment of her, dumping her so mercilessly after I'd got what I wanted. But not Emma. I only had to click my fingers and she would be mine. That was the beauty of the troubled backstory I had fed her. I could behave exactly how I wanted and she would put it down to me having a childhood as disturbed as her own.

'What are you doing here?' she said, clasping and unclasping her hands.

'You know why,' I said, my tone deep and menacing as I backed her up against a wall. 'I had a visit from the headmistress today. Have you been spreading rumours? Trying to get me the sack?'

Her mouth dropped open upon hearing the accusation, and I grabbed her arms and shook to elicit a response. 'Well? What have you been saying?'

'N . . . nothing,' she said. 'I swear, it wasn't me. Luke, please. I'd never do anything to hurt you.'

'Really?' I said, expelling a bitter laugh. 'Tell that to my dog. I only had him a year. Don't try denying it. I know it was you who let him out of the car.' The truth was, I had been glad to see the back of him.

I'd never liked that dog; it was my mother who thought I would benefit from having a pet. But women were attracted to animal lovers, and on this occasion I was happy to use him as leverage if it wiped the smile from Emma's face.

'It was an accident. I didn't know he was on the back seat. I saw you go into the shops. The car was unlocked and I was getting into it when he jumped out.' Her chin wobbled as she struggled to word a response. 'I panicked and ran away. I thought he'd just go home.'

'But he didn't run home, did he? He ran straight under the tyres of a car.'

'I'm sorry,' she wailed, her face twisted with angst. 'I feel awful for what happened. But you hurt me, Luke, more than Mum, Theresa, anyone I know. And the worst thing about it is that I . . .' She gasped for breath as tears lined her lids. 'I don't know what I've done wrong.'

'You were cheap,' I said, looking her up and down with disgust. 'After the way you behaved, did you really think I'd be interested in anything more?' A warmth spread from within as I watched her features crumble. This was what I'd wanted when I'd tapped on her window pane. 'Look at you, following me around, like you're trying to replace my dog. You almost lost me my job today. You'd better stop what you're doing or you'll come to regret it.'

'Please. You don't mean that,' she said, making no effort to escape as I edged myself closer to her. My words were saying one thing, but my body was communicating something else. Her expression was wracked with confusion as I lay my hands on her shoulders, grazing her cheek with the knuckles of my right hand, just as I had that time we'd met in my classroom after lessons had ended.

'Oh, little puppy,' I said, 'how many times must I kick you before you stop coming back for more?' I pressed my lips upon hers, teasing her mouth open with my tongue. For a few tantalising seconds we entwined, my fingers caressing the back of her neck, eliciting a soft moan. 'Is this what you want?' I whispered, planting butterfly kisses on her skin. She arched her neck to meet me, closing her eyes as my hands caressed her back. Pulling away, I tutted as she wrapped her hands around me, trying to draw me near. Grasping her wrists, I pushed her away. I wiped my mouth to remove all traces of her from my lips. 'Like I said, cheap. Harass me again and I'll call the police.'

'No,' she screamed. 'You can't do this to me. I won't let you. I . . .' but her words were cut short as I wrapped both my hands around her throat, pinning her up against the wall. 'You don't call the shots here, I do. Say one word to jeopardise my job and I'll leave you so nobody will ever look at you again. Understand?'

Emma spluttered a cough as I released my grip, the fear in her eyes telling me all I needed to know. I was the one in control, not her, and if I wanted her I would click my fingers and watch her come running. Not that I would be calling anytime soon. I had another prize in mind.

Closing the back door behind me, I disappeared into the night, leaving a broken little girl behind.

CHAPTER FORTY-SEVEN
EMMA

2003

The floorboards creaked from my movement, and I climbed on to my bed, gripping my phone as the mattress bounced lightly beneath my weight. I sat, legs splayed amongst the remnants of things I had collected over the school year. A piece of paper Luke had scribbled on, then thrown in the bin. A pebble from the gravel yard of his home. I knew I had been taking a risk in returning, but I ventured there only when I knew Luke and his family were away. Shame fell heavy as I remembered clambering through his open bedroom window on the ground floor. If he only knew! That would have blown up in my face for sure. Yet it had been a bittersweet torture, lying on his bed and spending time amongst his things. Inhaling his scent from the pillow on his bed. It made me feel closer to him. Less alone. I returned my gaze to the bent-up photo I had found in his bedroom drawer. I had taped a picture of me over the girl he was standing with. My gaze fell on the old clipping from the local newspaper about the school art exhibition I was excluded from. My bedspread was covered with things that whispered his name. I clutched the cordless phone in my hand, my fingers stiff from repetitively dialling his mobile phone.

It had been easy to disguise my tears from my father, blaming my puffy eyes on a bout of hay fever. Not that he had noticed. Since Mum left, he wasn't really present any more. There had been all sort of questions asked after she disappeared, but the rumours had died down now. Mum had been vocal about leaving us well before she took the plunge, but even now, I struggled to accept she had gone for good. It was me, it had to be. I drove everybody away. Today was the first day in ages that I had attempted to cook a healthy meal. Fed up of moping around, I had cycled to the shops and bought all the ingredients myself. But now the food lay uneaten in the bottom of our rubbish bin.

How could Luke be so cruel? I licked my lips, still sore from the pressure of his kiss, my tongue finding a small cut inside my gum. It had been just the same that night in the beach hut, rough and uncaring, not how I imagined my first time to be. Yet, I longed for him just the same.

He had told me I was beautiful, made me feel as if I counted in this world. But it was all lies, just to get what he wanted. He never really loved me at all. My guts churned at the thoughts of his departure. Why would he have kissed me if he didn't care?

I took little comfort from the thought. He was slipping away, and his kiss was just a parting shot. It scared me just how empty my life would become without him. Up until now I had fooled myself that there was still a chance for us.

Following him in town, poring over his things, I knew it wasn't normal behaviour. Sometimes I could justify my actions because I loved him. I knew then that I'd rather kill myself than face the thought of being without him. My heart felt as if it was breaking into tiny little splinters, and I could not take the pain any more.

I gathered my thoughts. Would that make him come to his senses? Make him fall in love with me again? It reminded me of the daisy game

I used to play, plucking the petals as I recited the words, 'He loves me, he loves me not, he loves me . . .'

I stifled a yawn. It was the middle of the night and I had school in the morning. How was I going to face school, when all the gossips in the common room now talked about me? I rubbed my throat where he had gripped me tightly, yet in some masochistic way I had welcomed his contact. It was rough and unloving but the best someone like me could hope for. My relationship with Luke was the worst kind of torture. Mum's departure had cut me to the bone, but at least it had been quick, with little promise of return.

CHAPTER FORTY-EIGHT
EMMA

2017

Busying myself in the changing room, I carefully tidied the array of dresses that my indecisive bride had abandoned. Given it was her fourth visit, I was relieved she had finally made a decision. I checked my watch. Alex's meeting with Theresa weighed heavily on my mind, stealing my focus from the job at hand. My trance was broken as the bell rang over the door.

'Only me!' Theresa said brightly as she shrugged off her suit jacket. 'Sorry I'm late. Oh, are you with a client?'

'Just left,' I said, feeling my throat constrict as I spoke. 'You look good. Been shopping?'

'I thought I'd make more of an effort, although I'm not sure about these heels. Cuppa tea?' Theresa breezed past me into the kitchen.

Did I imagine it or had she been unable to meet my gaze? Why was she suddenly making an effort with her appearance? Suspicion coiled around me like an ugly snake, and I busied myself as I tried to hold back the spiteful comments lacing my tongue. 'No thanks . . . I've been trying to ring Alex, but he's not answering his phone.'

The tinkling spoon came to a halt from the kitchen, and her response took a couple of extra seconds to come. 'I wouldn't worry. He's probably with a client. Oh, Ems, have you seen the scissors? I need to snip off some tags but they're not in the drawer here.'

'No,' I said, almost snorting at her desperation to change the subject. But Alex was a worry not so easily shifted. He had been growing distant; when he smiled it felt like he was putting on an act. But just the same, I found it hard to believe that he would betray me with my sister.

'Are you sure you're OK?' Theresa asked, sipping her tea. She stared intensely, her eyes feeling like they were searching the very corridors of my mind.

'I'm fine,' I said, unwilling to elaborate. My heightened anxiety had forced me to log into the nursery's webcam three times already, just to make sure that Jamie was doing OK. My thoughts went round and round on a loop and by late afternoon I was feeling sick and emotionally drained. I had yet to bring myself to eat, but I was equally worried that if I started I would not be able to stop.

'These shoes are killing me.' Sitting on the chaise longue, Theresa crossed her legs and rubbed the heel of her right foot. 'We've got Bridezilla coming soon. You know how demanding she is. If you're not up to it then I'm sure I can manage her on my own.'

'Don't be silly,' I said, my nose in the appointment book as I worked out next week's shifts. 'I've got this.'

'I hope the sun shines on her wedding day,' Theresa said, 'otherwise she'll be blaming us for the weather too. God, I feel sorry for that fiancé of hers. Still, he must be as much of a wanker as she is, to want to spend the rest of his life with her.'

'Not appropriate,' I said, raising a smile. I often felt like the big sister in our relationship. Theresa had floated through life with a string of boyfriends, never actually committing to any one thing. We had all been thrilled when she'd finally settled down. Charles was considerably older, not what you called good looking, but I'd had a feeling at the time that his bank balance made up for the shortfall. It was just a shame he had such a roving eye. Theresa didn't like to talk about him, and I didn't push the subject.

'Where would I be without you?' she said, her smile freezing as she glanced towards the door. 'Brace yourself. She's here.'

I took a deep breath. Flapping a polka-dot umbrella, a wide-hipped woman barged through the front door. I had some beautiful dresses for curvy brides, but Victoria had been putting on weight at a ferocious rate, and the problems began when she tried to blame the ill-fitting dresses on me. She had not held back, citing 'shoddy material' as one of the reasons the gowns grew tighter with each fitting. I thought of my father's saying, the one he used when my mother was in a bad mood: *If the cat had kittens it would be my fault.* At the time, I didn't understand what he meant. Now I was fully aware, as everyone in my life blamed all their problems on me. I plastered on a smile as I greeted Victoria, determined to make this appointment a pleasant one.

'I'll do the meet and greet, you get the dress for her highness,' Theresa whispered, probably because she could see that I was not up to pleasantries today.

Victoria was her usual vocal self, her mother cowering behind her as she barked orders in her wake. 'You sit there,' she scowled, scraping back her plum-tinted hair which had grown frizzy from the rain. 'No, not there, stupid, here where the light shines properly. I want you to tell me exactly what you think.'

Tell her what she wants to hear, more like, I thought to myself as I bustled between the dresses on the hangers looking for the tag with her name. I doubted anyone had ever dared tell Victoria what they really thought. I comforted myself that it was her final fitting, and I had pre-empted her weight gain by asking the seamstress to let her gown out a couple of inches more.

'Here we go,' I said, carrying the weighty gown in both arms. It was beautiful, one of our designer dresses that had cost me an arm and a leg. At over two thousand pounds, it was my first brand-new rental, and it appeased Victoria that she could hire a designer dress at a fraction of the cost of buying it. 'Do you want to try it on?' I said, wincing as the words left my mouth. It was just one of those things you said, but I knew she'd pick up on it straight away.

'Of course I do,' she said, rolling her eyes. 'I've got to make sure it fits. Three years I've been planning this day. Three years and of all the companies I've dealt with I've never used one as unprofessional as yours.'

My smile tightened because I knew this was a lie. I had many contacts in the wedding industry and what Victoria didn't realise is that we all discussed our clients. She had given every one of them a similar speech in the hope of a discount. I tugged at the zip, in no mood for her sniping comments today.

'Here, let me give you a hand,' Theresa said as we extracted the gown from its protective covering. It sparkled beneath the light and I found myself looking forward to seeing it on the new bride. The Prosecco was on ice, and fairy lights twinkled on the centre platform, all waiting for her special moment. But it was lost on Victoria as she greedily grabbed the dress from my hands.

'Gently,' I said, being rewarded with a red-faced glare.

But as she pulled the gown from its encasement, she emitted an ear-piercing squeal. 'What's this? My dress! What have you done to my dress?'

My head swivelled from Theresa and back to Victoria. This had to be a record. Usually her complaining began when she tried the gown on. My eyes widened as Victoria plunged her fingers into what looked like torn material. 'What the hell is this?' she raged, pulling at the slashed fabric and waving it in my face.

My mouth dropped open. I was dumbfounded. Surely I was not looking at a dress that had been ripped to shreds?

'Let me see that,' Theresa said, taking the dress from Victoria's grasp. I held the hanger as she spread it out between us, her fingers trailing down the jagged rips in the satin.

'I say, someone's taken a knife to it,' Victoria's mother piped up, like Miss Marple in the background.

But as I peered closer, I could see that the implement that had been used was more likely scissors. Someone had speedily cut through as many layers as they could. I looked down as sprinklings of diamante dropped to the floor. 'This can't be right,' I said, my words fading as my sister and I exchanged horrified glances.

'My dress, my beautiful dress!' Victoria emitted a low howl of despair and plump tears streaked down her face.

I could not blame her for her outburst. It was a week until her wedding, and the dress that she had so painstakingly chosen was now reduced to a tattered mess. However, it was just as horrific for me, given how much money I had invested in buying it. I felt sick, and shocked I had not noticed the damage sooner. 'It must be a different gown,' I said, grasping for answers. 'The seamstress must have sent me back the wrong one. This can't be yours, it can't. There's got to be a mistake.' My words tumbled out, and I continued speaking quickly until I stopped making sense. I fought for air, feeling the world close in on me as everything in my life went wrong.

Victoria's face reddened until it was almost puce. Her fists clenched, she grabbed me by my shirt, giving me a violent shake. She pressed her face against mine. 'What. The fuck. Have you done. To my dress?' she snarled.

I closed my eyes to the spittle landing on my face, my teeth rattling as this larger-than-life woman took hold. Throwing the gown to the floor, Theresa came between us, releasing Victoria's grasp. I left her to deal with the mess and, with my arms swinging by my sides, strode into the back room with as much dignity as I could muster. Slamming the door behind me, I slid to the floor, giving in to the tears that had built up in uncontrollable waves. It had happened again. My tormentor had returned to haunt me, breaking down each segment of my life until I had nothing left to give. Theresa's voice carried from the other room, saying that she did not know who could have done this. But I did. And he wasn't going to stop there.

CHAPTER FORTY-NINE
EMMA

2017

I don't know how long I was sitting on the floor before Theresa came to find me. Curled up in a ball, I had wrapped my arms around my knees, feeling like a child once more. Tentatively she approached me, her face clouded in concern.

'Sweetheart, are you OK?' She gently touched my shoulder, helping me rise to my feet.

Pins and needles spiked my legs, and I leaned on the kitchen counter for support. I felt dazed, as if I had been in a car crash and lost all sense of time. But the only car crash here was my life. My tongue felt glued to the roof of my mouth, and I swallowed, my words croaky as I spoke. 'I . . . I don't feel very well.' I clung tighter to the counter as the memory returned. 'The dress,' I said, recalling Victoria's angry face, her thick fingers digging into my shirt. 'Is she . . .' I stared at her, open-mouthed. 'Is she gone?'

'Here, let me get you a drink,' Theresa said, pushing a glass beneath the tap and guiding me to sit at the table. 'When's the last time you've eaten? How about a sandwich, eh? You need some food inside you.'

I sipped the lukewarm water, closing my eyes as it slipped down my throat. A wave of dizziness overcame me, and the glass trembled as I set it back on the table. I rubbed my eyes with the butts of my palms, trying to clear my field of vision. 'Victoria?' I said. 'I take it she's gone?'

'It's OK, I've sorted it out. Silly cow threatened to sue, but her second choice still fits her, and she's a bit happier now she's hiring it for free.'

A rustling noise ensued as Theresa poked her head in the fridge. 'Here,' she said, taking a tuna sandwich from its wrapper and laying it before me. 'Eat.'

I narrowed my eyes as I came to my senses. 'You know who did this, don't you? Luke. He's the one responsible.'

'That's not possible,' Theresa said, shaking her head. 'We lock up every night. I've checked. There's no sign of a break-in.' She shoved the sandwich towards me. 'I checked the dress when it came back from the seamstress yesterday. It was perfect.'

I frowned. The look on Theresa's face made me wonder. 'You don't think it was me, do you?' I forced myself to take a bite of the sandwich, knowing she wouldn't respond until I ate.

'No,' she said, a smile rising to her lips as she watched me eat. 'At least . . . not knowingly. You've been under a lot of pressure lately. I'm just scared that it's getting to you.' She touched my hand. 'This thing with Luke. I'm on your side.'

I paused mid-chew. 'What's me being stressed got to do with the dress being slashed?' My eyes flitted towards the door. 'And why are you here with me when there's nobody in the shop?'

'I've closed for lunch. Look . . .' she said, pursing her lips. 'I'm just saying . . . you don't have to prove anything to me.'

I swallowed, feeling my strength return. I stared at my sister as I got to grips with her words. 'You think I damaged the dress then blamed it on Luke so you'd believe me? Why would I do that? You know what a big mouth Victoria has. This is going to ruin our reputation.'

Theresa snorted. 'Nobody pays any attention to her. Besides, I sorted it.'

I rolled my eyes. 'Don't try to placate me. It's awful what happened. If it was me getting married and my dress was in shreds, I'd go mad.'

'No, honestly, I sorted it. I told her I have CCTV of her assaulting you. She's lucky I didn't call the police. I think that's enough to make it go away.'

'But we haven't got CCTV,' I said, for once wishing that we had. 'That camera in the corner is fake.'

Theresa gave me a wry smile. 'I know that and you know that, but *she* doesn't know that, and that's the way it's going to stay. Trust me, we can sweep this all under the carpet. Thank God the backup dress fitted her. Bridezilla will have her perfect day after all.'

'Even though I sabotaged the dress to begin with? You don't really believe that, do you?'

Theresa nodded towards the sandwich, and I took another bite. This was the way it had always been. Trading off information for food. She had encouraged me to eat in whatever way she could.

She shook her head. 'Of course not. It was a silly thing to say. But what *is* worrying me is your inability to cope with it. You've had far worse things than this come your way. You should have fought back, pushed the silly woman away.' She toyed with her silver necklace, a sure sign she was uncomfortable with what she was about to say. 'I just think that you should consider getting counselling. Alex . . . he spoke to me this morning. He knows you're not eating. He's worried about you. We both are.'

I opened my mouth to speak, but Theresa raised her hand.

'We weren't going behind your back. Please. Don't tell him I told you. I'm just trying to help the pair of you.'

I took a sip of water, dismissing the judgemental voices swirling around my head. There was no point in airing my suspicions about Luke. It was safer to tell her what she wanted to hear. 'Maybe he's right,' I said. 'Sometimes I feel like the whole world is against me.'

Theresa gave me a gentle smile. 'Don't be daft, it'll all be OK. Now, how about I make us both a nice cup of tea? I've got some chocolate biscuits hidden in the cupboard.'

Food was the last thing I needed, but I found myself nodding just the same.

CHAPTER FIFTY
ALEX

2017

I stared at the envelope, bile rising in my throat. The feeling of helplessness washed over me. It was the same alien emotion I'd encountered when the doctors had told me my chances of fathering a child were slim to none. Just like my infertility, this situation was out of my control. I had given my work address to the company who carried out the DNA results as there was no way I could risk Emma finding out what I had done. Having excused myself from the office, I stood outside in the dying sunlight, turning the envelope over in my fingers. The car park was reasonably quiet and, although this was not how I had pictured finding out, I could not wait until I went home.

I thought of Jamie's birth, the fierce pride that had burned in my chest at the sight of my son. Now I was reduced to this, holding on to a secret too awful to share. It was I who'd told Emma to sleep while I took over the night feeds. I who had comforted Jamie during teething when his red swollen gums caused him pain. I who taught him how to feed himself, raised out my hands beside Emma as he took his first step. Dada was the first word he had spoken. I tightened my jaw, determined to remain in control. If it came to it, I thought I would be able to get over the fact that I was not blood related, but Emma's deception would cut a much deeper groove into my soul. I turned the envelope over as I tried to gather enough courage to read the results inside. Wouldn't it be easier to tear the damn thing up and forget that it ever came? We could move to Leeds, start again and carry on believing that Jamie was mine. Did I need to know if Emma had lied to me about her relationship with Luke? It was all in the past . . . wasn't it? I leaned against the cold concrete wall, wondering if that was the case. How could it be in the past as long as Luke was living in York? Regardless of what he'd said, I could be placing Emma in danger. That's if she was telling the truth. I wanted to believe her but, every day, evidence was mounting against her, leaving me in fear of what she might do next. After all that had happened, was she capable of looking after our son? Our son. My grip on the envelope tightened as the wind threatened to whisk it away.

Fumbling with the flap, I finally ripped it open, my body rigid as I shook the letter free. I closed my eyes, taking what could be my last breath as Jamie's father, praying for a satisfactory conclusion. But my prayers went unanswered as I glared at the cold and impersonal string of words.

> The alleged father is excluded as the biological father of the tested child. The alleged father lacks the genetic markers that must be contributed to the child by the biological father. The probability of paternity is 0%.

'No,' I moaned, feeling like someone had ripped out my heart and crushed it in front of me. 'It can't be.' In the distance, a car door slammed and I quickly shoved the letter back into the envelope before pushing it deep into my jacket pocket. All these years Emma had lied to me. My own wife. I felt a wave of nausea as reality hit hard. I closed my eyes, seeing the text on the back of my eyelids. *The probability of paternity is 0%.* What a mug I had been. No wonder she was scared of Luke coming back. He was not the monster she portrayed, he was the father of her son. I had spoken to him myself. As for Theresa, of course she had told me the truth – she was Emma's sister. And now if I was in any doubt . . . the DNA result spoke for itself.

The question was, what did I do next? Where did that leave me with Jamie? Would Emma turn on me just as she had with Luke? I may be listed as the father on his birth certificate but, if it went to court, what legal rights did I actually have? Then again, would Emma really cause trouble when it emerged that I knew what she had done? Ugly thoughts raised their heads as I tried to assemble a plan. Dipping my hand into my pocket, I pulled out my vaporiser, closing my eyes as I inhaled. The artificial tang of tobacco and aniseed hit my throat, and I exhaled a cloud of white smoke. There were no clues, no evidence of Emma's attempt to murder Luke on our land. I was not afraid to play dirty. I would do whatever it took to protect my son.

I swallowed, the unpleasant taste of my betrayal making itself known. I could not believe I was thinking of Emma in this way. Her face flashed in my memory. I loved my wife. What had happened to always standing by her? She had problems, I'd known that from the day we met. But nothing like this. What good was a marriage without trust? How could she love me if all she did was lie? Opposing thoughts bounced around in my head as I paced the path, trying to work out my options. I had to get back inside. People would be wondering where I was. But how on earth could I carry on as if nothing had happened? Unless . . . I could say I'd received a phone call and there was a family emergency at home. If I did not speak to somebody soon I would combust. I couldn't tell my mother, the disappointment that she wasn't blood related to her only grandson would be too much for her to bear.

My phone buzzed in my pocket and I realised I had a missed call. As I checked my call log, the answer appeared before me. Theresa had helped me once already. God knows, people I could confide in were thin on the ground. I rubbed my chin as I mulled it over. Could I relay the full extent of Emma's lies? I felt like I had to. I needed help. I could not do this on my own.

CHAPTER FIFTY-ONE
EMMA

2003

Life had taken on a slate-grey hue in the months since Luke and I had split. What was the point? It was the end of the line. There was nothing more I could do. I slid my phone from my pocket, the late-spring sun casting a reflection on the screen. Sitting on my picnic blanket in the grounds of Colchester Castle, I was reminded of everything I had lost. How I had driven Luke away. Because he was right; it was my fault. He had been cruel just to push the point home. I looked through my texts one last time before I deleted them.

Emma: I miss you. Xxx
Emma: I'm sorry. Can we meet? Xxx
Emma: Please Luke, I still miss you. Please text me. Xxx
Emma: I don't want to live without you. Xxx
Emma: If you don't speak to me soon, I'm ending it. You'll never see me again.

Emma: Don't you care about me at all?
Luke: If you don't stop harassing me then I'm calling the police.
Emma: What about our night in the beach hut? You said you loved me.
Luke: I'm sorry but it's all in your head.
Emma: What??!! Why are you denying it? I meant what I said. I won't tell a soul.
Emma: Luke?
Luke: It's been six months. LEAVE ME ALONE. Final warning.
Emma: Fine. I'll leave you for good. See how you like having my death on your conscience.

I pressed the delete button, my heart sinking like a stone. My constant calls, the presents I had sent, nothing seemed to warrant a response. This was the final test. I had to get home quickly to carry out my plans. Dad was at some award ceremony by the archaeological society. He had not thought to ask if I wanted to go, but these days it was an effort for him just to get dressed and leave the house. What would he say when he came home to a pile of ash? Because when I left this world, I was going out with a bang. I might have seemed quiet and introverted, but my demise would light the skyline today. I bit my bottom lip, ready to send one more text, feeling every bit as pathetic as Luke said I was. I just couldn't leave it alone, and I prayed that this last gesture would bring him back to me.

Emma: I'll be at home alone at 2pm. The house will go up in flames, with me inside it.

I waited for a response but none came. By 2.30 p.m. I was sitting in my bedroom, the smell of white spirit stinging my eyes. Luke was right.

How many times would I let life kick me in the teeth before finally lying down? Mum, Theresa, Dad, Luke, they had all deserted me. My life had become one painful episode of loving people and watching them leave. My wounds were raw, my energy depleted. I wasn't strong enough to face life on my own. My shoulders shook as I sobbed, and I blinked away the tears to focus on the box of matches in my hand. The match fizzled into life as I struck it against the coarse surface of the box. Emitting one last desperate sob, I threw it on to the saturated floor.

CHAPTER FIFTY-TWO
EMMA

2017

As I strolled around the aisles of the supermarket, I thought how lucky I was to have my sister in my life. I knew that guilt still plagued her from not being there when I'd needed her the most and it had been hard, growing into a young woman with just Dad to guide me. Theresa did her best, popping back to see me when she could, but she was uneasy at home. She and Dad were not exactly close, and she always seemed to be counting the minutes until she could leave. She had more than made up for it since then, though, and Jamie's birth had been the balm that had healed many wounds.

My eyes scanned the cake section as I searched for a sponge of the right consistency. Only food could silence my inner voice, the one that plagued me from morning to night. It was growing louder now; the incident with the slashed dress had frightened me. I had tried to distract myself by filling my thoughts with my family, my business, even my choice of clothes. But now as things began to fall apart, the voice of my subconscious became so loud and fierce I wondered if other people could hear it too. Theresa had insisted I finish early, leave reporting the vandalisation to her. But I knew she wasn't going to call the police. She thought I had done it. I could see it in her eyes. Our seamstress would be able to replace the torn material, salvage the ripped dress. But my relationships with my loved ones were not so easily mended. I could have kicked myself for spying on Alex and Theresa that morning, especially since she had told me their meeting was born out of concern. But not enough was being done about the threat towards me. A cold feeling of déjà vu rose up inside me as I struggled to be believed. Surely the people closest to me must know that I was telling the truth? But Alex seemed more concerned about whether or not I was eating, asking me to mirror him at the table and provide a good example for our son, though he could not watch me all the time.

When I was young, the dinner table was a battleground, my bad habits a small act of defiance. And now I was rebelling again, except the only person I was hurting was myself. I threw three tubs of ice cream into my trolley, kidding myself that they were for Jamie. I liked the different textures and sensations of sweet and sour so I threw in a twelve pack of salt and vinegar crisps as well. Sometimes they felt like jagged glass as I swallowed, barely chewing while my eyes roamed the table for more. The only semblance of self-control I held was against bingeing on alcohol. I had grown up around Mum's drinking binges whenever Dad was away. I wouldn't allow it. Not when I was looking after Jamie.

Blaming my mother was easier than taking responsibility myself. I held traces of her in my mind, her pretty scarves and long flowing dresses which hung beautifully on her thin frame. When I thought of my childhood, memories of her were scattered everywhere. Yet I struggled to reach the good ones that were buried deep inside: Mum attending the school play, coaxing the teachers into giving me the lead role; her eyes shining with tears as she sat beside Dad, watching me sing on stage. That had happened, hadn't it? I hadn't just made it up.

I scanned my items at the self-service checkout, vowing that this relapse would be a fleeting one. Something to take the pressure off while I got my life back on an even keel. I hummed as I scanned, anything to quieten the voice that would resurface later on.

Puberty happened to my body long before my mind caught up with it. I loved flicking through my mother's magazines. I would stare at the images of emaciated models and ultra-thin pop stars worshipped by my peers. Each page, each image reinforced the answer that had been staring me in the face all along. I was not popular because I was not like them.

Diets were futile, leaving me with a growing sense of failure, making me despise myself even more. I just could not stick to them, preferring starchy foods and calorie-laden crisps and chocolate to fresh vegetables and fruit. That's when I read an article about a celebrity who was a self-confessed bulimic. It stated that she kept her stick-like figure by throwing up after every meal. It felt like a revelation. I stared at the article in wonder, a smile touching my lips. I could eat whatever I wanted and would never put on a pound. Looking back, I can see how naive I was.

Shoving my fingers down my throat did not come naturally, but as I closed my eyes, I would imagine my favourite celebs doing the same thing. They must have found it difficult at first, I told myself while I purged. I learned how to mask the smells and always kept the bathroom spotlessly clean for when I gripped the porcelain bowl. I liked the feeling of emptiness, and it soon turned into an obsession. My reward was seeing the weight drop off my face, and hearing the approving voice of my mother in my mind.

At the beginning it was euphoric, watching my body change. For the first time in my life I had sculpted cheekbones, a smooth stomach, and I felt free. But my hair had lost its shine and the knuckles of my right hand were raw from grazing my throat. My menstrual cycle was erratic. I was cold and tired all the time, and I could not keep up with the demands I placed upon myself. I was a failure yet again and found comfort in food. I began to have cravings, telling myself that I deserved it, that I could rid myself of the calorific value later and flush it all away. If only it were as easy to flush away the emotional turmoil that went with it.

The guilt was soon forgotten when I was tucking into the forbidden food. Like an animal preparing for hibernation, I would pull out my secret stash. After the initial euphoria, all I was left with was loathing and self-hatred. The cycle would start all over again. It was a mental battle I could not win.

A shopping bag on each arm, I left the supermarket, thoughts of my husband filling my mind. His kind face, his soft smile. Talking to Alex had gone a long way to aiding my recovery. When we first met, he did not allow a day to pass without telling me how valued I was. He guided me into getting proper counselling, driving me there and picking me up. Slowly I began to recover and the strength of my self-destructive voices began to weaken. But now they were back, along with a man hell-bent on revenge. Something told me I was in for the fight of my life.

CHAPTER FIFTY-THREE
ALEX

2017

It was a twenty-minute walk from my office in Colchester High Street to Emma's shop on the outskirts of town. I had spent the whole time looking out for her, despite her texting to say she had gone shopping and would be taking the bus home in her own time. I had swiftly replied, texting that I would pick up Jamie on the way home. I didn't tell her that I was finishing early for fear that she might ask for a lift. I could not bear to talk to her. Not yet. As the bell jangled over my head, Theresa met me at the shop door, turning the sign to Closed. 'I got your text. Sorry about the short reply, I've been busy.'

'Emma said you had a problem.' I took in the tight, worried expression on her face. 'Everything all right?'

'I could ask you the same thing,' she said, kicking off her heels.

'I'm a five-hour car journey from all right,' I said solemnly, following her as she padded through to the staffroom. I emitted a heavy sigh. 'I don't know where to start.' The envelope containing the DNA results felt like it was going to burn a hole in my pocket. I knew I should be talking to Emma, but I was afraid of what I might say. My sadness had turned to anger and right now it felt like our confrontation could end up with me packing a bag and taking Jamie with me. I took a seat at the table in the kitchen room. 'Sorry to bother you again so soon, I didn't know who else to talk to.'

Standing on her toes, Theresa stretched above me to reach two glasses in the cupboard overhead. The smell of her perfume kissed my senses, a sweet and summery scent. I loosened my tie and opened the top button of my shirt. The room was sweltering, so different from our chilly bungalow.

'You're welcome here any time,' Theresa said, pulling down a bottle of whisky from the shelf. She silenced my protests with a wave of her hand. 'I know you're driving, but one won't do any harm.' After topping up my whisky with water from the tap, she handed it to me.

'I can't,' I said wearily, 'but you go ahead.'

Ignoring my protests, she pushed the glass into my hand before taking a seat beside me. 'Just one, you look like you need it. Best we don't stay too long, eh? Emma's not been herself today. We had an incident with a dress, and I found her talking to herself, virtually a puddle on the ground.'

I raised an eyebrow, trying to muster up some sympathy as Theresa recalled what had happened that day. Nothing surprised me any more. 'Who do you think slashed it?' I asked.

Theresa sighed, taking comfort in the contents of her glass. Given that she lived in a flat above the shop, she did not need to worry about driving home. 'The thing is,' she said, her lips narrowing, 'the only person here this morning was Emma. Josh wasn't working today. The scissors went missing this morning.' She jerked her thumb back at the drawer behind her. 'They're kept in there. After Emma had left, I did a quick search of the shop, and I found them in her desk drawer on the shop floor.' Silence fell as I absorbed her words.

'You think whoever slashed the dress used the shop's scissors to do it?'

Theresa nodded. 'They hacked the material like they were in a hurry. I found some white satin fibres stuck between the scissor blades. We only really use them for removing tags. And what were they doing in her desk?'

'You'll have to ask her that, not me,' I grunted, knocking back a mouthful of whisky. I was still numb from reading the DNA results; cut-up wedding dresses were the least of my worries.

'Listen to me blabbering on. You said you needed to talk. What's happened?'

My chin wobbled as I tried to speak and I was horrified to feel tears rising behind my eyes. I wished I could play the hard man, but the thought of my son not being mine produced pain like I'd never experienced. Soon I'd be picking him up, and I would be forced to confront the truth. My left hand dropped to my pocket, and I pulled the envelope out.

I felt a warm, comforting hand as Theresa rubbed my back. 'Hey, what's wrong?'

'Read it for yourself,' I said, relieved to be able to share my burden. I rubbed my eyes until I was satisfied they were dry. 'God, I hadn't realised just how stressful it's been, keeping this all inside.'

Theresa's eyes darted from left to right, her lips silently moving as she scanned the page.

'Jesus!' Theresa murmured. 'You had a DNA test? I take it Emma doesn't know?'

I shook my head. 'And that's the way it has to stay, at least until I figure out what to do. Luke is the father. He has to be.'

'Are you sure? I remember she was looking into sperm donors around that time. How do you know it's not someone else?'

'There's a lot more to it than that.' I straightened in my chair as I regained my composure. 'But you've got to promise me; you can't let this go any further.'

She cupped my hand and gave it a squeeze. 'It won't. I'm here for both of you, and this is my sister we're talking about. I only want what's best for her.'

Sliding my vaporiser from my pocket, I began to suck on the plastic tip. Emma hated me using it in the shop, but I was desperate for a cigarette. Theresa rose from the table and walked to a dial on the wall. I knew she was hiding her shock, trying to stay strong to support me. I was grateful to hear a little click as she turned the heat down. She returned, bringing a pack of cigarettes with her.

'Here,' she said, throwing me a lighter. 'Just don't dob me in.'

'But the dresses,' I said, despite taking a cigarette from the pack.

'Sod it, nothing a bit of air freshener won't cover up.'

I closed my eyes as I inhaled, enjoying the kick that only a real cigarette could bring. If Emma could see us both now, flicking cigarette ash into a saucer on the table. She'd be horrified. I glanced at my watch, conscious of the time, and, pulling myself together, explained how Emma had tried to send Luke into an early grave.

'I don't believe it,' Theresa said, aghast. 'Not Emma. She would have said something. She would have told me.'

'She compartmentalised the whole incident; put it all behind her.' I exhaled, feeling empty like I had nothing left to give. 'I only found out because I insisted on selling the house. She was adamant that he was dead, but when she went back to dig the grave, there was nothing there.' I rubbed my chin. 'He can't have just disappeared into thin air. Unless . . .'

'Unless it never happened,' Theresa said, her face solemn. 'Maybe she's made it up to take the blame for everything that's going on.'

'But you're forgetting,' I said, taking another drag of my cigarette. 'Jamie's been fathered by another man.' I struggled to find the words. 'This is going to sound crazy,' I said. 'But I met Luke in Leeds. He tracked me down somehow and asked to meet up. He lives there now and he wanted me to tell Emma to stay away.'

'What?' she said, slamming her tumbler on to the table after emptying its contents. Unscrewing the lid from the whisky bottle, she refilled her glass. 'How is that possible?'

I shrugged. 'None of this makes any sense. I haven't told Emma yet. I need to know what I'm dealing with. The last thing I want is her having a full-on relapse.' I clasped and unclasped my hands. There was no escaping it. Despite everything she had done, I still loved my wife. What a fool I was.

I ran through my meeting with Luke and our conversation in the bar. The confused expression on Theresa's face would have been comical, had the subject matter not been so devastating.

'We've got to find out if the man you spoke to is actually the real Luke Priestwood,' Theresa said, stubbing out her cigarette. 'He's got an older brother, I remember him from school. I think he's got a sister too.' She clenched her hands, a frown crossing her face. 'All this stuff that's been happening, I thought it was Emma, but maybe they're setting her up to make it look that way.'

'But why now?' I asked.

'Why not? Think about it. Maybe Emma was telling the truth and she did kill Luke. What if they found the body, or are trying to draw her out because he's still missing and they're worried she's responsible for his death?'

'It's possible, I suppose. Luke's brother could be posing as him, using his identity. He had a scar on the back of his head, said it was from when Emma hit him with the shovel.' I felt a pang of guilt. I had been quick to point the finger in Emma's direction. At least Theresa was trying to vindicate her sister. I checked my watch for a second time. 'I'm sorry to put this burden on you and leave but I've got to pick up Jamie from nursery.'

'She's my sister. I'd be more upset if you didn't tell me,' Theresa said. 'Leave it with me. I'll put some feelers out for Luke, see what I can find out about him. But there's something we need to do first.'

'What's that?' I said, rising from the table and emptying the cigarette butts into the bin. I stood at the sink and rinsed the saucer. Theresa would clean up the rest, make it look like we had never met.

'We need to dig up the land.' She nodded in agreement with herself, her face set in determination. 'Yes, that's what we'll do. Hire a digger and go deep. Because if there is a body buried in there and you sell the house, my sister's going to jail.'

CHAPTER FIFTY-FOUR
ALEX

2017

I drove across the Strood to home, my thoughts battling against each other as I worked out where my loyalties lay. I glanced in my rear-view mirror. There was only one answer to that question, and he was asleep in the back seat. Clinging to his teddy, Jamie was dressed like Paddington Bear in his blue dungarees and red wellington boots. All he needed was a brown luggage label. *Please look after this boy, thank you.* My heart warmed at the sight of his cherubic face. He had truly been a precious bundle, a gift from God. I came to a decision. None of this was his fault. Regardless of the DNA results, he was my child, and he could rely on me. I would never let him down.

I returned my focus to the road, which was still wet from the afternoon tide. A flock of seagulls flew in the periphery, catching the glint of the sun on their backs. The nearer I came to home, the stronger the sense of timelessness became. Had I expected things to be different, just because my world had blown apart? I drove past the long green hedgerows, the tractors and cyclists, the people who had remained the same. My inner world had collapsed, yet life went on as usual. I wondered what had driven Emma's father to settle in East Mersea, when the west side of the island was filled with community life.

I had been delayed as I picked up Jamie because the nursery worker had chatted to me as he gathered up his things. It meant I would not be able to come home early and check on Emma as I had planned. I knew why she had insisted on going shopping on her own. She needed time to stash the food she would gorge on when I was asleep. I had supported her when she attended counselling and celebrated the times she was well. But stress was a part of life, and a relapse was always just around the corner. I had searched for support and information online so many times, but the administrators of online help groups were painfully guarded, open only to the sufferers themselves. Where was my support? All I wanted to do was to understand. People focused on the victims but what about their other halves? I was not immune to her pain. I learned to turn a blind eye to the packages of food hidden at the back of our wardrobe, the clues that signalled a relapse. I knew that she was not taking a shower when she disappeared to the bathroom after a meal. I knew that it was hurting her inside. Theresa had been a lifeline when it came to helping me understand, explaining the twisted narrative that had brought Emma her own private hell. My stomach contracted miserably as I parked the car on our drive. What I would give to wave a magic wand and put an end to all our problems. We loved each other, I knew that. But would a move to Leeds be enough to drive our demons away?

Carrying in my precious sleeping bundle, I was met with the smell of cleaning fluid drifting from the bathroom. I gently placed Jamie on the sofa, unplugging him from his wellington boots and covering him with the woollen throw. I found Emma at our kitchen table, having cleaned away the evidence of her binge and now barely able to lift her gaze. Her hair had come loose from its clip and mascara was smeared down her face. She looked gaunt and dishevelled, far from the immaculate image she usually presented to the world. I frowned. She had cleaned up the kitchen but forgotten about herself. My eyes darted to the cooker to find she had not made anything for dinner. It wasn't that I minded, but any deviation from her routine sparked new worries. She was getting worse. I needed to fix this as soon as I could.

'Jamie's asleep in the living room.' I was still hurting from the results of the DNA test and spoke in clipped tones.

'Is that the time?' she said, gazing at the clock on the wall, and I wondered just how long she had been sitting there.

'You sort Jamie out; I'll make us spag bol. Have you eaten?' I said, glancing in her direction.

'I got something in town,' she replied.

I shrugged a response. 'Fine, suit yourself.' I knew that I should comfort her, talk to her about her day. But my feet seemed glued to the floor, a part of me hanging on to the male pride which was telling me to walk away. My phone dinged with a text, and I slid it from my pocket. It was Theresa.

> Hired a mini digger. Being delivered this evening. Keep Emma off the land until we sort this out. x T.

I stared at the phone, relief sweeping over me as the woman I trusted took control. I failed to see how there could be a body in our land, but at least I knew that I was not in this alone.

CHAPTER FIFTY-FIVE
EMMA

2017

I sat on the lid of the toilet seat, absorbing the happy sounds filtering through our family bathroom. I had bribed Jamie into having his nightly bath by allowing him to use the colour-changing bubble bath Theresa had bought him last week. Clapping his hands together, he squealed with delight as orange and pink bubbles exploded between his fingers. 'Look, Mummy,' he said, taking a handful and blowing them in my direction.

'Oh, you naughty little boy,' I teased, exaggerating my movements as I pretended to shield myself from the invasion of bubbles. Skimming a handful from the bath, I plopped them on to his hair and watched as he gave himself a Mohican. But my thoughts tugged at my consciousness, and I picked up my phone to check my notifications, feeling a tingle of excitement as I realised I had received a response. I had not expected a reply this soon. Theresa was the wizz on social media whereas I barely looked at my Facebook account these days. My profile picture depicted a sunset, and my middle name was displayed instead of my first. On this occasion I was grateful for the anonymity, given who I was making contact with. I shoved my phone into my pocket and grabbed the towel that was warming on the rail. 'Right, little man, time to get you into your onesie. Daddy's cooking your favourite tonight, spaghetti bolognese.'

Scooping him out of the bath, I remembered the expression on Alex's face when he came home. I had been lost in thought, weak from my exertions. The incident with the slashed dress had shaken me, and the disbelieving look on Theresa's face had mirrored Alex's as he stood at the kitchen door. Last night I had heard scratching at the window, but I had been too scared to get up and look. I had not forgotten Luke's threats to break me apart. It wasn't just my house that felt like it was being invaded. My relationships with the people closest to me were too.

I brought Jamie close to me as he zipped up his X-Men onesie, and he squeaked in protest as I hugged him tightly.

'Mummy, you're hurting me,' he said, and I blinked back the tears blurring my vision.

'Sorry, poppet. Mummy just loves you so much, that's all.'

'I love you too, you're the best mummy in the world!' Planting a kiss on my cheek, he grabbed his teddy before running out to the hall to monitor his father's culinary efforts. I checked my watch. It was almost time for me to go. The meeting had been set up at short notice, but I would not back out now. I checked my face in the mirror, now scrubbed clean with a light application of tinted moisturiser. I should have dressed up, but I couldn't. I wasn't that person any more. Jeans and a thick woollen sweatshirt would have to do.

I quickly replied to the Facebook message, saying that I'd be there soon. After one last glance in the mirror, I pulled on my puffer jacket in the hall, popping my head into the kitchen to tell Alex I was going out. He seemed surprised by my departure, and when he asked when I was coming back I shrugged and said I wouldn't be long. My excuse of an evening appointment with a client was met with some suspicion, and as he looked me up and down, I told him that the bride seemed more comfortable with casual dress. Telling him I was catching the bus, I bade him and Jamie goodbye, satisfied that I was doing something to get myself out of this awful situation. After what happened in the car park, I still could not bring myself to drive. I knew my attention would not be on the roads today.

I bounced in my seat as the bus chugged across the Strood. Twilight had taken hold, casting the landscape in dull and colourless uniform grey. The tide had withdrawn, and an array of yachts bobbed against the lull of the water that gently lapped at their sides. I gripped my handbag tightly, trying to muster up courage for what lay ahead. For so many years, thoughts of Luke had terrified me, the mention of his name enough to send me into a tailspin. But time was running out. The executioner's axe was swinging over me. If Luke didn't hurt me, then I would end up hurting myself, swallowed by acts of self-destruction. Now, more than ever, I needed to be brave.

CHAPTER FIFTY-SIX
EMMA

2017

I wondered if it was a crime, pretending to be someone I was not. It wasn't as if I could afford to get into trouble with the police. It was nothing short of a stroke of luck that I had found Noelle online. Either she hadn't gotten married, or she had kept her maiden name. Luckily, there weren't that many Priestwoods around Colchester. Once I'd found her advertisement online, I was able to get in touch on Facebook. She had lost some weight since our schooldays, but I recognised her straight away. I had no idea how she would react to me, given our brief encounter in our youth. After being dumped by Luke, I had tried to talk to her in town. But she had turned on me, screaming to leave her alone. I just hoped that today's contact would provide a more favourable reaction. All I had to do was to befriend a mutual 'friend' and say I was interested in signing up to her network marketing business.

My nerves jittered as I walked into Wetherspoons, wondering if she would recognise my face. I had changed so much from the girl I used to be. Meeting Alex had turned my life around. It felt like a rebirth, going to university and living a normal life. It was only when I shared a house with other students that I realised my disruptive upbringing was far from the norm.

She had asked to meet in the Playhouse pub in Colchester. My profile picture had left her with little clue to my identity, but when I entered the bar I recognised her straight away. She had kind eyes behind her designer glasses and I could see a tiny bit of Luke in her. She was slimmer but not as tall as her brother, and her hair was a couple of shades lighter: brunette with a touch of sun-kissed blonde. The lines around her eyes suggested someone who was optimistic by nature. With her black dress and red court shoes, she made me feel underdressed. She extended her hand, gripping mine in a strong pumping action. I remembered my close encounter with my angry bride, imagining what Noelle would do with those fists if she were angry enough to take her frustrations out on me. But still, I felt a pang of sympathy for her. I knew what it was like to live without a family member, to feel the ghost of their presence, unable to move on. As we sat, I looked from left to right checking we had a quiet space.

'You don't remember me, do you?' I asked, mirroring her smile.

'I have to say your face rings a bell, but not your name. You're local, aren't you?' Noelle said, tilting her head to one side.

'Mersea Island,' I said quietly. 'I knew your brother, Luke, from school.' I waited for an outburst, or at the very least some mumblings of disbelief. Instead, she took out her business folder, spreading a set of leaflets on the table in front of us.

'Oh there's lots of interested clients in Mersea Island, you should make a killing out there. There's lots of people keen to supplement their income selling aloe vera, especially when it works so well.' She spoke in full business patter mode, barely stopping for breath. She had either not heard my comment about her brother or she was deliberately choosing to ignore it. Being a businesswoman myself, I could see that her focus was on getting me to subscribe to her network marketing team. By the end of her presentation, her fingers were positively twitching as they held the pen for the sign-up form.

'Have you heard from Luke lately?' I said, my gaze falling to the paperwork on the table.

'Why do you ask?' she said, her smile fading.

I glanced at her, trying to mask the guilt I felt inside. 'Oh, no reason. I heard he went off the radar and I was just wondering if you'd been in touch.'

It felt like the air was being sucked out of the room as she scrutinised my face. Like a worm baking under the sun, I squirmed under the heat of her gaze.

'Has Luke sent you? Because if he has, I don't want to know.' She snapped the paperwork from the table, giving me nothing to look at as I tried to divert my eyes. Her chest was heaving now, as if she were short of breath.

'I told you, I'm an old friend. Why, is there a problem with that?' I straightened in my chair. I had been assaulted once already, I did not want to make a habit of it.

But Noelle wasn't having any of it and tucked away her paperwork before getting in my face. 'You're not interested in these products at all, are you? Mum told me to be careful meeting strangers online.' She shook her head. 'Has Luke sent you? Run out of money, has he? Is that it?' But each word seemed difficult for her to express as her breath became strained. She fumbled in her bag, the colour draining from her face as she searched for something inside.

I was grateful for the precious seconds that gave me time to work out what to say. I had not expected this response at all. Luke's family had supported him when he'd taken out the injunction against me in school. Noelle was chalk white with fear. What had happened since then to turn things around?

With obvious relief, she pulled a blue-tipped asthma inhaler from her bag. It was similar to the ones my dad used to use before his emphysema was diagnosed. Giving me a weary glance, she attached it to her mouth and delivered two short puffs of air.

'I'm sorry,' I said, 'I didn't mean to waste your time. Luke didn't send me, but I *do* need to know where he is. Does he still live in Colchester? Have you heard from him since he disappeared?' My words fired out at an alarming rate. I told myself to slow down, but I couldn't help it as my anxiety took hold. Was he alive or not? I wanted to shake her until she told me what I needed to know.

She gathered up her things, almost toppling over her chair in her haste to get away. Grabbing her bag from the floor, she pulled a set of car keys from her pocket.

I rose too, ready to follow her out. But Noelle had other ideas. She spun on her heel to face me. 'Why are you following me? I don't know where he is, and if I did, I wouldn't tell you. The best thing you can do is steer well clear of him.'

I followed her as she made her way out, under the steady eye of the barman. Her feet pounding the pavement, she beat a retreat towards her parked car. Anger flared inside me as I trotted beside her in an effort to keep up. 'It's a shame you didn't think that way when he was taking an injunction out against me.'

Noelle came to a dead stop, a glimmer of recognition in her eyes. 'You're . . .'

'Emma Hetherington. Luke taught me in school.'

'He did more than teach you, from what I remember,' she said, her brows knitting together in a frown.

I flushed. 'Yes, well . . . that's in the past. I'm married now, trying to get on with my life.'

'Well then why are you following me?' My time up, she continued her walk to the car.

'Because I'm scared,' I blurted. 'Please. I need your help. He's tearing my family apart and I don't know what to do.'

Noelle stilled for a second time. She leaned against her car, her fingers digging into her bag, gripping the inhaler for another puff.

'Get in,' she said, nodding towards the passenger seat of her grey Ford Focus.

I pushed away an empty Coke can with my foot and settled in the passenger seat. My nerves were bubbling up inside me as I wondered if this was such a good idea after all. What if Noelle drove off and brought me straight to Luke? I could be walking into a trap. I took a deep breath.

'I don't want to bring any trouble to your door,' I said, encouraged by the sympathy in her eyes. 'But I need to know where Luke is. I'm scared he's come back.' I filled her in on the recent events, omitting the incident four years earlier.

'I don't know where he is,' Noelle said, tapping her fingers against the steering wheel. 'And I don't want to know. Luke's . . . well, he's bad news. I'm sorry we didn't believe you before. We underestimated him.'

'When's the last time you heard from him?' I said, my eyes on the footwell of her car.

Noelle exhaled a lungful of breath. 'Three . . . four years ago? I'm sorry I shouted at you, but you put the wind up me. The last thing I need . . . the last thing *my family* needs is to see Luke again.'

I gave her an imploring look, desperate for a semblance of help. 'Can you tell me what happened? Give me some idea of what I'm dealing with? Luke said he had a difficult childhood. Maybe if I knew more about him I'd know what I'm up against.'

'Pfft,' Noelle said. 'Tough childhood my backside. When did he tell you that?'

'When we met,' I said. 'I used to talk to him after school.'

'And were you by any chance telling him about *your own* difficult childhood?'

'Yes,' I said. 'But what's that got to do with anything?'

Noelle's mouth jerked upwards in a sardonic smile. 'He was mirroring you. Luke's an expert manipulator. That's what makes him so dangerous.'

'But why?' I said, gesticulating my confusion with my palms splayed wide open. 'Why is he doing this?' Outside, a bus rumbled past, followed by a string of cars. Noelle seemed to be mulling over my question, working out if she could trust me with the response. She looked at me glumly before responding, her elbow on the inside window frame as she leaned on her right fist.

'He's a sociopath, pure and simple. The world revolves around his wants and needs. The rest of us are just here for his amusement.'

I frowned. 'But he said that he was abused. Did he make the whole thing up?'

Noelle looked me in the eye, her expression resolute. 'The only abuse here is how he's bled my parents dry over the years, manipulating them into parting with their money. A university education, the latest gadgets, a brand-new car.' She glanced around her own worn-out vehicle. Through the crack in the windscreen she probably couldn't afford to repair. But her face held nothing but concern as she mentioned her mother's ill health. 'I'm sure it's the stress that's caused Mum to become ill. She got divorced five years ago and it's been tough for her, having to adjust – especially financially. She's virtually penniless. The last thing she needs is Luke turning up at her door.'

I bit my lip as I realised the implication of her words. 'He lied about everything. Luke said he came from a single-parent family, just like me.'

'It's messed up, isn't it? He's always had a fascination for schoolgirls. It's wrong, all wrong.'

'So why did I get the blame for what happened in school?' I said.

A faint smile rose to Noelle's lips. 'You're not exactly snow-white, love. I was forever looking out my window and seeing your face in the street below. Besides, he was my brother. I only saw the worst of him after he was kicked out of school.'

'For what happened to Sophie?' I said. Sophie Smith was the girl in the year below me who had replaced me as the focus of Luke's attentions. That was why I had kept up monitoring his whereabouts, long after I accepted he had finished with me. It was also why I had written an anonymous letter, telling her parents what was really going on. It had taken me a long time to gather up the strength to fight him, after he'd threatened me in my own home. But I could not stand by and watch him destroy another life.

'That used up the last of my mum's money, paying them both off so they wouldn't call the police. Mum was such a sucker for Luke's sob stories, blaming everyone else, saying he was misunderstood. After the money well ran dry, he disappeared. But not before he got his own back on me.'

'You?' I said, wondering if I had heard her right. 'What did you do?'

'Tried to stop him. Told him I was going to the police. He tampered with the brakes of my car.' She lifted the left sleeve of her black dress. A long white scar ran down the length of her inner arm. 'That's a result of the accident. I have nerve damage. It's permanent. But it's nothing compared to what could have happened that day.' She gazed at me, her eyes filled with renewed conviction. 'That's what I mean when I say he's dangerous. He's got unfinished business with you. That's one angry hornets' nest you don't want to be poking.'

'It's too late for that,' I said flatly, my stomach churning at the thought. 'I think he's already here. That's why I asked if you'd spoken to him, so I could at least know what frame of mind he's in.'

Noelle's head swivelled from left to right as she checked the street outside. 'Then I suggest you get as far away from him as possible.' Leaning over me, she grabbed the car door lever and pushed the door open. Straightening herself in her seat, she turned over the car engine and waited for me to depart. 'I'm sorry, but you're on your own.'

CHAPTER FIFTY-SEVEN
EMMA

2017

Alex met me at the front door, looking over my shoulder before letting me in. I had witnessed him experience the whole gamut of emotions since I'd confessed to burying Luke in a shallow grave. He was usually so easy to read it was painful. From shock to fear to fierce protection as he tried to work out what to do for the best. Today his anger was evident.

'Where have you been?' he said gruffly, closing the front door behind me. 'Because I know you weren't meeting a client at the shop. I've been ringing non-stop. Then I got Theresa to check and she said you weren't there.'

I tried to brush past him, but he grabbed me by the forearm. 'Emma, did you hear what I said?'

I stiffened. 'What's the point? You won't believe a word I say.' My eyes flicked to the grandfather clock as it chimed in the hall. 'Is Jamie in bed?' It was only eight o'clock, but I knew he was tired from his exertions in school. I hated missing kissing him goodnight.

'He's asleep,' Alex said, loosening his grip. He followed me into the kitchen, where the smell of garlic and tomato still hung in the air. I took in the dirty frying pan and the unwashed plates piled in the sink.

Pushing up my sweatshirt sleeves, I turned on the tap. We didn't own a dishwasher because there was no room in the kitchen to plumb it in. It had always seemed unnecessary, given there were only three of us at home.

'For God's sake, stop messing around with the dishes and look at me!' Alex shouted, making me jump.

Shutting off the tap, I slowly turned to face him. My eye twitched in a nervous tic as I absorbed the anger emanating from his body. 'What do you want?'

'What do I want? You're joking me, aren't you? I've been worried sick. Why don't you start by telling me what's going on?'

'I'm sorry,' I said, feeling like I had not slept in a month. 'I went to see Luke's sister to find out if he's alive, but she doesn't know where he is.'

'What?' Groaning, Alex rubbed his forehead with his hand.

I folded my arms, my back against the kitchen counter. I hated seeing him like this, but all the fight had left me. I didn't want to argue any more. 'I had to do something,' I said. My words were slow and deliberate. It was as if I'd had too much to drink and were pretending to be sober. I could not look Alex in the eye, for fear that I might laugh out loud. It was something that would probably frighten me later, but for now, detachment felt preferable to facing up to what I had done. 'Anyway, she couldn't tell me much. She's too scared of him to find out where he is.'

Alex threw me a glare that conveyed he was not entirely convinced. 'Please tell me you haven't done anything to hurt her.'

'Of course not,' I said. 'What do you take me for?' I tried to give him a reassuring smile as I realised the irony of my statement. It quickly dropped from my face as I took in the extent of his anger. He was in a foul mood, and nothing I said would ease it.

'So, everything you said about meeting a client was a lie.'

I could have turned the tables on him, asked how his coffee with Theresa had been, but instead I turned back to the sink and immersed my hands in the hot soapy water. The bubbles felt nice on my skin, and I squeezed the sponge as I ran it over the plates. I did not want to think about Luke, or Noelle, or the binge I'd partaken in today. I was not sure my mind could cope with it. But Alex stood over me, filling the air with hushed accusations. *It was my fault I had dragged the family into this. All I did was tell a lie. I didn't take his feelings into consideration for a second; did I love him at all?* I allowed his words to flow over me, waiting for him to run out of steam. I knew he was keeping his voice down because Jamie was asleep, and I wondered if it would be better for him just to let it all out.

By the time I had washed and dried the dishes, his outburst had come to an end. A one-sided argument could only last so long, particularly when the object of your frustrations remained unresponsive. Slowly I felt the fog in my brain clear, and I dried my hands before taking a seat at the kitchen table. 'I'm sorry,' I said. 'I know I've put you through a lot. I won't go behind your back again.'

Alex sagged in the chair, his energy spent. 'When you didn't answer the phone at the shop I thought the worst.' He took a deep breath, his face carrying some extra worry lines that weren't there before. 'What's going to happen when we go to Leeds? I mean, sure, we can move away, but are we still going to have a marriage at the end of all this?'

Tears pricked my eyes, real emotion finally worming its way into my heart. 'Please, Alex, don't say that. I thought I could meet Noelle and ask her if she'd heard from him. I don't think I'm being unreasonable. It's driving me mad, not knowing if he's dead or alive, if everything that's happening is down to him, or if I'm slowly losing my mind.' My chin wobbled as I spoke, and I wiped a tear from the corner of my eye. 'It's killing me inside.'

Alex's head hung low on his shoulders, and when he raised it to meet mine, all traces of anger had dissipated. 'You can't afford to draw attention to yourself. Leave it to me. I've been working in the background, making enquiries.' He spoke slowly and carefully, as if he was talking to a four-year-old child.

I nodded, grateful that he was taking control. My head was swimming in confusion and I no longer felt like I could make the right decision for myself. I grabbed his shirt sleeve, hating myself for being so needy. 'Please don't leave me. I don't want to be here on my own.'

'Of course I'm not going to leave you,' he said, leaning over to place his hands on mine. 'But you have to let me sort this out. Did his sister mention when she last saw him?'

I shook my head. 'Not since before I . . . before what happened in the paddock. Her family have broken all contact. Her mum is very unwell. Noelle seems to think that further contact from Luke could finish her off. She said he's caused the family nothing but heartbreak over the years.'

'Then it's all the more reason for you to be careful. First Jamie and now this . . . Don't go stirring things up.'

I rose from my chair, my situation becoming grimmer by the minute. 'I'm going to peep in on Jamie,' I said, feeling like I was carrying the whole world on my shoulders.

CHAPTER FIFTY-EIGHT
EMMA

2003

The antiseptic tang that assailed my nostrils told me I was not at home any more. I tried to bring my vision into focus as I blinked. My chest was tight and I felt like someone had poured a bag of grit into my eyes and throat. A warm hand squeezed mine and for a second my heart fluttered as I wondered if Luke had come to my rescue after all. The last thing I remembered was being dragged out of my smoking house by a pair of strong hands, and it made me melt to know he cared after all.

'Hey, are you OK?' Theresa said, and I rubbed my eyes, disappointment bringing instant tears as I realised that Luke was not there.

'Shh, don't try to talk,' she soothed, squeezing my hand. 'You're lucky to be alive. You gave us an awful fright.'

My eyes grew wide as I looked around the hospital room. A curtain shielded my bed. On the locker beside me were a bunch of carnations and a punnet of grapes.

'Dad's in the men's ward. He dragged you out of the fire. It's not done his lungs much good.'

I groaned. How could I have been so selfish? Why hadn't I just taken some pills instead of the need for all the drama? I knew why. Because I still thought Luke would come to save me, and the flames would light up the sky like a beacon.

'Luke,' I croaked, forgetting my promise to keep quiet about us.

'Oh, babe,' Theresa said, 'I know. Everyone does. It's all come out.'

I licked my dry cracked lips as I tried to force out the words, feeling grateful that the sorest part of my body were my lungs and throat. I could have been scarred for life. How could I have been so stupid?

'Shh, just listen,' Theresa said, looking as if she had not slept all night. Devoid of make-up, her face was pale and gaunt, her unwashed blonde hair scraped back into a ponytail. 'You're not in any trouble, but the police are waiting to speak to you. I don't want you to get a fright when they turn up.'

'Police?' I croaked, fear spearing my heart. Had something happened to Luke? I imagined him rushing over to save me, a car accident maybe. Had he been killed? Had the police found my texts on his phone? I bit my lip as a wave of anxiety threatened to engulf me.

'It's OK. It's all been sorted. You should have spoken to me. I know I've not been about lately, but I'm only at the end of the phone.' She glanced through the crack in the curtain before lowering her voice. 'They need to serve you with a harassment warning. Luke went to the police about it when he heard you were in hospital. He said you've been stalking him for months. I spoke to him on the phone. He said he's sorry it's gone this far but he had to report it to the police to stop you hurting yourself again.'

'But he . . .' I took a painful breath, barely able to believe her words. 'He kissed me . . .'

Theresa's gaze fell to the floor. She didn't believe me. 'I know things have been tough since Mum went, but I thought you were feeling better about things. Dad said that you were improving. I had no idea that all this stuff was going on.' She sighed, quickly checking her phone before sliding it back in her pocket. 'You were lucky. That white spirit you used – Dad bought it from one of his cronies in the pub when he was redecorating the house but he was going to throw it out because it was so watered down.'

I tried to swallow, my throat tight from breathing in the fumes. How much worse would I have been if it were full strength? But then again, I wouldn't be here at all. Tears pricked my eyes as I tried to come to terms with Luke's betrayal. He had only just called the police, which meant he was covering his back; he had no intention of saving me at all.

Oblivious to the reasons behind my distress, Theresa kept talking. 'There's a bit of fire damage to the house but nothing that can't be fixed. The best thing you can do is to accept the warning and say no more. Luke said he's willing to forget about things if you are, wipe the slate clean, although you won't be in his class any more.' She gave my hand another squeeze. 'We're going to get you some counselling. I know you've not been eating properly. But we'll sort it. Everything's going to be fine.' She let go of my hand to pick up a cardboard gift bag that had been on the floor. 'Here, I got you a present,' she said, pulling a Steiff collectable teddy bear from its tissue-paper wrapping.

'Thanks,' I said, stroking its fur. I had stopped collecting teddies at the age of eleven. With an aching sense of loneliness I realised that I couldn't confide in my sister about Luke now even if I wanted to. Theresa was a stranger to me. She didn't know me at all.

CHAPTER FIFTY-NINE
ALEX

2017

My flesh crawled as Theresa's text came through.

See you in one hour.

I replied with the thumbs up emoji, not trusting myself to say any more. It was one o'clock in the morning, and I tried to understand Theresa's reasoning for meeting at this hour. After being made aware of Emma's encounter with Luke's sister, she had insisted we bring forward the dig to tonight. I suppressed a shudder. The place gave me the creeps during the day, God knows what it was going to be like down there at night. I gently shook Emma by the shoulder, not willing to slip away without making her aware.

'Emma,' I bent over, my lips close to her ear. The last thing I wanted was to wake Jamie as he slept. My son and I had eaten our supper just the two of us, me wondering if this is what it would be like should our marriage come to an end. Taking Jamie at weekends, while Emma had him weekdays. In my eyes, it was a fractured upbringing; he deserved so much more.

'Mmm?' Emma said, her words thick with sleep.

'I've got to go into work. There's been a flood in the Colchester office, and the caretaker can't get hold of anyone else.' It seemed as good an excuse as any, and she accepted it readily before turning to go back to sleep.

I parked as close as I could to the field. I could have walked the whole way, but I had told Emma I was going to work, so needed to take the car. I was grateful for the full moon as I trudged along the muddy path. All I could hear were my boots being sucked in by the mud and the rustle of nocturnal creatures startled by my night-time visit. I could feel their eyes on me, watching my every movement. I gripped my torch tightly, my senses on edge as I listened for every sound. The moon reflected against the frame of the digger, casting the metal in a blue-grey hue. As I approached it, I could not believe what I was about to do.

'Boo!' Theresa shrieked, jumping out from behind the machine. She was wearing a long black coat and woollen hat, and I had not seen her approach.

I clasped my hand to my chest as she dissolved into fits of giggles before me. 'You nearly . . . gave me a heart attack,' I gasped, and despite the grotesque situation, I found myself laughing just the same. But it was dark humour, mingled with a sudden sense of dread. It was several seconds before we gathered our strength, ready to focus on the task ahead.

'If you don't laugh, you'll cry,' Theresa said, handing me the keys. 'Know how to work one of these things?' Leading me to the cab, she showed me the controls. She flicked a switch, casting a spotlight on the ditch. With the help of the mini-digger, it wouldn't take long to get into the drain.

A sudden flapping noise rose from the oak tree overhead. I ducked as a white feathery creature screeched its disapproval before flying away.

'It's just an owl,' Theresa said. 'God, you really are a city boy, aren't you?'

I tried to laugh it off, but this time I struggled to raise a smile to my lips. Goosebumps rose across my flesh as I thought about the implications of our actions. Granted, I had apparently spoken to Luke, but what if we uncovered something? We could be digging up a grave. How would I feel if I unearthed the corpse of a man Emma had killed? Could I look at her the same way again?

I turned the keys in the ignition. The rumbling sound of the engine provided comfort, anything to break up the hoots and screeches of this dark observing world.

With Theresa instructing, I tore the bucket of the digger into the soil. I breathed in through my nose, strong, steady breaths, stopping to survey the land as we dug down the first foot. Just as Emma had described, there was no trace of any corpse, and I grew a little more relieved with each scoop. Soon we reached three feet down, and I was making short work of it with the digger. I tried not to imagine Emma with her shovel, the tang of metal against the earth as it sliced through the soil. But she had described the moment with sickening clarity, and the image came just the same. I was ready to call it a night when we'd dug four feet down, but Theresa insisted we keep going, just in case. I couldn't imagine Emma digging this far down with a shovel. Could her adrenalin have fuelled her? Just how accurate had her memory been? On I dug, the controls vibrating under my grip, the machine screeching as it swivelled left to right, dumping the black, insect-infested soil. Under the light of the moon the world took on a surreal aspect, and I was working on autopilot when Theresa shouted at me to stop. Her call was loud and piercing, easily heard over the rumble of the digger.

I switched off the engine, my hands still buzzing from the vibration of the controls. Theresa was pointing frantically into the bucket, which held the freshly dug soil. Something in there was white, glinting in the moonlight, and I jumped out for a closer look, my legs feeling like jelly as I walked. Our breaths laboured, we approached the bucket, aiming our torches for a clearer view.

I felt like I was in a scene of a horror movie as I approached the digger bucket. My legs and arms moved under their own steam as if they weren't a part of me any more. It would have been easy to convince myself I was dreaming, that any minute I would wake up to find that none of this had been real. But there was no reprieve as we peered into the dirt, both rooted to the spot. Theresa was not laughing now, instead her mouth forming a perfect O. In this moment, I knew that my life was going to change for ever.

'Steady,' Theresa said, as I almost lost my footing in the mud. We stared at the subject of our torch beams, each waiting for the other to make the first move. Neither of us wanted to touch the bone jutting out of the soil.

'It could be an animal,' I said, realising I was whispering, and not knowing why.

'Look,' Theresa said, diverting her torch to the bottom of the pit we had just dug. A long thin bone lay on top, attached to what looked like a skeletal hand.

It took every ounce of my strength not to drop my torch and run. 'Christ,' I said, my stomach turning over as a sudden wave of nausea took hold. 'I must have beheaded it with the digger.' The taste of tomato-flavoured bile rose in my throat, and I swallowed it back, fighting to keep the contents of my stomach in place.

Theresa's face had lost all colour, even her lips had paled from shock. Closing her eyes briefly, she took a deep breath, pulled back her jacket sleeve and checked her watch. 'Right. We have to finish this by hand. Do you want me to get into the hole?'

The last thing I wanted to do was to volunteer, but Theresa was shaking, and I would not be much of a man if I looked on. 'I'll do it,' I said, forcing my feet towards the digger bucket. 'But first, we need to get rid of this.'

I worked through the mud with gloved fingers as Theresa looked on, carefully plucking the bone from the digger bucket. My heart hammering, I brushed away patches of dirt to reveal a human skull. I stared into its hollowed eyes. Its sockets were thick with mud. Wisps of hair still clung to the bone, finding life as the cool night breeze took them. 'God,' I said. 'It's him. It's really him,' I breathed the words, my voice hollow with disbelief. Thoughts flowed like ice water through my veins. I shuddered. My wife. A murderer.

'Emma must have buried him deeper than she thought,' Theresa said.

I nodded. Emma had been telling the truth all along. She had killed Luke, and now she was driving herself insane, punishing herself over and over for her crimes. I heard something rustle behind me and saw Theresa holding out a bin bag. At least she had come prepared. I had not planned on what we were going to do if we actually discovered a body, or the remains of one. I stiffened at the thought of Jamie at home with Emma. I could not afford to waste time. We had to finish this.

Pulling a sheet from the bag, Theresa offered it up to me. 'Place it in here,' she sniffed, and I realised she was crying. 'It deserves some respect. I'll find a way of disposing of it later on.'

Gently I wrapped the skull in the cloth before placing it into the bag. 'I can't ask you to take this,' I said. 'It's implicating you in a crime. You could go to prison for a very long time.'

'Only if we're found out,' Theresa said. 'This is our secret now. Besides, I'm implicated already. It was me who hired the digger, don't forget. There's no walking away from this – for either of us.'

A thought struck me. 'If this is Luke . . . then who was I talking to in Leeds?'

'I don't know.' Theresa was ashen. She wiped her tears with the back of her hand, streaking her skin with mud. 'I can't think about that right now. Please let's just hurry up so we can both get out of here.'

Reluctantly I jumped into the ditch, trying to push back the feeling I was climbing into my own grave. Above me, the machinery loomed, and I almost expected the wail of police sirens to scream into life. But there was nothing apart from the soft rustle of the oak tree overhead, and Theresa sniffling in the background. I clawed at the ground until I recovered the remains of the skeleton. I worked automatically, disassociating myself from my task in order to carry on. So much had happened that my brain was barely able to take it all in. Using my torch, I searched for pieces of clothing, any extra clues to the identity of the skeleton beneath my feet. But there was nothing but bones and scraps of white material. Theresa and I exchanged a glance as I handed her the last of the remains. Her breath thick with the exertion, she reached out a hand to pull me up from the hole.

A light sprinkling of rain began to fall on my face. Time was running out. 'Cover it in as quick as you can, then we'll pull some branches across.' I admired her strength as she took control and told me what to do.

'I can't believe that's all that's left,' I said, watching as Theresa carefully wrapped our finds. 'No shoes, no personal effects. I'd have thought there would have been more.'

'It's been here years. They could have disintegrated, or maybe Emma disposed of them elsewhere so he wouldn't be recognised.' She glanced over her shoulder at me. 'C'mon, you need to get moving. We can talk about this later.'

'But where are we going to put him?'

Theresa gave me a knowing look. 'Leave that to me. The less you know about it, the better.' She closed the bag and stepped back out of the way. 'Emma's my sister; this is my mess too. I should have been there for her.' She looked at me as if to ask why I was still standing there. 'Quickly. We don't have much time.'

I wiped a bead of sweat from my forehead before shrugging off my coat and throwing it on to the fence. The wind cooled my face, and I welcomed the light mist of rain that accompanied it. Hot from exertion, my mind was working overtime as I climbed into the cab of the digger. The bucket swung as my hand slipped on the controls, my fingers slick with rain and mud.

'Steady!' Theresa shouted, jumping out of the way.

'Sorry!' I said, pausing to take a breath before drying my hands on my coat. I set to work, churning over the soil and filling in the empty grave. I tried not to imagine how Emma had felt as she shovelled dirt on top of Luke's body. Disgust rose within me. I wanted to pack my things, take my child away from this awful place and start again. But I had so many unanswered questions. Who was the man I'd met in Leeds? Surely that meant that someone else was in on the secret too? They could be watching us right now, waiting for Emma to lead them to Luke. I shivered, grateful that Theresa had arranged to dig at night. She was reliable, someone I could trust. Unlike my wife. Throughout the haze of revulsion, one question loomed clear in my mind. Yes, I wanted to leave, but did I want Emma to come with me? And could I trust her with my son?

CHAPTER SIXTY
ALEX

2017

Dawn streaked the sky as the rising sun bled on the horizon, signalling the beginning of a new day. With a heavy heart, I climbed down from the digger, dreading the muddy trudge back to my car. My legs felt like lead as I approached Theresa, who was kneeling on one knee over the wrapped remains. Overwhelmed with guilt, I laid my hand on her shoulder and squeezed. 'I'm sorry,' I said. 'I should never have involved you. I honestly didn't expect to find anything.'

I noticed fresh tears on her cheeks as she rose, and she bowed her head as she wiped them away. It was her all over, wanting to appear strong and in control. 'It's so sad,' she said. 'To end up like this, reduced to a pile of bones in an unmarked grave.'

I sighed, unable to keep my opinion to myself another second. 'I know Emma's my wife and I love her, but how could she?' I glanced down at the remains. 'This was a real person, a human life.'

But Theresa did not have the answers any more than I did. Her shoulders shook as she sobbed, and I drew my arms around her. 'Shh, it's going to be OK. We'll sort this out, I promise.'

She wrapped her arms around me, the warmth of her body providing comfort. I closed my eyes, breathing in the scent of her hair. Silence fell, and we drew back from each other. I cleared my throat.

Having sensed my hesitance, Theresa stepped away, heat rising to her cheeks. 'Sorry,' she said, wiping away the last of her tears. 'It's not like me to fall apart like this. You go home to Emma. It'll be morning soon. She'll be wondering where you are.'

'I don't know if I can do this,' I said. 'Act like nothing's happened.'

'You have to. What choice do we have? At least now you can sell the house without worrying about what they'll find.'

But it was not that easy, and we both knew it. Time after time I had prayed Emma had got it wrong and this would all be proven to be a mistake. But now, with the evidence of a body, there was no disputing the facts. I was living with a stalker who had murdered her victim. Her mental health was already declining. What if I said the wrong word, threatened to take Jamie away? Was this the fate that awaited me?

As I drove towards home, I could not imagine what Theresa was going through, with those skeletal remains in the boot of her car. Just what had she planned? What would she say if she were stopped by the police? It did not bear thinking about. But right now my worries were closer to home. The sight of light in our bedroom made me grip the steering wheel tight. What was Emma doing up at this hour of the morning? Was Jamie OK?

I quickly flung off my wellingtons and protective trousers before changing into my shoes. There was nothing I could do about the mud lining the sides of the car, but at least I looked reasonably clean. I opened the front door, only to be met by Emma, wide-eyed and staring, with Jamie clinging to her side.

'Daddy!' he cried, running towards me, and I quickly checked him over before taking him in my arms. He clung to me tightly, burying his face in my shoulder. 'Hey, it's OK,' I said, trying to provide reassurance. 'Everything's going to be all right.'

'Mu . . . Mummy said there was a bad man outside,' he stuttered, each word piercing my heart.

I glared at Emma, trying to keep my tone low. 'What the hell's happened?' I said, rubbing Jamie's back as I soothed him. But Emma stared at me vacantly, tears springing to her eyes. 'Emma!' I said, trying to snap her out of whatever trance she was in.

She pointed to the door. 'It was Luke. He was outside.' She turned, leading me out to the kitchen. Every light in the house was switched on. 'Here,' she pointed at the kitchen window. 'I saw his face in the window.'

Her eyes were wild, her hair windswept. I glared at her mud-caked feet in disbelief. 'Have you been outside?' I said, fear creeping up my back as I thought of where I'd been just minutes before.

'We need to call the police,' she said, staring over my shoulder through the window. 'I heard noises. He's out there. It's only a matter of time before he comes back.' She grabbed my arms, making Jamie tighten his grip. But the more I tried to reassure our son, the louder Emma became.

'Can't you see?' she said, grabbing my forearm. 'He's been doing all these things and blaming me!'

'Pull yourself together, you're frightening Jamie,' I said, yanking my arm from her grip. I had just had the most horrific night of my life, and now it seemed never-ending. How could I tell her that the noise that she heard was most likely the digger Theresa had hired? Holding on to my son, I checked the doors and windows were secure. 'Has anyone been in the house?' I said, trying to establish what had happened in my absence. I was rewarded with a quick shake of the head. I carried Jamie back to bed and wrapped him up in his blanket. Dawn had seeped through the sky as soft shafts of golden light touched his bedspread. 'Where were you, Daddy?' Jamie said, his words punctuated with a yawn.

'At work. But I'm back now. What happened? Did Mummy have a nightmare?' I said. It was the only thing I could think of, to chase his worries away.

Jamie shrugged, drawing his teddy to his chest as the memory filtered in. 'Mummy woke me up 'cos she was shouting. But when I looked for her, there was nobody here.' His bottom lip trembled. 'I was scared.'

'We're here now,' I said, fingering his soft blond hair from his forehead.

'Mummy said there was a bad man outside. She was trying to chase him away. I don't want the bad man to get me.'

I inhaled deeply, trying to push my rising anger down. The only bad man was the one in Emma's head. I couldn't afford to leave Jamie alone with her any more. 'You get some sleep,' I said. 'Mummy was just dreaming. Daddy's going to look after you. I'm never leaving you alone again.'

Jamie raised his little finger for the most solemn of vows. 'Pinky promise?' he said, and my heart melted as I joined my little finger in his. 'Pinky promise.' I kissed him on the forehead before I rose, and left his bedroom door slightly ajar. I had made a vow to my son, and I would not let him down. I had seen the evidence with my own eyes. Held the skull of the man Emma had murdered. As soon as she left the house, I was going to Leeds and taking Jamie with me.

CHAPTER SIXTY-ONE
ALEX

2017

I found Emma in the bathroom, furiously scrubbing at the soles of her feet. Puffs of steam clouded around her, and she seemed oblivious of my presence. How long had she been awake? Had she slept at all? Anger and pity fought for dominance as my emotions twisted inside me.

I drew an intake of breath at the sight of her red raw skin. 'Emma, stop it,' I said, taking the nail brush from her hand. I passed her a towel before turning off the tap, wincing as I almost burned my fingers.

'We need to call the police,' she said, drying between her toes.

'And have another social services report made?' My words were firm. 'Just what happened tonight? Jamie said you left him alone again. How could you?'

'Luke . . . He rang the house phone. At first I thought it was a silent call, then I heard a voice on the other side. Next he started banging on the front door and then the back. It was driving me mad . . .' She raised her hands to her temples as if her thoughts were causing her pain. 'Then

I saw him at the window. I'd had enough, so I ran outside to have it out with him. But he was gone.'

'Will you listen to yourself?' I said, shaking my head. 'Running outside in your bare feet leaving Jamie on his own?'

'It was only for a minute. I did it to protect him.'

'It was only for a minute in the car park, remember, when you almost got him killed? You're acting crazy. Isn't it time you told me the truth?'

'The truth?' she said, looking at me as if I were speaking a different language. 'I've told you everything.'

I almost laughed out loud. I could have told her about recovering Luke's body, that it couldn't possibly have been him at the door. And who had fathered Jamie, a ghost? But she was not in the right frame of mind to take it in. I thought about my son asleep in his bedroom and the pinky promise I had made. Right now, he would be safer without her, at least until we sorted this mess out. Emma had lied from the beginning. Now she was saying that Luke was back, even though Theresa had what was left of his body hidden God knows where. I had to accept the truth. Emma was unwell, a danger to those around her. It stopped here.

She followed me into the kitchen. 'You don't believe me, do you? You think I'm making it all up. How am I meant to protect my family if you don't listen to a word I say?'

I stepped back as she leaned on the kitchen counter, suddenly aware of the block of knives near her hand. One of the knives was missing. I tensed, waiting for her next move. I would not be her next victim. She followed my glance to the knives behind her. 'So you're frightened of me now? What's going on with you?' she said, her voice shaking. 'I wouldn't hurt you. I'm just trying to make you understand.'

I ran my fingers through my hair. I needed her to calm down, to recover the situation so we could both carry on with our day. 'I'm tired,' I said. 'I'm going to bed.'

'What about Luke? We need to sort this,' she said.

'We will. Tonight when you get back from work. I promise.'

I hoped to leave it there, but Emma followed me into the bedroom. 'Work? You want me to go to work?'

I nodded, undoing the buttons of my shirt. 'It's best we keep things normal for now. Go to work, give Josh a call, see if you can get him to come in. Then, when you've got cover for the shop, we'll go to Leeds. Sort out the sale of the house from there. After tonight, I'm not spending another night in this house.'

Emma sighed wearily. 'I suppose we could rent somewhere until it all goes through.'

I felt like a shit for lying to her, but I had no choice. 'I don't have to be in work until later. Let Jamie sleep in. I'll take him to school on my way.'

'OK,' Emma said, hanging up her clothes in our wardrobe. 'I'll talk to Theresa when I get in, tell her we're leaving early.'

I turned away, unable to look her in the face.

I didn't expect to sleep, and it felt like minutes had passed when the alarm on my phone rang at nine. It was a relief to see that Emma had gone, leaving me a note to say she would ring me later on. I pulled back the duvet, a sudden thought making me freeze in my tracks. Jamie. What if she had guessed my plans and already taken him from me? An image flashed through my mind, of Emma disappearing with my son. I had vowed to protect him yet here I was, asleep in bed. I padded across the hall, my heart thundering in my chest. Would he have left without making a sound? Emma was paranoid and upset. Stories of mothers killing their children came to the forefront of my mind. Time seemed to slow down as I pushed open Jamie's bedroom door.

CHAPTER SIXTY-TWO

EMMA

2017

I rubbed my eyelids, which were still sticky with make-up from the day before. I strained to remember if I had showered this morning. Had I even brushed my hair? My focus had been on keeping guard on our home. I didn't know how Alex could sleep after everything I had told him the night before.

Had I known he'd be called into work I would not have taken a sleeping tablet the night before. It had brought with it fierce nightmares, and when I first heard the phone ringing from the hall I struggled to differentiate reality from my dreams. I had jumped out of bed, my heart beating wildly as I crashed through our bedroom, knocking over our bedside lamp and almost falling to my knees. I had half expected the ringing to stop by the time I got to the hall.

'Hello?' I breathed, trying to calm my voice in case it was Alex on the line. Yet even as I awaited a response, I knew he would have called my mobile phone. Just when I decided it was another silent call, a voice spoke from the other end. It was faint and muffled, torn by the backdrop of the wind. I held my breath as the words were delivered . . . 'Let me in, little puppy, your master has come home.'

'No,' I gasped in horror, using both hands to slam down the phone. It was only then that I heard the banging noise coming from our front door. I stumbled through the darkness, flicking on every light to ease my discomfort. But as soon as I approached the door, the thumping stopped. It wasn't Alex, it couldn't be. But I felt his absence keenly and had summoned up enough courage to approach the door when a dreadful rapping noise of fists on glass filled the air. My heart beat like a jackhammer, and I could physically feel the sudden rush of adrenalin pumping through my veins. I jumped as a sharp rap rebounded against the back door. I needed my phone but my mind was hazy, and I could not remember where I'd left it. I leaned against the wall as I tried to focus my thoughts. I needed a weapon.

Running into the kitchen, I had every intention of grabbing a knife, anything to protect Jamie. That's when I saw a hooded figure pressed against my window. I screamed, dropping the knife to the floor.

Just like before, I blinked and the figure had gone. Anger rose from within me. I picked up the knife and gripped the handle tight. Thinking back, I don't know what possessed me. I had felt trapped in a nightmare, my thoughts disjointed, but my resolve was fierce. I had to strike first, because this time Luke would not be satisfied with sex or telling my husband all. Murder was the only form of punishment that would satisfy him now. I opened the back door and ran into the night with the knife held high, screaming at Luke that I was ready for him. But the only sound was Jamie crying from inside the house. I jogged around the house, returning to the kitchen door, realising too late that I had left it wide open.

'Mummy?' Jamie spoke from the hall, tears streaming down his face. Shoving the knife in the drawer, I locked the back door, realising what I had just done. I had frightened my son to death and acted like a madwoman. 'It's OK,' I said, my hands trembling as I pulled him towards me. 'I've chased the bad man away.' That's why he was crying, wasn't it? Because he had heard the banging too? As a key was shoved in our front door, my heart stalled in my chest. It was Alex. He had looked at us in bewilderment and I heaved a breath of relief that I had put the knife back in the drawer.

Looking back, it was hardly any wonder Alex had reacted with suspicion. Jamie had clung to him, terrified, and only then did I realise my feet were caked in mud. I tried to tell him about Luke, but his eyes were alight with anger and disbelief. He made me feel like I was losing my mind. Numbly I walked into our bathroom while Alex took Jamie back to bed. It was only later when we had spoken that I realised my husband was right. We could not wait any longer. We needed to leave tonight.

I was ready to leave for work by 7 a.m., quickly peeping in on a sleeping Jamie before I went. Shame washed over me as I recalled what had happened the night before. What had I been thinking of, leaving him alone and vulnerable in the house like that?

I got into work, my shoulders drooping as I tried to carry on with my day. I knew Alex would take a dim view of me leaving Jamie alone, even if it were just for seconds. I took a slow breath as I pushed my anxiety down. Lately, I was going through periods of lucidity then falling into what felt like clouds as I withdrew from the world. Anxiety was taking me over, and it frightened me to the core. I had not been able to bring myself to tell Alex the full extent of my issues. I tried to remember when I had last kept down a meal. As if on cue, my stomach rumbled to tell me it had been far too long. I smoothed down my print dress, catching sight of a dropped hem. My eyes trailed down to my feet and only then did I realise I was wearing odd ankle boots. Both brown, both suede, but the one on the right had a fringe on the side. I exhaled a moan. What was happening to me?

The jingle of the bell above the door set me in motion.

'Hello, anyone here?' It was Josh. But as I walked out to greet him, his face fell.

'Emma, are you OK?' he said, his face creased in concern. He was dressed in his usual work clothes: black trousers and a shirt. Unlike me, Josh had made an effort with his appearance.

'I'm fine,' I said, trying to sound more positive than I felt. 'What are you doing here?'

'You texted me,' Josh said. 'Don't you remember?'

A vague memory infiltrated my mind. I brought my fingers to the side of my forehead, wishing the clouds would clear. 'Oh yes, I forgot. I was going to ask you to cover some extra shifts. Are you up for it? I'm leaving soon, but I need cover for the shop.'

'Yes, I texted you back, saying I was on my way in.'

'Thanks,' I said. 'I'm glad you're here.'

'I can work as many hours as you like,' he said. 'When do you need me?'

'The thing is, I'm going today. I've not been . . .' I swallowed. 'I've not been very well. I'm taking a break in Leeds. We're going to rent somewhere until the sale of the house goes through.'

'Want to talk about it?' he asked, eyeing me curiously.

I shook my head. 'Not now. I'm sorry to leave you both in the lurch.' The phone rang, bringing an end to our conversation.

I checked my watch, it was only nine o'clock. I wanted to ring Alex, see if he was up, but the thoughts of his disapproving voice were enough to make me wait. Today would be Jamie's last day in nursery. I could check him on the webcam and see how he was getting on. Tonight we would pack for Leeds, and tomorrow we would begin our new life. Just one more day, that's all I had to get through. One more day and we could start again. But the thought felt like a lie. Life was not a fairy-tale, and my happy ever after would not be so easily granted.

CHAPTER SIXTY-THREE
EMMA

2003

'Tea for Two' was an unusual name for a place that served mainly coffee. Regardless of the name, its customers did not seem to mind. It was one of my favourite haunts, when I could afford it. Lots of students came here because of the cut-price drinks. Balancing my cappuccino on the narrow window counter, I craned my neck to watch the baristas at work. My stay in hospital had clarified my thoughts, making me see Luke for the predator he was.

My vision had been filled with his face as I tried to sleep at night. Every time I'd close my eyes, he would be there, but not in the way I wanted. I had imagined him hovering above me with a pillow, his face twisted and angry, just like before. I could believe it – almost. But there was something I needed to know. Was the man I fell in love with just a figment of my imagination? Had Luke presented what I wanted to see? The answers came when I was sorting through the charred remains of the pathetic fire I had lit in my room. Embarrassed by my own stupidity, I had peeled back my photo from the picture of Luke that I had stolen. The girl beside him was pretty, young and blonde, with a face I had not recognised the first time round. It was only when I sought clarity that it sparked a memory in my brain. Now here I was, trying to gather up my courage as I watched her work. She could not have been much older than me – eighteen, perhaps; maybe more?

By the time her customers had cleared, the remnants of my drink had gone cold.

'Can I get you anything else?' she asked, rubbing a damp cloth over the counter and gathering up a sprinkling of crumbs. Dressed in black trousers and long-sleeved shirt, the badge pinned to her chest identified her as 'Vicky'.

'Just five minutes of your time,' I said, slipping her photo from my pocket. 'This is you in this photo, isn't it? You and Luke?'

She froze as she caught sight of the image, her eyes locking on to his face. 'Where did you get that?'

'In his bedroom,' I said, slightly shame-faced. 'Please. Did you go out with him?'

'Why do you want to know?' She cocked her head to one side. 'No . . . Surely not. You're just a kid. How old are you?'

'I'm sixteen,' I said, mildly offended.

'Well, take my advice, honey, steer well clear. He's not called Mr Love 'Em and Leave 'Em for nothing.'

'It's too late for that,' I said, staring at my empty cup.

'Vicks, can you give me a hand?' A bearded man popped his head from behind the counter.

'Give us two secs, boss,' she replied. If anything, she seemed relieved to be called away.

'I can't get involved, sorry,' she said, before taking my empty cup.

'Please,' I said, touching her sleeve. 'I just want to know what he's like.'

'He's a bastard, that's what he's like.' Her forehead scrunched as she paused for thought. After a few seconds, she leaned forward, keeping her voice low. 'For most people, a relationship begins when you date someone properly. Maybe that first kiss, or something more. For Luke, it's the first moment he sets eyes on you. Seducing you, gaining your trust – the lead-up is his favourite part. As soon as he's broken you down and got what he wants, he switches off. It's like that person you fell in love with just isn't there any more.'

'So it wasn't just me,' I said.

'Far from it. He's had loads of teenage girlfriends; a proper little heartbreaker, he is. But take my advice, keep away from him. He's got a nasty temper when he's provoked.'

'But if I don't stop him he'll just keep on doing it,' I said, knowing I couldn't just leave it at that.

The girl straightened. 'I'm sorry, love, but he's not my responsibility.'

My brow furrowed as she walked away. Unlike her, I couldn't just let it lie. I had been lucky, I survived the fire I had lit. I couldn't allow him to hurt anyone else, not when I was equipped with the truth. But the police had been called, I'd been served with a harassment warning. Who would believe me now?

CHAPTER SIXTY-FOUR
ALEX

2017

I exhaled in relief as I caught sight of Jamie shoving his feet into his furry brown slippers as he sat on the edge of the bed.

'Guess what?' I said, smiling widely. 'I've got a surprise for you.' There was nothing more Jamie loved in the world than a surprise. As for me, I'd had more than my fair share.

His face lit up with excitement as he ran towards me, bouncing as if he had springs in his feet. 'What is it? Is it ice cream?'

'It's far better than ice cream,' I said, bending on one knee to accept his hug. 'We're going to Nanny's today, and she's going to buy you all the ice cream you want.' I knew Mum was counting off the time until she got to see Jamie again.

Jamie had responded with a squeak of excitement before a dark cloud crossed his face. 'What about Mummy? Is she coming too?'

'Mummy's going to follow on,' I said, feeling a pang of regret. Was I doing the right thing, leaving without telling her? I could not have this argument in front of our son.

'Mummy had a knife. She was going to get the bad man.' Jamie raised his hand in a stabbing motion, filling me with terror. Any remnants of doubt dissipated in that second. I needed to get Jamie away and fast. I checked my watch. Soon she would be logging into the school webcam to check that he was there. 'Did you see anyone apart from Mummy last night?' I asked, the response being a quick shake of the head. 'I think she just had a scary dream,' I reassured him.

'Playing with knives is dangerous,' Jamie said, repeating a phrase I had drummed into him many times before.

'That's right,' I said. 'Mummy was very naughty, and she won't be doing it again. But she feels very bad for frightening you, so perhaps we won't talk about the knife any more. Now, what say we get you dressed for Nanny? She can't wait to see you.'

I quickly flung our belongings into a suitcase. I could come back for the rest later, when I had Jamie safely tucked away. Mum was only too pleased to help. Not that I could tell her everything. Within half an hour Jamie had eaten and the packed cases were in the hall. I took one last glance around the house I had dreamed about leaving. I had never envisioned it would end like this. I found a piece of paper and scribbled a note.

> Emma,
> I've taken Jamie to Leeds for a break. Theresa knows everything. She will help you to sort yourself out. When you're feeling better, you can follow on, but right now some time apart would do us all good. Jamie said you had a knife last night, and that you left him alone because you were going to stab someone. Is this

really how you want your son to see you? You need to face facts. You need help.

I'll call you later. Please, for the sake of our marriage, see a doctor. I know everything and I'm willing to work through this. But you have to make the first step.

Love,

Alex

After strapping Jamie in the back seat of the car, I dialled my mum's number. 'Hi, it's me,' I said, trying to sound happier than I felt.

'Oh? You don't usually call me this early. Everything all right?'

I smiled. That was my mum, straight to the point. I imagined her with a cuppa and a magazine in front of the television, waiting for *Loose Women* to start.

'Not really, but it's nothing to worry about. Listen, would you be able to put Jamie and me up for a few days? I'm leaving now.'

Her demeanour brightened. 'Of course, I'd love to. There's lots of room here.'

It was true; Mum still lived in my childhood four-bedroomed home. 'I thought you'd say that. Hopefully, there won't be any traffic hold-ups. We'll probably stop for a break along the way, but if I leave now I should be with you by around two.'

'Wonderful. Just enough time for me to pop out and get some shopping. I know how much Jamie loves his ice cream.'

'Don't go to any trouble, Mum, and not too much junk for Jamie. He'll be bouncing off the walls.'

I could sense her hesitation on the other end of the line. 'And Emma . . . is she coming too?'

I peeped in through the car window at Jamie, who was no doubt listening to my conversation. Leaning against the door, I briefly turned my back to him. 'Maybe later. We've had a bit of a falling out. Listen,

Mum; I'll explain everything when I get there. I have Jamie strapped in the car, and we're ready to leave. Can you do me a favour?'

'Of course,' she said.

'If Emma rings, say you've not heard from me. The last thing I want is her turning up on your door.'

'OK, but I'd like to know why—'

'She's not been well,' I interrupted. 'Problems with her nerves.' I was speaking on my mum's level now. It was a phrase she had used many times before. 'If she knocks on the door I don't want you to answer it. She's not thinking clearly. I don't want you to let her in.'

'Really, I can't do that, turn my back on my daughter-in-law,' Mum scoffed. 'Surely we can sort this out.'

'We *will* sort it out, but you have to promise me. Don't answer the door to her, or anyone you don't recognise.'

'Very well,' she said. 'But I want to know everything that's been going on.'

'You will,' I said, not necessarily meaning it. Some truths were too horrific to deal with. I opened the car door and climbed in. It was time to walk away.

CHAPTER SIXTY-FIVE
EMMA

2017

'Sometimes it's not so much you choosing the dress as the dress choosing you,' Josh said, sounding like a natural. I watched through the crack in the door from the back of the room as he coaxed our newest client.

'We have lots of different types to select from,' he said. 'Silhouette, A-line, fitted, flared, you name it, we've got it. You've a figure that's crying out for a fitted dress.' He looked the woman up and down with the eye of someone who knew what they were talking about. 'Then you have waistlines to consider . . .' Material rustled as he worked his way through the hangers. 'We have Empire, natural or asymmetrical. Then you have to decide which neckline you want – halter, strapless, sweetheart or V-neck.'

'Gosh, I didn't know there was so much to take into account,' the young woman's mother said. Josh dazzled them with a smile, acting like an old hand. 'Some people just like to come in and pick something off the hanger, but we like to look for the wow factor, something that will blow people away. A lot of our gowns are preloved, but they're all bang on trend. Take this rail, for example,' he said, flashing his potential bride a smile. 'We've got glamorous to simple, sparkly to vintage and everything in between. I could keep going, but I think the best thing to do is to try on some fitted dresses and see where you go from there. The wedding's not for another nine months, is that right?' he asked, and the young lady responded with a nod of the head. 'Well, you don't look like someone whose size fluctuates so at least we don't have to worry about lots of alterations.'

My shoulders dropped as I relaxed a little. At least my business was in safe hands. Which reminded me, where was Theresa? She was meant to be helping this morning but was yet to make an appearance. I had tried both her phone and Alex's but received no response. Come to think of it, Jamie was yet to show up on the CCTV. It was eleven o'clock. Surely Alex had woken up by now? I quickly checked the diary, which was free of further appointments.

After clearing it with Josh, I popped outside to knock on Theresa's flat upstairs. It had come with the lease of the shop and, at the time, provided her with a home. I was so sorry for her after her divorce; I couldn't imagine what it must have felt like, being cast off like a bag of old clothes. Now, as I knocked on her door, butterflies flapped mercilessly in my tummy. Alex was deliberately blanking me. What if I was the one who would end up being alone?

Relief swept over me as she answered, but it was short lived when I caught sight of her red-rimmed eyes. Still wearing her pyjamas, she led me up the narrow set of stairs to her one-bedroom flat. A thick, cloying smell hit the back of my throat as I inhaled, making me temporarily forget my concerns. 'Sorry about the mess,' she said, pulling back the living-room curtains. White streams of dust-moted light flooded in. It served to highlight the takeaway cartons, peeling wallpaper and piles of clothes littered around the room. I had been so busy with the business I had not visited Theresa's flat in months. I hadn't even asked her how she was. 'Are you OK, Sis?' I said, casting a concerned eye over my sister, who was hastily finger-combing her hair.

She shook her head. 'I wasn't going to say anything. The divorce papers came through today. I'm officially single.' She gave me a watery smile. I berated myself for being so selfish.

'Come here,' I said, reaching out to give her a hug. But it was brief as she turned away, making an excuse to open the window.

'I'm OK. It's what we both wanted. It just makes me angry when I see everything that he has and . . .'

'You're stuck in this shitty flat,' I finished her sentence.

She smiled, despite herself. 'Careful, Sis, you're beginning to sound like me. But yes, I'm halfway through my life, and I've sod all to show for it.' She picked up a pile of unironed clothes from the sofa and made space for me to sit down.

'I hate to see you like this,' I said. 'You've always been the one who keeps me afloat.'

Lost in her misery, she didn't seem to hear me. 'You know what hurts the most? I put off having children for years because he wanted to wait, and now he's dumped me for his pregnant girlfriend. Time is ticking. Who's going to want me now?'

I took her hand and gave it a squeeze. 'We pretty much gave up on having kids and now Jamie's in our life. He's a big part of yours too, isn't he?'

Theresa nodded as she stared at a photo of Mum, which was hanging crookedly on the wall.

'Are you missing her?' I said, trying to put my problems aside.

She responded with a one-shoulder shrug, as if she did not trust herself to speak. There must be more than the divorce upsetting Theresa. Her flat had not fallen into decay overnight. But our conversation was cut short as her mobile phone rang on her table. My husband's name flashed up on the screen, and we met each other's gaze. Why was he ringing her and not me? Theresa snatched the phone, quickly disappearing into the kitchen. Just what was going on?

CHAPTER SIXTY-SIX

EMMA

2017

I waited in the living room as my sister spoke in low tones to Alex on the phone. As I took a step back, I was drawn to the stagnant, earthy smell coming from her open bedroom door. I turned around, wondering what she had in there that would cause such a stench. I didn't notice Theresa's voice fall silent until I was at her bedroom door.

'Everything all right?' she said, an edge to her voice.

I jumped. 'You gave me a fright. Yeah, sorry, it's just that . . . well, I think the place needs a bit of an airing. I was going to open your bedroom window. There's quite a pong coming from there.' I glanced down at the muddied boots outside her bedroom door.

'It's nothing, just a problem with the drains,' she said, leading me back to the sofa. 'I'll get it sorted, but I need to tell you something first.'

'I should really be getting back to Josh,' I said. 'I only called in to see if you were able to make it to work today.' Then I remembered that

Alex had called, and I read the concerned look on her face. 'Is something the matter?' I said, gripping her forearm. 'Jamie . . . is he OK?'

'They're both fine. Alex rang from a stop-off at a petrol station. He wanted me to talk to you.'

I frowned, taking a seat beside her. 'Why didn't he call me himself?'

Theresa rubbed her face as if this was the last thing she needed to be dealing with, on top of everything else. 'He's taken Jamie away for a few days. He's asked me to come and stay with you while you sort yourself out.'

My heart flipped in my chest. *Taken Jamie away?* 'I don't understand. Where's he gone?'

'He didn't say. He's going to call you later once Jamie's settled. He told me what happened last night, how you were running around the house with a knife, scaring Jamie half to death.'

I rose, my fists curled by my sides. 'It wasn't like that. I was trying to protect him. Luke was at the window. I saw him.'

'Settle down,' she said calmly. 'He's not left you or anything, he's just taking a break. It's been very stressful for him too, you know, and he's got his new job to consider. If he blows that, then none of you will be going anywhere.'

'He had no right taking Jamie like that, not without my permission.'

'Emma, this is me you're talking to. I know you better than anyone, and you're not an easy person to live with. Your eating disorder, all that stuff with Mum, and now Luke. People do have limits, you know. I think you forget that sometimes.'

I looked around the dirty flat, at Theresa's dishevelled appearance. I had come here for my own reasons, but was shocked to see what a state she was in.

'Sorry,' I said quietly. 'Perhaps you *should* stay for a couple of nights while I give Alex some space. We can talk things through; we could do with a proper catch-up.' It would be good for her to have some company, and I was scared to be alone in case Luke returned. Alex had disturbed his game-playing last night, but I had nobody to protect me now. I checked my watch. 'I'd better be getting back. Do you need a hand cleaning up before I go?' I eyed the bedroom. If there were a drainage problem, surely it would be coming from the bathroom instead? Whatever it was, she didn't want me to know about it, or perhaps she was just ashamed I had caught her out.

'No, you get back to Josh, I'll take a shower and join you in an hour. And, Emma, don't try ringing Alex. He's back on the road now. It might not be safe. He said to tell you that Jamie's fine and he'll speak to you soon.'

I nodded dumbly, the guilt making me feel like my heart had been wrenched from my chest. I knew I had frightened Jamie last night, and for that I was thoroughly ashamed. To be honest, I had frightened myself. I was on an emotional see-saw, experiencing cycles of lucidity and aggression, with a hazy fog of confusion in between. The slashed dress, the incident in the car park . . . had I orchestrated it all myself? It was a chilling prospect. But I had received phone calls . . . hadn't I? I knew it was him. I had not imagined a hooded face at the window. It had been dark outside, but it was Luke . . . it had to be. I said my goodbyes to Theresa, my thoughts tormenting me. Perhaps if I saw a doctor, cleared my head, then these torturous feelings would go away. I needed to eat, to make myself strong. I had to fight for my family if I had any hope of winning them back. And somewhere in my mind was the thought that I was not the only one with secrets. Theresa was hiding something too.

CHAPTER SIXTY-SEVEN
ALEX

2017

I hadn't intended to call Theresa, but the further I got from home, the guiltier I felt. I thought about how I'd feel if I was the one back in Colchester, completely oblivious of the fact my son had been taken away. I knew Emma would be checking the webcam and would panic when he didn't show. Yet again I found myself relying on my sister-in-law to bridge the ever-widening gap between my wife and me. I could only hope that she would make her understand.

Mum's house in the suburbs was warm and welcoming. Deep luxurious carpets graced the floors, and floral sofas dressed with plump cushions and soft throws made the living room a very inviting place. I inhaled deeply as the enticing aroma of freshly baked Victoria sponge teased my senses. It felt good to be home. Jamie loved it here too, and it did not take long for him to settle in. I wished that we'd moved here earlier, but Emma had expressed reservations. She'd needed time to dig up the body on our land, of course. I wondered what Theresa had done with the remains and felt my appetite fade. Shuddering, I directed my focus to Jamie, who was sitting on the living-room floor. Wearing a huge smile on his face, he tore open the wrapping on the present my mother had bought.

'A Nintendo DS!' he squealed, taking it from the wrapping paper, pausing only to give Mum a hug.

'You shouldn't have gone to so much expense,' I said. 'He's only four, he'll barely be able to play.'

But my words fell on deaf ears. Mum was positively glowing in his presence. Despite our regular phone calls, it had been hard for her, living so far away. It was a part of our relationship that Emma could not understand. Mum and I were close, but it was not something Emma had experienced, and once I saw her rolling her eyes as Mum called us for the third time that day. I caught my thoughts. What was I doing? Trying to justify leaving my wife? I had a good reason. I had unearthed more than a body last night. Simmering resentment had risen to the surface too. But I could fix this. I had to. We were over the worst. Emma would be by my side when she was well enough to join us.

'If I can't treat my only grandson then who can I treat?' Mum said smugly. She was only five foot one, and with her short permed hair and colourful clothes, she was the sweetest person you could ever meet. But Mum was like me: fiercely protective of her brood. I knew she was desperate for the truth. 'Besides . . .' She lowered her voice. 'You made it sound like he's going to be here for some time. I didn't want him getting bored.'

I knew the remark was a request for further information, but I was still raw from recent events. 'I'll fill you in later,' I said, with as much reassurance as I could muster. I slid my mobile from my pocket, activating the screen to bring up a recent missed call. 'I've got a phone call to make, can you watch Jamie for five minutes while I take it outside?'

'Of course. I'm not going anywhere,' she said, throwing me another enquiring look.

'Thanks. There's some business I need to take care of that can't wait.' I pocketed my phone and walked into her small garden.

Before we had left for Leeds I'd conducted a hurried online search and hired a private detective to dig into Luke's whereabouts. Since our grim discovery in the field I had come to my own conclusion. But I still needed to know the identity of the man I had met in the pub. There might have been a grain of truth in what Emma had said about seeing someone at the window, but it was surely beyond a coincidence that the man calling himself Luke Priestwood had contacted me. I returned the missed call, nibbling my bottom lip as I was put through. The private detective, a man by the name of Edwin Burrows, sounded more like a grandfather than one of the all-action types who usually portrayed such roles on TV. Pleasantries over, he launched into the reason for his call. 'I thought you'd like to know that I've tracked down your Luke Priestwood. Seems he's been keeping tabs on you through social media.'

I frowned. I had been waiting for him to tell me there was no trace of him.

'Are you sure it's definitely him?' I said, scratching my head.

'Without a doubt. I've checked out his credentials. He taught art in Colchester before leaving under a cloud. He's worked various jobs since then. His credit history's nothing to write home about. He's had a few relationships; doesn't seem to hang on to them for very long.'

'And now?' I said, trying to come to grips with this latest revelation.

'He works in the York art gallery, but I wouldn't bother visiting, he's on leave for the next couple of weeks.'

'How?' I said. 'I mean, you said he was keeping tabs on social media. I'm not on Facebook and neither is my wife.'

'But her sister is,' Burrows said. 'I friended her myself. Seems she's not too fussy about who she accepts. You should have a word with her, she's sharing images of your son online and saying how much she's going to miss him when you move. They're innocent enough, but she should change her privacy settings and only friend people she knows.

Anyone can hide behind a fake name and a phony profile picture. She's too trusting by far.'

I ran my fingers through my hair as life took another twist. How I'd missed having normal friends, good company, an ordinary life. It was all within my grasp if I could just figure out what was going on.

My forehead creased as an image flashed in my mind. If the man I'd spoken to really was Luke Priestwood, then who had we just dug up? I thought of Theresa, insisting we keep digging. Of her tears as she gently wrapped the skeleton in the cloth. A sudden sense of urgency bloomed. I had to get hold of Theresa and find out what the hell was going on.

CHAPTER SIXTY-EIGHT
EMMA

2017

Despite Theresa's reassurances, I felt forlorn. I had wanted to leave work, catch a train and get to Leeds to see my son, but an influx of customers gave us all a busy afternoon. Theresa had advised me to give my husband some space, assuring me that she wasn't letting me out of her sight. But the day had dragged on as I continuously checked my phone, waiting for Alex to call.

Now, with evening drawing in, I was finally back in Mersea. Theresa's holdall thumped against the front door as she entered the living room. I'd told her I'd be going to Leeds as soon as I had cleared it with Alex. There was no way I could stay away from my family for very long. Besides, Luke was closing in, and I didn't feel safe here any more. I picked up Alex's letter from the kitchen table and read it three times before it sank in. What did he mean, 'I know everything?' How was that possible? How could he possibly know?

'Storm Jessie's in full flow. I reckon we'll lose a few roof tiles tonight,' Theresa said, her eyes dancing around the room. She carried the same nervous look that accompanied every visit, but I could not think about that now.

I shrugged, the weather the least of my concerns. The house seemed so cold and unwelcoming without Alex here to light the fire and stir some warmth into the place. I unwound the silk scarf from around my neck and hung my coat on the back of the kitchen door.

Theresa caught my glance. 'Why don't you sit down. I'll rustle us up some supper.'

'You're my guest, I should be doing the cooking,' I said half-heartedly.

'I'll end up eating lettuce leaves if that's the case,' Theresa said. 'Sit yourself down.'

'Thanks,' I said, pulling the latch tight on the kitchen window as memories of Luke's face filtered in. Soon a pot of chicken soup bubbled on the stove, something Theresa had concocted from the leftovers in our fridge.

I took two bowls from the cupboard and laid them on the table. 'Alex is right. A fresh start is just what we need,' I said. I had to think positively. I would go to Leeds and win back my husband's trust. I would book myself into a clinic if I had to, as long as I was close to my family. I slipped two soup spoons from the drawer and placed them beside the ceramic bowls.

Theresa's face took on a serious aspect. Taking the bread knife from the block, she began slicing the tiger loaf she had bought on the way over. 'I'm going to miss you when you're gone.' Her face grew more serious as she sawed at the bread. 'I always seem to end up the one that gets left behind.'

There was a depth of emotion behind her words. I knew she felt she had been given a raw deal.

I poured the soup, waiting for her to join me. 'There's something I wanted to tell you. I'd been waiting for it to be finalised, but now seems like a good time.' I looked over my shoulder. 'Come, sit,' I said. 'It's good news. I've cut you into the business.'

Dropping the knife, Theresa carried the bread from the counter to the table. 'I don't understand,' she said, her face pale.

'Dad should never have cut you out of the will. My inheritance – I spent it on the business in the hope that it would grow so we could split it one day.' A smile broadened my lips as I relayed the good news. 'I've signed over fifty per cent to you. I've easily enough money to start another shop in Leeds. The Colchester branch is yours to run. I've had the papers drawn up. You can rent your flat to Josh if you like, give yourself a pay rise and buy a house of your own.'

'I . . . I don't know what to say,' she said, her mouth falling open.

'You don't have to say anything. It's yours.' Dad's legacy had left a bitter aftertaste, and I was relieved to be able to put things right. The fact that Theresa was my half-sister was never discussed – she was only a baby when Dad took her and Mum in. But it had obviously been a deep-rooted issue for him, and I wondered if that was why she had left home at such a young age. As a child, I was too wrapped up in myself to notice, but now I wondered, had she felt like an outsider all along?'

I sipped a spoonful of soup in silence. This was not the reaction I expected. The back door rattled on its hinges. Outside, the storm had taken hold. Usually I would be figuring out how I was going to expunge myself of calories, but I could see Theresa's thoughts were troubled, and I leaned across the table, touching her hand. 'Sis,' I said, flinching as she withdrew. 'What's wrong? I thought you'd be pleased.'

'I don't deserve it,' she said. Her eyes reached mine, but they were cold and troubled. 'I'm sorry, I can't accept your gift.'

My heart flickered in reaction to the intensity of her gaze. It was as if a mask had dropped from her face, and her true expression was revealed. I clasped my hands together, the fingers of my right hand touching my wedding ring on the left. Suddenly I felt very alone.

Theresa cleared away the bowls, even though I had barely touched a drop. There was no coaxing me to eat tonight. No gentle words.

'Dad cut me out of the will for a reason. I don't deserve anything from you.'

I winced as she gathered up the dishes and cutlery from the side and threw it all in the sink. Pots, pans, everything went in, and I pressed my palms against the table to rise. 'We're some family, aren't we?' She emitted a humourless laugh. 'Some people have skeletons in their closet. Ours has a whole graveyard.'

'I don't understand,' I said, feeling bewildered. But she barely heard my words as she mumbled under her breath.

'I thought things would improve after you left, that maybe you didn't need to know. God knows, you and Alex have enough troubles of your own.'

I rose from the table, watching her hang her head as I rested my hand on her shoulder. 'Sis, what is it? What's wrong?'

She swallowed, and her face seemed pained as she faced me. 'It's Mum. I know where she is.'

CHAPTER SIXTY-NINE
LUKE

2003

The light of Emma's bicycle had now been replaced by one of a scooter. The tinny sound of the 50cc engine tore through the night as she drove to the beach hut to meet me. I had only half expected her to come. It seemed that there were a few kickings left as far as Emma, my little puppy, was concerned. Despite everything I had done, I only had to click my fingers and she would appear. Her phone had been singed in the fire, along with all the things she had stolen from my room. Of course, I knew what she had taken, having made a careful inventory before telling her my house would be empty for the day. It paid to think ahead, and it had worked out beautifully when I had gone to the police and reported the items stolen. That and my concerned chats with my colleagues were enough to convince them that she was at fault. It was fortunate that I had conditioned her to delete her texts, when all I had to show them were insistent requests to meet up from her. Yes, that side of things had worked out very well. I had enjoyed our little games, but now I had needs to be met, and she was becoming a real thorn in my side.

The bike engine extinguished as she parked it around the corner, and minutes later she was at my door. Just like before, she was red faced and flustered, but I sensed something different in her expression this time. Gone was the neediness I had enjoyed feeding off in the past. Tonight her dark eyes regarded me with contempt. That I had not expected.

'Thanks for coming,' I said, walking past her to slide the bolt across the beach hut door. 'We don't want to be disturbed, given your brush with the law,' I explained with a half smile. 'You've taken a chance turning up here.'

'I've been waiting to have it out with you for a very long time,' Emma said, her words low and menacing. 'I wouldn't have missed it for the world.'

Gone were the floaty skirts and the tight tops. Her long, slender legs were encased in a pair of flared jeans, a quilt patchwork jacket zipped up over her T-shirt. She'd had quite a transformation since the fire and it wasn't just her wardrobe. It led me to wonder if I had kicked this puppy for the last time.

'If you're looking for burn scars there aren't any,' she said, catching my lingering gaze. 'No thanks to you.'

'Oh, please,' I said, narrowing my eyes in a look of disdain. 'I knew I'd never get rid of you that easily – and besides, you lit the match, not me.'

'I'm glad my dad found me in time. You weren't worth dying for. I must have needed my head seeing to, getting tangled up with you. You're nothing but a predator.' She gave me a look of unveiled disgust. 'As if you're capable of loving anyone but yourself.'

I took a step towards her, closing the gap between us. 'You couldn't get enough of me. Remember? On this table, how I hitched up your skirt and—'

'What did you call me here for?' she said, taking a step back. She was looking less sure of herself now, her eyes telling me it hadn't been such a good idea to come here after all.

'I hear you've been trying to befriend Sophie Smith. I want you to back off. Stay out of my business.'

I felt a flicker of anger rise from within as a smug smile appeared on her face.

'I'm just biding my time until I catch you in the act. I might not be able to follow *you* about, but there's nothing to say I can't look out for her.'

I stabbed the air with my finger. 'I'm warning you . . .'

'And I'm warning you,' Emma said, surprising me by answering back. 'She's only fifteen. Leave her alone.'

'She's sixteen soon,' I said. 'And if you don't stop getting in my way I'll call the police, tell them you've been harassing me again. You could get sent away this time.'

Sudden laughter erupted from Emma's mouth, dark and throaty. 'And what are you gonna do? Report me for protecting her from becoming your next victim?' She shook her head. 'Do you know what you've put me through over the last year? Do you? You were my first kiss. Then you took my virginity. Two things in the world most precious to me. But I let you have them because I thought you were special. I thought you cared. It was bad enough that you dumped me so callously, but then you fixed it so I couldn't talk to anyone about it.'

Her chin wobbled as she spat out the words. 'I had to bottle it all up, because confiding in anyone could explode in my face. I'd be called a slapper – sixteen years old and sleeping with my teacher. But it didn't stop the whispers in the girls' toilets after class. You drove me to attempt suicide. But you weren't happy with that. After you called the police, I *knew* nobody would believe me. I was a silent victim. But not any more.'

She prodded me in the chest. 'You lay a finger on Sophie, or any other girl in school, and I'll catch you out and I'll tell, I swear it. I'll tell everyone. I won't rest until they put you behind bars.'

'Oh no you don't, you little bitch.' Grabbing her hand I twisted it around her back. She screamed as I led her to the table, pushing her face down hard on the wooden surface. Leaning over her, I exerted every ounce of my strength to show her she was sorely mismatched in this fight. 'I've lots more evidence against you. Remember that time you broke into my bedroom? Climbed inside my bed? I've got you on CCTV, and I've manipulated the date. So all I have to do is call the police and say you've been back.' I ground my pelvis against her hips, my erection straining against my jeans. 'This is why you've really come back here, isn't it? Because I'm happy to give you a repeat performance if you like.'

'No, please,' she whimpered, completely at my mercy.

'Because if you say one word about me to anyone,' I leaned over her ear, spitting the words into the side of her face. 'I mean one fucking word, I'll come back to get you. Maybe not now, but sometime in the future. Just when you're least expecting it.' I licked her face and she squirmed beneath my touch. 'You can spend your whole life looking over your shoulder, because nobody messes with me and gets away with it. And I'll make it good. I'll make it so nobody believes you. You may think you can come in here and start calling the shots, but you remember one thing.' I pulled her arm back another inch until she screamed. 'I can fuck you up any time I like and nobody will believe you.'

'I'm sorry,' she whimpered, tears flowing freely down her face. 'I'll leave you alone. Please, let me go.'

I backed away, my arousal evident. She rose from the table, and with her tear-streaked face and dishevelled hair, she looked half-woman, half-girl. As she pulled the bolt across from the door, I blocked her escape with my arm.

'Do we have an understanding?'

Emma nodded, a small sob jolting her words. 'Y . . . yes,' she said. 'You won't hear from me again.'

CHAPTER SEVENTY
ALEX

2017

My throat was scratchy and sore, and I recognised the early signs of a cold, no doubt a by-product of my night-time excursion with Theresa. I looked back on those hours from a distant perspective, as if they hadn't happened to me at all. I supposed that was how it was becoming with Emma. A coping mechanism when the horrors of her actions ran deep. As I paced Mum's garden, I couldn't help but feel that I was missing something. I had thought I was doing the right thing, taking Jamie out of harm's way. But was Emma that much of a threat? None of my friends in Leeds knew of my troubles, and I did not want to upset Mum by telling her the truth. The only people who knew Emma's secret were Theresa and me. Emma said she was a victim, Theresa said the exact opposite. Who should I believe? A few weeks ago, there would have been no question. I would have sided with Emma.

Yet every time I felt compelled to believe her, something happened to change my mind. If the DNA test had turned out differently . . .

Lying to me about Jamie was a betrayal too far. I still found myself wondering if we could work around it. Jamie was the best thing that had ever happened to me. I had been desperate for a child and I knew I had piled the pressure on. How could I be angry about that?

On Mum's radio in the kitchen, a George Benson song played. 'Nothing's Gonna Change My Love for You' . . . Our first dance. I felt a guilty pang as the tune filled the air. It was as if the world was conspiring to bring me back to her. I had meant every word as I hummed it to her on the dance floor. Why hadn't I been honest with her and told her that I knew there was more going on between her and Luke than she was letting on? Internally, my emotions played out a game of tug-of-war. I took a breath as I found my mother in the living room. I had to get a grip. I had Jamie to think about now.

'What's wrong now?' Mum said, concern growing as she took in the expression on my face.

'I've got to go back to Mersea,' I said, keeping my voice low. 'Can you keep an eye on Jamie for me? I think Emma's in trouble. I should never have left her.'

'I wish you'd tell me what's going on,' she said. 'Alex, are you listening to me?'

'There's no time,' I said. 'I think her sister wants to hurt her. I can't get through on the phone. Please, Mum.'

She exhaled in frustration. 'What am I going to tell him?'

I kissed her on the cheek before opening the front door. 'Tell him I've gone to get his mum. I'm bringing Emma back.'

CHAPTER SEVENTY-ONE
EMMA

2017

My eyes widened at the force of my sister's revelation. 'Where is she?' I said, the thought of my mother setting my nerves on edge.

'I'm sorry,' Theresa said flatly, 'but she never left.'

My gaze fell on the living-room door, as if I had expected her to make an appearance. But I knew from the tone of Theresa's voice that it was not likely to happen. I had not wanted to believe what my father had hinted at all these years, that the real reason he had built the bench at the foot of the oak tree was because he needed a place to visit my mum. I hadn't been digging a vegetable patch the day Luke came to challenge me. I'd long suspected that there was more to Mum's disappearance than either Dad or my older sister were letting on. It felt like there was some sort of conspiracy between them and, over the years, I'd grabbed on to the one explanation that made sense. I was finally confronting my secret fear that my mother had been buried on the land adjoining our house all along. Mum's leaving had been so sudden, coinciding with Theresa's departure shortly afterwards. I hadn't wanted even to consider the thought that she was no longer alive, but the way Dad behaved gave me plenty of cause for concern – and doubt. The missed birthdays, the Christmases that passed without a word, I couldn't help but wonder why Mum had not got in touch. Sometimes I silenced the niggles, but when Dad became ill and we came back to Mersea, I could no longer ignore my suspicions. The faraway look in his eyes, his mumbled regrets in his last days before he passed away, all conspired to give me no choice: I had to unearth the truth, once and for all. 'She's dead, isn't she?' The words came out as a whisper. 'He buried her next to the tree.'

The glint in Theresa's eye cast a chilling reminder. I had seen that look many times in my youth, and her resemblance to Mum caught me off guard. 'It was the day Dad said she left,' Theresa recounted, unable to meet my gaze. 'Mum had been drinking and she was in one of her moods.'

'I remember,' I said, clawing back the image from the bowels of my memory. 'She caught me bingeing and shoved my head down the toilet to teach me a lesson. Then Dad came home and he sent me to my room.'

'I'd just come in when their argument kicked off,' Theresa said, her fingers tightly clasped around each other. 'Dad's arms were all scratched from where Mum had attacked him, and next thing I knew she was going for him with a knife. She would have killed him . . . He . . . he had no choice.'

'No,' I said, bringing my fist to my mouth as the pain and fear of that day came back all over again. My bravado left me. I wasn't ready for the truth. 'I don't want to hear it. Please, don't say any more.' I tried to turn away but Theresa rose from the table with me, gripping my forearm and gently stilling my movements.

'I can't leave it there, not now. We need to get this out in the open so we can both move on with our lives. Surely you had your suspicions?'

I sighed, feeling something shift from deep inside. The clues were there. I remembered what she had been like that night. It was their wedding anniversary and Dad had been gone all day. But regardless of her behaviour, she did not deserve to die. 'Did she . . . suffer?'

Theresa shook her head. 'It was an accident. Mum launched herself at Dad just as he turned to leave. I saw the glint of a knife in her hand and screamed at her to stop. Dad pushed her away to defend himself, but she was drunk and stumbled.' Her eyes turned to the living-room door, to the real reason she could not bear to be in this house. 'She fell on her knife. Within seconds she was dead.' She paused, the memory of that awful day etched on her face. 'I wanted to call an ambulance, but it was too late by then. We had two choices. Call the police and risk Dad being falsely accused of murder, or cover it up.'

'I . . . I don't believe it,' I stuttered, yet somewhere inside, I knew it was true.

'Dad was covered in scratches. The police might not have believed it was self-defence. He did what he had to do, to keep the family together. Do you remember? How I stayed with you for ages, telling you everything would be OK?' Theresa sniffed as a tear trickled down her face. 'You were playing some God-awful music to drown out the sounds of their argument.'

'Pink Floyd,' I mumbled, remembering how she had come into my room and reassured me. There was an edge to her voice that had made me scared that day. Now I knew why.

'I never knew where he buried her . . . until he was dying. He told me he was scared. Scared to die because Mum would be waiting for him.' Her fingers relaxed on my arm. 'Then he said it was my fault, that I shouldn't have got involved.' She shook her head. 'I think he was trying to pass on the blame before he died. Writing me out of the will just reinforced it.'

'And you're sure she didn't suffer?' I said numbly.

'No,' Theresa said softly, plump tears gathering in her eyes. 'It all happened so fast.'

'It was an accident,' I whispered. 'You should have told me. You didn't need to shoulder this on your own.'

'I waited for the right moment but it never came. Dad paid me off. He couldn't bear to look at me because I knew the truth. I was scared you'd feel the same way about me too.'

'That's crazy,' I said. 'I remember what Mum was like. That day when she shoved my head down the toilet, I thought I was going to drown. Dad should never have let things get that far.'

'He never was very good with confrontation.' A bitter laugh escaped Theresa's lips. 'You know, I used to lie in bed at night, thinking about Mum. I wanted to see her one last time. But then I look around this house and realise she never left. She's in the floor, in the walls. She's waiting for a peaceful burial in a marked grave. Dad couldn't bring himself to do it but I can.'

CHAPTER SEVENTY-TWO
EMMA

2013

I frowned in irritation at the knock on the door. 'Blooming postman,' I muttered. 'Can't I get a minute's peace?' Snapping shut my laptop, I rose to answer the insistent rap. Alex had finally gone to work and I had snatched a spare moment to research a subject that had been banned from discussion. Lately all I could think about was getting pregnant. I reminded myself to delete all trace of my visits to the sperm-donor website when I was done.

As I twisted the door latch, my breath stilled at the sight of the bright-yellow bouquet of flowers before me. 'Luke,' I said, my breath cut short at the sight of my old teacher. I gripped the door, preparing to slam it in my unwanted visitor's face.

A bemused smile crossed his face. 'Now, Emma, is that any way to treat an old friend?' He had aged since my school days but was every bit as intimidating. Dressed in a shirt and trousers, his style had hardly changed from when we first met.

I had thought about this moment many times, and what I would say if I saw him again. But now that he was here, I struggled to find the words. 'What do you want?' I said, a sudden rush of dread like ice flooding my veins. 'My husband will be back any minute.'

'We both know that's not true,' he replied, pushing past me into the hall. His voice trailed behind him as he let himself into my home. 'I thought you could do with some cheering up, after your dad dying. He made the nationals, you know; a big name in the archaeology world.'

'I . . . I didn't say you could come in,' I stammered, following him into my kitchen. I rubbed my neck, the ghost of his breath still heavy on my face.

He rested the flowers on the table, as if he knew his way around. He said something about a reunion, and I realised he had a bottle of red wine in his other hand. I couldn't get over his gall. After everything he'd said about me stalking him, he'd turned up at my house like nothing had happened.

'I want you to leave,' I said, reversing against the kitchen counter. Luke advanced upon me, the tang of his aftershave assailing my nostrils. His eyes were intense, carrying the flame of a long-buried anger.

'Don't be like that,' he said, his icy-cold smile freezing me to the core. 'I thought we could have a drink together. I just want to clear the air, take some responsibility for how things turned out between us.'

My chest tightened as my memory of our shared past re-emerged. I thought of our last meeting in the beach hut, when he had forced me across the table and threatened to hurt me if I didn't back off. But it had not stopped me. Because of my actions, Luke had lost his job. But why now? After all these years, had he only just discovered it was me who was responsible for his dismissal? His excuse for wanting to patch things up almost seemed reasonable, had it not been for that cold glint in his eye. 'You sent the sunflowers after Dad's funeral too,' I said, the words a whisper on my lips.

'Of course. Aren't you lucky, getting another bunch? Aren't you going to put them in water?' he said, looking me up and down. I wished I was wearing jeans and a jumper instead of the blouse and skirt I had chosen that morning.

I was glad of the excuse to turn my back on his gaze. I never thought I would hear Luke finally admit the truth, that a tiny piece of him enjoyed pulling my strings.

I swallowed to clear my throat, placing the vase of flowers on the side. 'Life goes on,' I said. 'I just want to forget about it now.' I watched his every move as he prowled around my kitchen, his eyes never leaving mine.

'Do you remember little Sophie Smith? It was strange, how someone tipped off her parents about the night we arranged to meet,' he said, tracing his finger over the backs of the chairs where Alex and I sat to eat. 'Why would anyone be so vindictive?'

'Things were different back then,' I said. 'As you said, it's time to move on.'

'It's a good idea in theory.' He smiled. 'But then some of us find it easier than others. Got a good job, have you? A husband, a nice home. Seeing that photo in the paper of you at your father's funeral really stirred things up for me. Made me wonder how far you'd come.'

My lips thinned as I failed to form a response. His mood was darkening and I was too scared I'd say the wrong thing. My eyes trailed to the knife block, but I tore them away as he caught my gaze.

'Forget about the drinks. Why don't we continue this conversation in the lounge?' he said, swiping at my arm.

'No.' Squirming from his grip I made it to the back door. 'If you won't leave then I will.'

'Fine, make a run for it,' Luke said as I twisted the key to release the lock. 'I'll just wait here until your husband gets home. Alex, isn't it? Perhaps he'll give me a warmer welcome.' His lips widened in a smile.

'I'm sure he'd love to hear about your school days. Does he know what a little goer he's married to? Gagging for it at the age of fifteen?'

'I'll deny everything. He won't believe you,' I said, standing with my back to the door.

But Luke was quick to respond, with a speech he no doubt had practised many times before. 'He'll believe the police,' he said, advancing upon me. 'I still have the copy of the harassment order against you. And then there's that video footage of the time you broke into my room. Shameless, you were. What were you thinking when you were lying on my bed?'

He rested his hand on mine, forcing my fingers to lock the back door once again. His skin was icy cold and I shuddered beneath his touch.

'I thought after I last saw you that I could let things lie. But we have a history, you and I,' he said, coaxing this time. 'Unfinished business.'

I cursed my inability to stand up to him. Suddenly he was the one calling the shots. 'I . . .' I broke off, desperately trying to find the courage to finish my sentence.

'You want to put all that behind us? Is that what you're trying to say?' he interrupted, his face pressed close to mine. 'You see I *want* to forgive you, but I just can't move on. There's an outstanding debt between us. I made a promise and I feel it only fair I carry it out.' He turned his head, his eyes roaming around my recently inherited home. 'I've not had things as easy as you. It's hard to get a job without a decent reference to my name.'

'What do you want?' I asked. 'Money? I've got a couple of hundred pounds I can give you, if you promise to leave me alone.'

A sly grin marred his features. 'Now we both know it's not money I'm after.' Reaching behind me, he pulled the clip from my hair and just like before, allowed it to swing free. 'This is what I want,' he said, his hands cupping my shoulders. 'You. Now. Once more, for old time's sake. Then I'll walk away from here and you won't see me again.'

'And if I don't?' I said, my heart thundering in my chest. I knew I should run away. Grab my phone and call for help. But my limbs felt like lead, my body frozen under his spell. I could not bear for him to tell Alex the sort of person I was. The sort of person that people walked away from. I couldn't allow the past to infect my happy home. I caught sight of my laptop and my thoughts raced as I recalled what I had been researching just moments before. Sex with Luke would last just minutes, and there was no love involved. I had pinpointed my fertility cycle and knew I was ovulating today. I turned over the idea creeping into my head. Perhaps something good could be salvaged out of all this mess. It was not like I was being unfaithful. I loved my husband. A baby would make our marriage complete, and with Luke out of my life for good there would be nothing to threaten our happiness.

'You want me, you always have,' Luke said, nuzzling my neck as he began undoing the buttons of my blouse. 'It was your jealousy that inflamed you, not concern for those other girls. We'll keep it our little secret. Nobody else needs to know.'

I caught another whiff of his aftershave, the same scent he used all those years ago. It felt like I was back there, a teenager once more. I could not bear to become the subject of gossip all over again, for my words to be disbelieved. My legs were trembling as I tried to work out what to do. He pulled up my skirt, then asked me if it was what I wanted, just like before. I nodded. He smiled because deep down he thought it wasn't true. But all I could think of was getting pregnant. I would not have given in for anything less.

CHAPTER SEVENTY-THREE
LUKE

2013

I thought I'd feel recompensed after my encounter with Emma, but the whole episode had been one big anti-climax. True, she had baulked when she'd seen me in her doorway, and bringing the sunflowers had been a nice touch, but as she fixed her clothes I had caught a look of triumph, as if she actually had wanted me to screw her after all. It had left a bitter taste in my mouth, and as I sat in my car outside her front door, my anger resurfaced. She was in there, thinking she had gotten one up on me. Perhaps she had, pretending to act frightened all along. Sex was not enough of a payback for everything she had put me through. Hell, maybe I had done the bitch a favour. Perhaps she wasn't getting it from her husband any more.

My fingers tightened on the steering wheel. I had always suspected that she was the one who had tipped off Sophie Smith's parents, and her failure to deny it answered the question that had been bugging me for some time. The anonymous letter Sophie's parents received had pinpointed our meeting in the beach hut that night. I'm only grateful that we were both fully clothed when they caught us. A large pay-off from my mother had at least stopped them calling the police. I became much better at covering my tracks after that. But my promise to Emma had not gone unforgotten, and I spent many happy hours thinking about inflicting my revenge.

I knew I should drive away, draw a line beneath it all. But my reputation had been smeared. Mud sticks. Emma's meddling had put an end to my career before it even began. If only she had died during the fire in her home that day. I remembered receiving her text, how hopeful I had been that she would carry it through. Then the searing disappointment when she was pulled out alive. But if at first you don't succeed . . . I surprised myself with the thought. Could I? Commit murder? As I sat there, I imagined how it would feel to finally watch the bitch burn. And why not bring her home down with her? The life she'd managed to build for herself that eluded me. *She* was unstable once. I could slowly break her down. Then, when she was alone, I would recreate her suicide attempt – but get it right this time. I smiled as my plan unfurled itself in my mind. Tomorrow. I would return to taunt her tomorrow, tease her about my future conquests, really stick the knife in. Her infidelity would ensure her silence, at least until I carried out my plan.

CHAPTER SEVENTY-FOUR
ALEX

2017

My eyes flitted from the road to the caller display on my dashboard as I tried for the third time to contact Emma. At least the hands-free system allowed me to drive, saving precious time. It would take at least another couple of hours to reach Essex. I groaned aloud. By the time I got there, the tide would be in, cutting Emma off from the outside world. It was not as if I could call the police. What could I tell them? Given Emma's state of mind, she could end up blurting out everything. Why wasn't she answering her phone? If I had any sense, I'd go back to Jamie and leave Emma behind. But I was like a moth drawn to the flame. No matter what she did to me, I would always return to her.

Using voice commands, I patched through another call. The phone answered after five rings.

'Hello?'

I sensed the hesitancy in Theresa's voice but tried to mask my concern. 'Hi, it's me. Is Emma with you? I've been trying to ring but her phone's switched off.'

'She's asleep. I turned off her phone so she could have some rest, bless her; she was in quite a state after you left, but she's OK now.'

'Can you tell her I'm on my way? I shouldn't have left. I should be with you around one in the morning.'

'Is Jamie with you?' Theresa said.

'No, he's back in Leeds. I'm just coming to pick up Emma and bring her back.' I took a deep breath, my throat raw from my oncoming cold. 'There's something I've got to ask you.'

'Me? What's that?'

Checking my rear-view mirror, I indicated and overtook the car in front of me. 'I hired a private detective to track Luke down. Apparently he's alive, and friends with you on Facebook. Why did you lie to me, Theresa?' My words broke off in a cough.

'What? I'm not friends with Luke. Am I?' Silence fell between us as she searched for answers. 'I use Facebook for work, I accept requests from lots of people . . . I don't know them all.'

The irony of her words hit home. How could people qualify as friends if you didn't know them? It was the very reason I hated the whole social media thing. You didn't know who you were talking to. Anyone could bung up a fake profile picture and snoop on your movements. But there was another question playing on my mind. 'If Luke is alive, then whose body did we unearth?'

Theresa hesitated. 'I don't think we should be discussing this over the phone. We'll talk about it when you get here.'

But I was not so easily deterred. 'I've been doing some research. Bodies don't reach the skeletal stage until after at least ten years in the ground.'

'For Christ's sake, Alex, this is not an appropriate conversation!' Her breath ruffled the line as she exhaled loudly. 'I'm sorry,' she said, trying to regain her composure. 'I've had a rough day.'

In the background I heard scuffling, a movement of furniture. I strained to listen, but it grew distant as Theresa walked away. 'Is that Emma?' I said. 'Put her on the phone. I need to speak to her.'

'It's just the storm. I told you. She needs her rest, and I don't think she should be going anywhere tonight. You can sort things out when you get here.'

'I could sort things out now if you told me the truth. What's going on, Theresa? What are you not telling me? Who was buried in that grave? Because it wasn't Luke, was it? Funny how you insisted we keep digging down after I wanted to give up. Why was that?'

'This is family stuff. It's none of your concern,' Theresa snapped, before disconnecting the call.

I thumped the steering wheel with my fist. What the hell was going on? I replayed our conversation in my head. Why did she ask if Jamie was with me? I patched a call through to Mum.

'Son? Is everything OK?' Mum said, answering the phone after one ring. I asked how Jamie was doing, making her climb the stairs to his bedroom to ensure he was safe. But Mum plagued me for answers, her voice brittle with worry.

I pulled a tissue from my pocket and paused to blow my nose. 'I'm not sure what's going on, Mum; all I know is that Emma needs me. She's with her sister, but something's not right.'

'Isn't there anyone you can call who can check on them? What about your local constabulary? We've got a lovely PCSO near us. They're so helpful. I'm sure if you give your local station a ring they might send someone out. When Mrs Connor wasn't answering the door, we gave them a call and . . .'

I exhaled a terse breath. I had heard the story about Mrs Connor and her fall a thousand times before. 'No. There's no need for police. I'm just checking that Jamie's OK.'

'Well, call me when you get there. It doesn't matter what time it is. I'm sure I won't sleep until you do.'

I ended the call, inching up the speed dial as I pressed my foot on the accelerator.

CHAPTER SEVENTY-FIVE

EMMA

2017

My eyes fluttered open as I awoke from my nap. It had been Theresa's idea, an hour's sleep to ease my nerves before working out my next steps. She had calmed my anxiety to get to Leeds, telling me to allow the dust to settle before galloping up there and upsetting everyone. But a black cloud loomed on the horizon. A succession of silent phone calls told me that Luke was close to hand. I hadn't expected to get any sleep, but when I woke, a whole hour had passed and the house was cloaked in darkness.

'Tizzy?' I said, shuffling blindly in the hall. I had reverted to her childhood nickname, seeking comfort as fear crept up my spine. I flicked the light switch with no response. She must have blown the fuse box, I told myself, trying to quell my rising panic. It was situated in the living room, and I groped the walls as I made my way there. I listened intently to the usual creaks and groans of the house under the oncoming winds, my heartbeat feeling as if it had doubled its pace. 'Tizzy?' I said a second time, and her lack of response made me want to bolt for the door. But I could not leave my sister. As I entered the living room, the figure before me rooted me to the spot.

'Theresa?' I said, my heart stalling as I caught sight of her. Tied to a chair, she sat in the centre of the room. I recognised one of my scarves, which was now wrapped around her mouth. I followed her line of vision too late as I turned to look behind the door.

A sudden searing pain took hold as a blunt object hit me from the side. My legs weakening, I gave in to the darkness, and the last thing I remembered was a strong hand clamping around my throat, a pair of cold blue eyes piercing my soul.

The next thing I knew I was squinting as the lights flicked on, the click of the trip on the fuse box returning me to consciousness. I caught sight of Theresa sitting across from me, her eyes wide with fear. 'Theresa,' I moaned, my head throbbing as white starry flashes speared my sight. I blinked, trying to focus my vision as footsteps broke the silence, coming in from the other room. I swallowed back a whimper. I had not imagined the face in the window. After all these years, Luke was still alive. He loomed over me, dressed in black, laughing in response to my terrified expression. It was a thin, brittle sound, his humour failing to reach his eyes. 'Oh come on, little puppy, you must have known this wouldn't end well.'

I swallowed, my throat tight as I realised my hands and feet were bound just like my sister's. I still held the memory of the pressure of his thumbs on my windpipe as he had clamped down hard and squeezed. All that time I had craved his touch, and yet it had ended like this.

Luke circled me like a shark as he explained the motive behind his presence. 'It's time for you to face up to what you've done.'

'What do you want?' I said, knowing that screaming was pointless. Out here in the windswept landscape, there was nobody to hear.

'What do *I* want? You tried to kill me. You must have known I'd come back one day. I planned it well, don't you think?' he said, his eyes flashing under the light of the bulb hanging overhead. 'The flowers, silent phone calls, slipping in after hours to slash that wedding dress.'

'It was you who let Jamie out of the car,' I said, the fear of that day rising up to greet me. Thank God Alex had taken him away.

'I can take credit for most of those things, but I wouldn't hurt a child. You can thank your own stupidity for that one.'

As Luke's words filtered in, I remembered back to that day: it was raining, I was late. Had I pressed the wrong button on the car key and blamed it on him instead? I hadn't been looking. My fingers were wet. All at once, I knew that I had been the one to blame.

Luke paced the room, taking pleasure from his captive audience. 'I have a lot of plans for *my* son. Only there's one problem with that, isn't there? Your husband's taken him away.'

I sucked in a breath, fighting against my bindings as I tried to break free. How did he know? I hadn't told anyone about what happened that day. Had he worked out the timings, come back for his child? The thought of Jamie brought my protective instinct to the forefront. I had to get away. I pushed my head back against the chair as I tried to wriggle free. I squirmed as Luke's face entered my field of vision, his breath tainted with alcohol and cigarettes. His proximity made me shrink back. I had to face up to the past because even if I got away, what would I say? Nobody would believe me, certainly not my husband, that much I knew. He had made his feelings apparent the minute he walked out the door.

'Theresa,' Luke said, tearing his gaze away from me as he turned to my sister. 'I was just having a little chat with Emma here. What's it they say? "Beware the person who stabs you then tells the whole world they're bleeding"?' He touched the back of his head, his gaze returning to me. 'If I only knew what a fucked-up little girl you were when we met. I lost everything because of you.'

Theresa struggled against her bindings as she muffled a helpless cry.

'Let her go,' I said, wincing from the pain of my sudden blow. 'Please. This has nothing to do with her. I'll take what's coming to me but you've got to let my sister go.'

'I don't have to do anything,' Luke said, walking towards her and loosening the scarf around her face. 'So what do you think, Theresa?' he said, a bemused smile on his lips.

She licked her lips, her eyes narrowed with determination. 'I think she's right,' she said, clearing her throat. 'Do what you want with her. Just let me go.'

CHAPTER SEVENTY-SIX
EMMA

2017

'There's no reason we can't wipe the slate clean.' I wriggled against my bindings. 'Please, Luke, just let me go.' My gaze fell to the container in Luke's hands.

He exposed his teeth in a narrow smile. 'How did it feel, falling victim when nobody believed you? Because that's how it was with me. No matter how much I protested my innocence, I still had to leave my job. Your infatuation clung to me like a stinking boil.' Placing the container on the floor, he began to unscrew the lid. 'Well, now it's time to give that boil a good lancing.'

The smell of petrol rose in the air, making fear chill the blood in my veins. 'No,' I said. 'Please. I don't deserve this.' I knew what was coming. Luke was recreating the fire I had lit in the past, only this time my father would not be there to save me. After listening to Theresa, he had replaced her gag. She had been frightened, that was all. Surely she had not meant what she said?

Luke jabbed his finger to his chest as he leaned over me, expelling spittle with his words. 'Did you really think I'd just forgive and forget?'

'What do you want from me?' I shouted, trying to buy some time. I knew he wanted to make this look like I had struck the match. I imagined Luke, encompassed by hatred and disgust, plotting to teach me some elaborate lesson with far darker things in mind.

'An eye for an eye, isn't that what the Bible says? You used to go to church, didn't you? Did you stop because of me? Perhaps now is a good time to say your prayers.' He picked up the container and began splashing its contents around the room. My eyes watered as the fumes filled the air.

'Wait,' I begged for the second time. 'Please, Luke, let my sister go.'

Theresa worked the gag loose from her mouth as she rubbed her chin on her shoulder. 'Luke, listen to me,' she said, her words suddenly commanding. 'I wish you'd approached me from the start, because I agree with you.' She nodded in my direction. 'Everything that went wrong in my life is because of her. You'll be doing me a favour, now she's signed over the business to me.'

Luke raised an eyebrow at this sudden act of betrayal. 'You're not serious,' he said.

But Theresa was not going to stop now. 'You said it yourself. She's poison. Why do you think I let you friend me on Facebook?' She paused, delivering the parting shot sure to win him over. 'She's not fit to raise a kid, but I am.'

I stared horrified as Luke nodded in agreement. 'So you knew that was me?' A ghost of a smile played on his lips.

'Yes,' Theresa said. 'But first get rid of any evidence you were here. Alex is on his way back, but the tide should hold him for now. When he gets here, I'll say I went out to the shops and when I returned, I was beaten back by the flames. It makes a lot more sense for her to be torched rather than the both of us. Don't forget, I can help you get Jamie back.'

'I don't even know if he's really mine, not for sure,' Luke said, which proved he had not really thought beyond this day.

'He is,' Theresa said. 'Alex had a DNA test done.'

'No!' I screamed, unable to believe what I was hearing. 'This is murder. Theresa, how could you!' But as he untied my sister, my words fell on deaf ears. I screamed and cried until I'd exhausted myself. It was like I wasn't there.

'Don't pour it on her directly,' Theresa warned, as he sloshed the last of the accelerant around me. 'We have to keep it like it was before.'

Luke delivered a sickening smile. 'See? We're being kind.' He pointed to the doors. 'I've sealed them up, so air won't get in. There's a wad of newspapers stuffed up the chimney too. You'll pass out from lack of oxygen long before the fire gets you.'

'Alex is coming . . .' I choked a cough as the acrid fumes infiltrated my airways and reddened my eyes. 'They'll put you away for life.' Clenching my fists, I fought against my bindings, feeling a small give in the rope. But it was not enough. This was not my Dad's watered-down white spirit being spilled on the floor. As soon as Luke added a spark, I would go up in a ball of flames.

'That's the beauty of it,' Luke said. 'Your long-suffering husband is going to turn up just in time to watch you burn. We had a drink together. Nice chap. Maybe we could become friends. I could let him see Jamie . . . every now and again.' He cocked his head to one side, regarding me like a crow about to pick at a worm. A row of white teeth glistening under the artificial light as he smiled. 'I did enjoy playing with you.' Giving the room one last glance, he stood at the door. 'Goodbye, Emma. Enjoy your time in hell.' Flicking back the lid of his lighter, he positioned his thumb over the wheel. I squeezed my eyes shut, hoping it would be quick.

CHAPTER SEVENTY-SEVEN
ALEX

2017

I sneezed three times in quick succession, making my car wobble in the road. My vision was blurred by a pair of flashing headlights as the oncoming driver's horn blared loudly in frustration. After breaking the speed limit, I was back in Essex, filled with a sense of dread. A beeping noise and a flash from the dashboard alerted me that I was nearly out of diesel. I groaned with frustration. All I wanted was to get Emma away from that house and the horrible memories that came with it. I would help get her better, nurse her back to health. I clicked down the indicator to pull into the next petrol station. Call it a sixth sense; I just knew something bad was about to happen. I checked my watch. The tide was still in. The island owned Emma now.

After paying for my diesel, I headed back on the road. Soon I was parked at the wrong end of the tide, willing the waters to part. I patched through a call to her phone. No answer. I ground my teeth as I tried

Theresa again. She answered almost immediately. 'Alex, I'm driving. What's the matter?'

'I can't get through on Emma's phone. Why isn't she answering?'

'I told you, she's asleep. Look, I'm going back there now. Where are you?'

'At the other end of the causeway. Where are you?'

'On Mersea. I'll be back at the house in a minute.' She sighed. 'Emma's not been herself today. I just nipped out to pick up some milk from the all-night shop.' I frowned, wishing she had not left Emma alone.

'Seeing as I'm stuck here,' I said, imagining Theresa on the other side of the tide, 'you may as well tell me what's going on. Because you're hiding something, aren't you?'

'My divorce papers came through, that's all. Listen, I've got to go. I'll talk to you when you get—'

'I don't believe you,' I said. 'I've confided everything in you. Isn't it time you did the same with me? Who did we dig up that night?'

'I've got to go,' Theresa said.

'Why? What's the hurry, Theresa?' But the only response was a dead dial tone. I exhaled a long deep sigh. She didn't deny that the body wasn't Luke. Judging by the state of the remains, they had to be at least ten years old. And then, just like that, the answer crept into my mind. Theresa sobbing over the skull. How she had carefully and gently wrapped it before taking it with her. There was never any question of me disposing of the body – because it meant so much to her. Emma and Theresa's mother had not walked out on them. She had been murdered. Was that what this was all about? Theresa genuinely loved Jamie, and now we were taking him away. I couldn't believe that Theresa would want to hurt her family, but something strange was going on. I gripped the steering wheel as I stared at the ebb and flow of the tide. If I risked driving through it, I could be stuck there even longer. But Emma could be in serious trouble. I might already be too late.

CHAPTER SEVENTY-EIGHT
EMMA

2017

The phone call from my husband had only served to pause proceedings. From what I gathered, he was stuck on the other side of the tide. Luke had stood over Theresa as she lied, his hand tightly gripping the back of her neck. I had not imagined the fear in her eyes.

'Please,' I whimpered, barely able to find the breath to form my words. 'I don't want to die.'

Theresa turned to Luke, stilling his motions.

'Wait,' she said, and relief swept over me as she saw sense. But it was short lived as she took a piece of paper from the dresser drawer and scribbled. 'We should leave a suicide note in her bedroom, just like before. We don't want this coming back to us.'

'But it'll burn in the fire,' Luke said, his eyes narrowing as he looked from me to my sister.

'There's a tin box under her bed. If you put the letter in there, it'll preserve it from the flames.'

'No! You can't do this!' I fought for my life as I squirmed in the hard wooden chair. I couldn't believe my own sister could turn against me in this way.

'Jamie will be safe with me,' she said, her words plunging me into despair. 'He deserves more than you can give him. I'm sorry. It's for the best.'

I screamed her name, but she didn't flinch, just reached out and handed Luke the notepaper. 'You've got to leave the second you light the fire. I'll call the fire service once it takes hold. There's an extinguisher in the kitchen,' she said. 'I'll make it look like I've been trying to put it out.'

Luke nodded and left to place the note in my bedroom. On his return he sneered in my direction, his enjoyment at my predicament plain to see.

'C'mon, we're running out of time,' Theresa said, disappearing briefly to the kitchen before returning with the extinguisher. Luke watched her warily, his expression revealing pleasurable surprise that my sister would betray me in this way.

'Please,' I cried, my throat raw from screaming. 'I'm sorry. Please let me go. I won't say a word . . .' I coughed, the smell of petrol cutting my words short.

Luke gave me one last ghoulish smile before standing at the door, still holding the lighter. He flicked the wheel and it burst into life, the small flame signalling what was to come. Throwing the lighter to the floor, he turned his back on me as flames sprung to life in the room. I could not believe they had both left me here alone. Within seconds, the room was alight. My home was like a matchbox, providing kindling for the fire. I prayed for Alex to reach me in time. Wouldn't someone see the flames? But by that time, it would surely be too late for me. My consciousness fought two battles, trying to understand my sister's betrayal while coming to terms with the fact that I was going to die. Tears streaked down my cheeks as flames licked the walls of the living room, spreading towards the furnishings until the circle was complete. I felt like an object up for sacrifice and lowered my head into my shoulder as I tried not to breathe in the acrid smoke. If I could just get away. My heart beat double time, the bindings tearing the skin on my wrists and ankles as I fought. But the fumes made my vision blur, and within seconds the room began to spin. I closed my eyes as searing heat engulfed me, only to be tugged awake as something pulled at my wrists. My eyes snapped open, the sudden movement making me cough. It was Theresa. After releasing the contents of the fire extinguisher, she was undoing my ropes. Was she trying to make it look as if I had taken my own life? Surely, anyone finding me would know my hands had been tied? I should have pretended I was unconscious, got away when her back was turned, but my lungs burned in my chest, forcing me to splutter as I heaved for air.

'He's gone,' she said, frantically undoing the knots that bound me. 'Sorry. It was the only way I could think to get rid of him. The police wouldn't have got here on time. Stay with me, please. I can't lose you too.'

Overwhelming relief washed over me as I realised she had been pretending to play along. If she had screamed at Alex to call the police then Luke would have killed her too. With the tide in, they would never have reached us in time. Tears glistened in the corners of her eyes as I struggled to speak. 'Come on,' she growled, tugging at the bindings.

'Just get me out,' I croaked, the crackle and hiss of the wooden floors almost deafening. The contents of our tiny fire extinguisher had only served to dampen the flames, not put them out. We'd have to move fast if we were to get out alive.

'Go!' she said, picking up the fire extinguisher and turning it back on. But the tiny expulsion of foam was not enough to fight the fiery war from within. I watched horrified as pictures peeled and curled from the walls, as everything I knew became blackened and disintegrated. My legs like jelly, I pulled the neck of my sweatshirt over my mouth, masking the fumes as the furniture took hold. A slice of fear rose up as

I saw Luke, his features contorted with anger, stumbling into the living room in front of us.

'Fucking bitches!' he roared, shielding his head with his forearms as he ran through the flames to get to us.

Disbelief scored my brain. He was unstoppable. Just when I thought I was safe, he was back. Drawing back his fist, he punched me hard in the stomach, making me drop to my knees in pain. The circle of flames was growing stronger now, burning my flesh, the fumes invading my lungs. I was wasting precious seconds. I needed to get outside, to claw back some air. Black circles spotted my vision. I was too weak to fight any more.

CHAPTER SEVENTY-NINE
ALEX

2017

After waiting what felt like a lifetime, I put my car into gear. Water still flooded the road, but as long as I drove steadily, I was confident I could get through. I held my breath as the sea splashed against my windows, the reflection of the moon appearing in hazy zig-zags before me. Having found purchase on the road and come out the other side, I put my foot down on the accelerator, aware that my drenched brakes could fail, but all I could think about was Emma and the need to get to her as quickly as I could. My heart sank in my chest. There was no sign of Theresa anywhere on the road. I raced through the traffic, aware of a blue flashing light in my rear-view mirror. I didn't care if they came up behind me, I was not stopping until I got to my wife. Thoughts spread through my mind like wildfire, my brain trying to work things out.

I pulled on the steering wheel as I negotiated a bend, sending stones flying from the ditch and rattling against the paintwork of my car. In the distance, the flashing lights were advancing as I sped down the twisty lane. That was good, wasn't it? But what if it were not me they were after? What if something had happened to Emma?

As I turned the corner, my worst nightmare became reality. The sky was flamed with red, and the sight stole the breath from my lungs. It was only then that I realised it was not the police gaining in the distance, but a fire engine – on its way to our home. But where was Emma? 'Please God, don't be inside,' I whispered, my words laced with dread. Pulling up my handbrake, I skidded on to our drive. Flames leaped from the top of the building, the heat beating me back. I focused my gaze on a man running in through the open front door. Was that Luke? What was he doing here? Stumbling over my own feet, I ran to the house, but the whole of the entrance was engulfed in flames. 'Emma!' I called, praying for a sight of her, but whoever had run inside was making no sign of coming back out. I scrambled around to the side of the house, trying to find a way in, but the searing heat beat me back every time. My heart hammered against my ribcage. I could not lose her, not now. I was getting her out – even if it killed me.

CHAPTER EIGHTY
EMMA

2017

Sweat slicked my skin, the heat of the flames making it hot and blistered. Fingers pressed into my flesh and shook my shoulder hard. Slowly, my eyelids fluttered open, and I realised I had passed out on the floor. I recoiled as I saw Luke beside me, blood pooling beneath his head. A horrible sense of déjà vu encompassed me, and the scene took on a surreal tone.

'Get up,' Theresa coughed, grabbing the fire extinguisher and turning it back on. The butt of the metal was streaked with blood. With one hand, she wrenched me from the ground. 'Out the back. I'll keep you covered.'

I stumbled through the smoke and flames towards the back door, my legs like rubber bands. Light bulbs popped and fizzed overhead, sprinkling us in glass. In the hall, the smoke alarm beeped beneath the full roar of the hungry fire. Hissing and spitting, it consumed all in its path, and soon we would be next. Plunged in darkness, I had only the flames to light my way. My lungs felt like they were caving in on me as I heaved for breath. I fought to stay conscious as my world closed in. I presumed Theresa was behind me until I heard Luke call her name. He was still going, still after us – still alive. I was in the kitchen now, and the scene took on a dreamlike quality as I turned around to find her. But my legs buckled beneath me as darkness closed in once more.

Looking up into the face of my husband I wondered if I was dreaming. A flashing blue light illuminated the night as he hovered over me. The cool night air touched my blistered skin, and I realised I was outside. For a second time I tried to call out Theresa's name. 'Thank God you're OK,' he said, answering my question. My lungs were burning as I drew in air, feeling as if I was breathing in hot coals. I grimaced as I tried to swallow, barely able to raise my head from the ground.

'Shh, stay where you are. The ambulance is on its way.'

I blinked through the pain of crusted eyes as I watched my house go up in flames. The roof had caved in, and I knew whoever was still in there would not be coming out alive.

CHAPTER EIGHTY-ONE
EMMA

Twelve months later

The playground seems different today, and I'm glad Alex managed to persuade me to visit Mersea again. I watch as Jamie reacquaints himself with the equipment, his face alight with pride as he negotiates the slide he was too scared to climb before. I hold my husband's hand as we stand side by side, watching him. I can't believe we made it, after all we've both been through.

Alex has felt the change in me too. The couple who were going to buy our house in Mersea went ahead and bought the land. It felt strange to see new foundations on the site where our old place used to be. Given what had happened, it was probably for the best. Too many bad things had happened there. Malevolence had seeped into the very framework, causing misery and misfortune to its dwellers. The deaths within would be enough to put most people off, but luckily our buyers were willing to put aside such reservations.

Our new home in Leeds is so bright and airy in comparison. I wake up bathed in sunlight, which sets me up for the day ahead. Josh has made such a success of managing the Colchester branch of Something Borrowed that he's had to take on extra staff. I've learned how to work the online side of things and am content with that for now. It frees up more time with Jamie and I love chatting with the other mums when I pick him up at the school gates. It feels good to envelop him in the warm hugs I was deprived of as a child. Alex's family have embraced me into the fold, none the wiser of Jamie's true parentage. Call it magical thinking, but Alex and I have come to an agreement. We are Jamie's parents. The DNA test results have been destroyed. I didn't deliberately set out to deceive my husband, because deep down I always saw Jamie as his. I'm still coming to terms with Theresa's death but have finally managed to free myself from the shackles of guilt and remorse that kept me bound. She's buried beside Mum in Colchester, and I'm visiting their graves later today. Josh has been so kind, placing flowers in my absence.

There's only one dark cloud on the horizon. In the quiet times, *he* creeps into my thoughts. Sometimes I think I catch a glimpse of him: a man sitting in a passing bus, a hooded figure in the distance. Other times I feel his eyes on the back of my neck. I know he's dead but I half expect him to return. I think of the day I almost killed him, how he taunted me about all those girls. I take comfort in the knowledge that he cannot prey on such innocence again. At least everything is out in the open now. I told the police the truth, and after months of investigation, Mum has finally been put to rest.

Releasing my hand, Alex hoists Jamie on to the swing.

'Higher, Daddy, higher,' he giggles, and this time I am happy to let him fly. I'm not going to waste another second of my life fretting. I sit in the swing beside him, push it back as I stand on my tiptoes and launch myself into the air.

AUTHOR'S NOTE

Thank you for reading *Silent Victim*. The subject of grooming and abuse is one I have encountered many times in my career, having worked in specialised roles dealing with vulnerable victims and sexual abuse cases. For each case I have handled, there are many more which have gone unreported owing to fear, unwarranted shame or social stigma.

I would urge anyone in such circumstances to find help, whether it be from the police, a family member, or one of the many helplines available to people in need. It is important for victims to know they are not alone, and equally important to report past abuse to ensure it doesn't happen again.

If you have enjoyed this book, I would be immensely grateful if you could write an Amazon review. Just a couple of lines can help new readers discover my work. Perhaps you could recommend my books to friends, family or your local book club. I'm also on social media if you'd like to get in touch. I do hope you can join me for my next offering.

ACKNOWLEDGMENTS

Thanks to:

The wonderful team at Thomas & Mercer, particularly to my editors, Jane Snelgrove, Sophie Missing and Jack Butler, who have given great thought into shaping this book to being the very best it could be.

Madeleine Milburn and her team, in my opinion the best literary agency in London. I feel truly blessed to have them at the helm.

The amazingly wicked group of authors I'm a part of. I'm very fortunate to belong to this scene.

Mel Sherratt, Angela Marsons and Lindsay J. Pryor, who have encouraged me from day one. A nicer trio of authors you couldn't meet.

The book reviewers and clubs who have championed my books and spread the word.

Last but not least, my friends and family. Your support means so very much to me.

ABOUT THE AUTHOR

A former police detective, Caroline Mitchell now writes full-time.

She has worked in CID and specialised in roles dealing with vulnerable victims – high-risk victims of domestic abuse and serious sexual offences. The mental strength shown by the victims of these crimes is a constant source of inspiration to her, and Mitchell combines their tenacity with her knowledge of police procedure to create tense psychological thrillers.

Originally from Ireland, she now lives in a pretty village on the coast of Essex with her husband and three children.

You can find out more about her at www.caroline-writes.com, or follow her on Twitter (@caroline_writes) or Facebook (www.facebook.com/CMitchellAuthor).